A GILDED

Drowning Pool

CECELIA TICHI

In the Val and Roddy DeVere "Gilded" Series

A Gilded Death

Murder, Murder, Murder in Gilded Central Park

A Fatal Gilded High Note

A Deadly Gilded Free Fall

A Gilded Drowning Pool

To Come....

Death in a Gilded Frame

Chapter One

New York City, June 12, 1899

A HORSE THAT KICKS can kill anyone near its hind legs. A stable hand, a groom, a coachman, or a careless owner will risk their lives if struck by the animal's lightning-fast speed and power. Some escape with broken bones. Others die.

I knew this from girlhood in the far West, where wild horses stomped and kicked in the picturesque distance. Close to home, my papa warned me to look out for the pinned ears or bared teeth. He made me watch a blacksmith hammer iron horseshoes at the anvil and nail a shoe into each hoof of my dear buckskin Quarter Horse, Comet, who did not seem to mind. Saddled, she took me riding in the streets and outskirts of Virginia City, Nevada, where Papa was a "Silver King" and the mining camps of Colorado were a thing of our past.

Comet came to New York City when I married, and Central Park's bridle paths suited just fine in season. So did Newport's Ocean Drive in the summertime. Comet was never a "kicker" until this spring of 1899, when her back legs struck hard and fast—and sent someone six feet under to the grave. It was judged an accident, nobody's fault. To be clear: her kick saved my life. (The deceased was interred in another state.)

On this warm Thursday evening, the twelfth day of June, my horse would stir a spat between my husband and me over an invitation to a country house in the Hudson Valley. My Roddy had just mixed one of his fabulous, mysterious drinks, this one called a Collins. We tapped our tall glasses and sipped.

"Delicious, Roddy." I sipped again. "I taste orange, Florida orange. The name of this must be the Florida Collins."

"Are you so sure?" My husband's blue eyes twinkled devilishly.

"Out West," I said, "we placed bets whenever we were darned sure. If I put one dollar on Florida, will I win?"

"Not so fast, my dear. How about the saying, 'The House always wins?'"

"So," I said, "will the House give this wagering lady a hint? Offer more favorable odds?"

My husband stroked his firm, clean-shaven chin, winked, and said, "Think north...far north." He tapped his glass and mimicked a shiver. "Think ice and snow, and two places starting with 'A' and 'Y.'"

"Don't tell me…Alaska? Yukon?"

Roddy grinned. "The Klondike Collins Cocktail, a tribute to the Gold Rush."

I held up my glass and peered at the bottom. "No nugget? A Klondike cocktail without a gold nugget…I withhold my bet."

"Then, let us bet on one another," Roddy said, leaning for the kiss I enjoyed. The evening was on course for a discussion of plans for this month. We could not foresee that a minor disagreement would soon balloon—and explode by midnight, though neither Roddy nor I could have foreseen homicide as we debated the invitation and my horse's hind legs.

"Please, Roddy, let's just send regrets," I said. "We will be in Newport by July, and I want the rest of June to work with Comet before we go. She is much better…gentled. But I cannot risk another…episode." I put down my glass.

My handsome husband narrowed his deep blue eyes and fingered the country house invitation. The "episode," as we called it, occurred less than two weeks ago. Roddy was not in the stable with me when Comet's back legs hammered and killed. Our groom and coachman could not account for the unprovoked kick, though I had my own ideas.

"So, how about it?" I prodded. "Regrets to the Kidds?"

"Not so fast, Val," my husband replied. He sipped and put his glass down. We sat together in our newly redecorated *Empire* room in this French chateau that my husband's parents had built before Wall Street sent them to the brink of bankruptcy. The Street's bulls and bears had butted and clawed until the senior DeVeres faced ruin because of poor investments. I had become Mrs. Roderick Windham DeVere of New York City before my dear papa's death, when the Mackle silver mining fortune came to me and meant that Rufus and Eleanor could once again hold their heads high. My turn as the mistress of the chateau also marked a timely change in décor, which my husband warily approved. The ink-dark upholstery and the fat, stubby legs of the Victorian *Empire* room's chairs and sofas gave way to sunny wallpaper and lightweight furnishings.

"I'm afraid there's more to this than several days at Kiddwood," Roddy said. My handsome husband held the invitation to Alfred and Mercedes Kidd's country house where he had spent long weekends in boyhood and, later on, in his bachelor days.

"Father hopes we will accept the invitation," he said. "It seems that something has gone wrong with the water flow at Kiddwood. It usually gushes this time of year, but it's been a dry spring up there, and Father asks me to see about the flow, since the Kidds' water comes from my parents' tract."

"Tract? What tract?"

"Property..." Roddy said. "Acres."

These words were as familiar as the reference was baffling.

"About a hectare," Roddy said. "Roughly, one hundred acres."

"Your parents own property in the Hudson Valley, Roddy? Property deeded to them? I didn't know."

My husband looked like a caught-out schoolboy. Why had the moment turned awkward on this mild evening with drinks and gentle teasing? Roddy and I conversed easily and believed in each other, as unlikely as our pairing was thought to be, a fifth-generation son of Old New York and the daughter of an Irish immigrant who reaped a fortune in the Colorado silver mines.

"Roddy," I said, "what about those acres?"

"Adjacent to Kiddwood," he said, "my parents completed the purchase of a hundred-acre tract they initially had optioned."

"Since when?"

"The purchase was rather recent. The option...as long as I can remember."

"I see."

But I did not "see" why this real estate fact should pop up just now. The invitation came with a jack-in-the-box surprise. "Roddy," I said, "the Kiddwood invitation and this tract that your parents own...it sounds like hospitality mixed with a chore...your father's chore. He is worried about water, is he? I thought the Hudson Valley had lots of water."

"Mainly, it does, Val. The streams flow down from the hills toward the Hudson River, but the Kidds' acreage happens to be flat and always relied on water from my folks' tract, even when they optioned it. The tract had waterfalls flowing over limestone cliffs where we played as boys, and some streams were diverted and piped to Kiddwood. The limestone could have been quarried for cement, but Father refused to consider it. He says there ought to be plenty of water for both properties, and the manager of the tract agrees."

"Manager?" I asked. "What manager?"

Roddy's cheeks slightly flushed. "Father says he hired a man to keep an eye on the tract to make sure the hardwood trees aren't cut for lumber...stolen. The manager makes monthly rounds and sends reports. Father asked me to take a look...to make sure the reports are worth the expense." He paused. "Also, a few rumors reached Mother about a vagrant in the area."

"What sort of vagrant?"

"Mother does not exactly know, but Mercedes Kidd sent a note about a stranger who was seen on the tract. She called him a vagabond."

"Vagabond on the tract and water problems as well," I said. "I would think your parents ought to see about this. Weren't they invited to Kiddwood this spring? They go every year, don't they?"

"They did, Val. For years, we all did. The two families have been close for a long time, and the Kidds' son, Clarence, is nearly my age, so we two spent the spring and fall weeks together, making mischief."

"What mischief?"

Roddy shrugged. "Typical boys' stuff...Clarence made campfires, and we climbed trees...blood brothers one day, bloody fights the next. I haven't seen him since law school, and I hear he has become quite the man of the world...

London clubs, ducal estates. Anyway, my parents visit Kiddwood every year, but mother's doctor advised against it this year because the trees and grasses could affect her health...."

Roddy said no more. In going-on four years of marriage, I had learned that Eleanor DeVere ruled social life with her health's **on** and **off** switch.

Further questions about the senior DeVeres' situation seemed out of order. Since my papa's death, the Mackle Trust allocated funds to the couple, and Roddy was named their trustee, which we agreed was wise. The two had lived prudently. Secured by blood in Society's topmost tier, Rufus and Eleanor chose to move into the suite that had been Roddy's bachelor apartment with its separate entrance around the corner. They gave up their stable and put several carriages into what Eleanor called "camphor mothballs." They also bypassed Newport, claiming the Maine air did wonders for health. Each July and August, Roddy and I took over the twenty-room DeVere cottage, Drumcliffe, on Newport's Ocean Drive.

"Perhaps your father could go to Kiddwood for a few days," I said. "Not to pry, but perhaps your parents plan to sell the tract? Or might their friendship with the Kidds be at risk?"

"I don't know, Val. Whatever it is, the issue most likely involves the 'between' season."

"Ah yes," I echoed tartly, "the 'between' season." The term was totally foreign to me before my marriage. Society's calendar marked winter and summer, but the "between" weeks of late spring or early autumn were set aside for travel to Europe for couture wardrobe fittings, or for pheasant shoots, or visits to ducal estates. Those staying in the U.S. hosted parties at country houses, such as Kiddwood.

Virginia City, Nevada, knew no such "between" season. Papa's Big Lode gave us our year-round homeplace, a Queen Anne Revival house on "B" Street with a wraparound porch. If my mama had lived, she would have loved the porch where we sat on cool evenings. When school was out, I joined Papa on business trips to San Francisco, and we often spent a few days in The City by the Bay, happy to go and happy to get back home. New York Society's shuttling took me by surprise, even as I fell into the rhythm of Newport summers and city winters.

"Roddy, let's thank the Kidds for the invitation but send regrets," I said. "I will write the note."

I expected my husband to agree. I would consult my shelf of etiquette books for all occasions, which Roddy's mother supplied for her son's Wild West wife. We had joked about the mother-in-law "gift" books. In truth, they were useful at times.

"So, I'll write the note?"

Roddy's expression said otherwise. His brow arched, and he pushed at the wave of light brown hair that found its way over his broad forehead. "What is it?" I asked. "What's the matter?"

"The Hudson Valley tract," Roddy said, "is a sensitive issue for my mother and father. A country house of their own always appealed to them, and they planned to exercise the option, purchase the property, and build a retreat. Then, the downturn…. You know the rest."

I did. The rest meant the West, when Rufus and Eleanor DeVere lurched to Nevada's famed "Silver City" in a last-ditch effort to replenish their sagging fortune by striking it rich in silver. Wall Street was their downfall, but visions of a silver bonanza fueled their next investment folly. Against all odds, it also led to romance between Roderick Windham DeVere, their law school student son, and me, Valentine Louise Mackle, born on St. Valentine's Day in a snowed-in mining town in Colorado's Rocky Mountains.

"You know all the rest," Roddy repeated, "every bit of it."

I answered, "I thought I did."

He took my hand. "Let's not fuss, Val. We are rock solid, and we both knew it from the moment I showed off at the Silver Dollar Hotel bar." His eyes twinkled.

"Showed off," I said, "and horrified your parents and intrigued my papa." I chuckled at this momentary time-out from the surprising conflict over my horse and the Hudson Valley tract.

"I took a chance, didn't I?" Roddy said, "…showing off a flashy drink I never risked until that fateful night."

Truly, the young gentleman from New York had earned a round of applause in the Virginia City hotel dining room where Papa and I sat at a dinner table beside visiting Easterners named DeVere. Across the tables, Papa cautioned the couple to steer clear of overblown mining stocks, while their son offered to show me a trick. The young gentleman marched to the bar, issued orders, and mixed a scotch whisky cocktail, then set it alight and poured the flaming mixture back and forth in silver mugs he gripped in each hand. ("Ladies and gentlemen," the young man had called out, "I give you the Blue Blazer.")

Roddy's blue eyes had blazed for me that night, and my gaze belonged to him from that moment on.

The Blue Blazer recipe, Roddy explained when he sat back down, came from *How to Mix Drinks,* a book that horrified his parents when they spied it among his tomes on torts and criminal law. Secretly, he had become interested in the recent invention of the mixed drinks called cocktails, but the DeVeres shut their ears, convinced that Demon Rum had seized their son. Filled with blind faith in the silver mines, Rufus and Eleanor set forth on the westward pilgrimage that unexpectedly restored the family fortune. Quite simply, to the senior DeVeres' dismay, Roddy's romantic letters and further visits to Nevada resulted in his marriage to this Wild West "gal" who had fallen madly in love with him.

The question to myself at this moment: what right had I—or Roddy—to know how Rufus and Eleanor spent the allotment accorded to them by the Mackle Trust? My husband specialized in criminal law, so estates and trusts were far from the docket in the gritty city courtroom where he defended taverns and saloons against the zealous Temperance crowd that vowed to extinguish all alcoholic beverages. (At the same time, Roddy's *bon-vivant* hobby now put him in high demand as a consultant and master cocktail mixologist, although solely on a confidential basis. *How to Mix Drinks* was a mere fraction of what my husband dubbed his "libation education." Rufus and Eleanor had jumped to the wrong conclusion when they hauled their son west to "dry out.")

The senior DeVeres had made their present-day choices, I felt, and their money and activities ought to be none of my business. Or my husband's.

Before I could dismiss the Hudson Valley invitation, Roddy said, "My dear, a few days at Kiddwood will let me reassure my parents. Meanwhile, the coachman and groom can tend to Comet...and Justice too."

Our coachman, Noland, was top-notch, and young Zachary, the groom, had a feel for saddle horses. Both men were alarmed that neither Comet nor Roddy's Arabian gelding, Justice, had been properly exercised and fed during the winter months when we boarded them in the South. The horses had gained weight and turned balky.

And now Comet kicked.

She was on my mind, her tawny coat and little ears, her dark mane and tail, her spirit and good nature...except for the recent episode. Mindful of my horse, I halfway heard Roddy praise the coachman and groom until I heard him say, "The point, Val, is that the water ought to be plentiful for both properties, even if my folks decide to sell or go ahead with their country house plan.'"

"Roddy," I said in a firm voice, "let us stay at home for the rest of the month. I want to work with Comet without interruption. Perhaps you could use the time to prepare court cases? And what about the bitters business?"

"My bitters partnership is on hold for the moment, as you well know, and the case against the Anti-Saloon League has been postponed," Roddy said drily.

I knew about the bitters delay. A legal tangle temporarily halted my husband's plan to produce cocktail bitters in partnership with a fellow law school alum from Chicago. The recent preparations became a hair-raising affair and best put out of mind for now.

"But let's stay in town this June," I said. "You can work on new cocktails, and I will tend to Comet. I prefer that we stay here at home for the remainder of the month," I said quietly and firmly.

"And I have made my preference clear," my husband replied. "I wish to look into the water situation in my parents' tract and see about the 'vagabonds' that might be trespassing. I prefer to accept the invitation to Kiddwood."

An onyx mantel clock struck eleven p.m., and neither of us gave an inch. Tense and tight-lipped, we prepared to go upstairs for the night, when we heard the doorbell and our butler, Sands, at the front door.

"Telegram, sir," our butler said with apologies for disturbance. He withdrew, and Roddy slit the envelope with his finger.

"What is it?"

Roddy's eyes narrowed as he mouthed the words.

"What does it say?"

My husband handed me the Western Union form. CONTACT POLICE ULSTER COUNTY FORTHWITH. BODY FOUND PROPERTY OF R DEVERE.

Chapter Two

"IT'S YOUR FATHER, RODDY," I stammered. "The 'R' means Rufus. The telegram is meant for your father, Rufus DeVere."

My husband bit his lip. "...a body...dead."

"Ulster County," I said. "Where is it?"

"Hudson Valley," Roddy mumbled. "It's the tract."

"The telegram has come to the wrong address," I blurted, but Roddy's glance set me straight. The 620 Fifth Avenue chateau housed my husband's parents as well as ourselves. The senior DeVeres lived around the corner in this building. "For your father, 'forthwith,'" I said, stepping back as if the message could scald my fingers.

Twelve tinkling chimes of the mantel clock announced midnight. "My parents turn in early," Roddy said, "so no point waking them now. Father rises before the crack of dawn. I will go."

In silence, we retreated upstairs, Roddy to his suite, I to my boudoir for a fitful, restless night. Awake at dawn, I learned from my maid, Calista, that Roddy had gone around the corner to his parents' entrance.

"Would you care for a tray this morning, ma'am?"

"Coffee and a roll," I said, "and the papers...and Velvet."

"Velvet, yes ma'am."

The rumpled covers and my tangled hair told Calista the first order of the day was to be an in-bed tray and the cheer of our French bulldog, who bounded in, jumped up beside me, sniffed, licked, and rolled over for a tummy rub. The white crest on her chest set off her soft, velvety dark fur. Her dear face and pointy "bat" ears had charmed us from the moment Roddy and I claimed her when she was about to be abandoned. All twenty-three pounds of her wriggled in delight, oblivious of such matters as a telegram and dead body somewhere in the Hudson Valley.

"Calista," I asked, "remember the atlas we looked at before we all went to Florida last winter?"

"Would you like it, ma'am? I'll get it for you." The breakfast tray was soon set over my lap, cleverly fitted with a side basket for newspapers. A quick scan of the *Herald* and *Times* showed nothing about a body found in the Hudson Valley, I buttered the roll and sipped the coffee, reliably rich butter and feeble coffee, the usual.

"Here it is, ma'am...shall I open it?"

I moved the tray aside. "Find New York, Calista," I said. "Let's see the Hudson Valley...and Ulster County."

Across my lap, jagged boundaries of counties filled a sprawling page as I traced a finger up the Hudson River. "Here it is," I said, "Ulster County...it says 'southeastern New York State, immediately west of the Hudson River.'"

Calista bent close.

I read aloud, "'Much of Ulster County lies within the Catskill Mountains...settlements grew into the village of...W-i-l-t-w-i-j-c-k, which the English later named Kingston.'" I fingered a black dot by the river. "That's the county seat, Calista. It's Kingston."

"Yes, ma'am."

My maid, Calista Adrianakis, was the soul of discretion, having worked for years as a stewardess on a coastal steamer. Trim, efficient, and tactful, she would not ask why an atlas of the U.S. and its Territories would be her employer's early morning request, but she had helped me in countless ways, and I owed her some explanation. "Calista," I said, "Mr. DeVere and I have been invited to a country house in Ulster County. There may be certain matters to consider, but for now, bookmark these pages and leave the atlas close by." I added, "Changes may be in store, and we will see."

My tense tone unsettled the dog, and Calista blinked. I said it was time to dress for the day, no more lounging. A shirtwaist and culottes skirt were the comfortable favorites. I would add a light jacket and be ready to exercise Comet later this morning on a bridle path in Central Park.

By seven a.m., Roddy joined me in our breakfast room, where the footmen, Chalmers and Bronson, served us each morning before attending to other duties. Velvet lounged at our feet, and I remarked on good morning weather for exercising my horse. Over Roddy's tea and my second cup of coffee, I complimented my husband's coat and tie.

"It's always best to avoid Mother's well-meaning scrutiny of my tailoring, Val. As it happens, she was not yet awake, but I wanted to get to the point with Father. I barely slept. You too?"

I nodded. "You gave him the telegram? Left it with him?"

Roddy sipped his tea. "I meant to, but it became… complicated."

"How so?" I paused while Chalmers approached for the breakfast request. The eggs and beefsteak felt like a foolish delay as Roddy pressed the footman about his steak. "Medium rare, Chalmers, not well done. And not rare. You understand? You will tell the kitchen?"

"Yes, sir."

I asked for oatmeal. "Roddy...the telegram?"

My husband rubbed his eyes. "Father became agitated, Val. Quite unlike him, he swatted at the telegram, grabbed at his cane, and walked about the drawing room in circles... limped, I should say. My parents' new butler tried to take charge, but Father drove him off."

"Mr. Stallings?"

"Their most recent English butler, direct from London last month. He withdrew to the pantry while Father kept muttering that he should have listened to Mother."

My starchy father-in-law in a tantrum would be comic had he not recently suffered with a bad knee...and had a dead body not been found on his property. The picture was grisly. "What does that mean, listened to your mother?"

Roddy paused while the noisy Junghans wall clock hammered eight beats and Chalmers refilled our cups and stepped away. "It seems my parents argued about the manager of the tract," Roddy said. "Several men applied, and Father interviewed them all. He gave the job to a man named Keith...Roland Keith. A lady friend of mother thought she had heard something unsavory about him."

"Which was...or is?"

"Father did not wait to find out. Keith said he had other job offers involving property management, and he pressed for a decision. His low fees seemed like a good bargain, so Father hired him...signed a contract without legal advice... and says he wished that his only son had gone in for contract law instead of crime and cocktails."

"He said that to you?"

"He did. Father was as riled as I have ever seen him, Val, more upset than when his Wall Street stocks crashed and the silver mines proved worthless. He is angry at himself, worried about his knee and lashing out. He signed with Roland Keith, no lawyer involved."

My husband's frown deepened. "Foolish cost-saving decision...cheap, penny wise...you know that saying. And there's the rest...."

Roddy broke off as our breakfast arrived, my oatmeal and his steak that curled and shriveled. He peppered his eggs and jabbed at the meat. I reached for the dish of raisins and brown sugar and stirred them in. The dog sat up and begged, but Roddy said, "No, Velvet." We each took bites. I waited.

"The 'rest,' Val, is Father's inquiry after the fact. He has learned about Keith's run-ins with the law here in the city. The man defaulted on mortgages, got sued, and still was hired to manage tenements on the Lower East Side. He was blamed for letting trash pile up when the weather was dry. One of the tenements caught fire. Children died."

"Horrid...and he was held responsible?"

"The victims were immigrant youngsters, so the law was indifferent. The destroyed property was another matter... very valuable. The tenement owner's insurance company filed suit but has since gone bankrupt. So, Roland Keith lives to profit another day...in the Hudson Valley. He keeps an office in the city but now manages properties in Beacon, Poughkeepsie, and now Kingston and vicinity."

"Vicinity," I said, "including your parents' tract? And Kiddwood too?"

"I have no idea whether the Kidds employ a manager. Perhaps in the off-season. I do not know."

Roddy sawed at the steak and said, "Overdone." He salted and finished his eggs and sipped his tea.

"The telegram?" I asked softly. "You left it with your father?"

Roddy put his knife and fork down and raised his eyes to mine. "With every intention, Val."

Minutes ticked by. "Meaning," I said, "that you did not do so?"

"Meaning," Roddy said, "that my father's knee has badly hobbled him. He is in no condition to travel to the Hudson Valley. He said Mother has mentioned a wheelchair, which makes him furious. His state of mind would put him in jeopardy in Ulster County. Whatever occurred in the tract, my father ought not to deal with it. For his own protection, he ought not."

"And so," I said, "you will communicate with the police 'forthwith.'"

"Immediately after our breakfast...." He peered at his plate. "Such as it was." He raised his eyes to mine. "I fussed over the beefsteak, Val, thinking it was easily managed. A medium rare steak, and what could go wrong?" Roddy touched his throat and loosened his tie. "So, this morning we will both try to rectify problems. You will exercise Comet and do your best to stop her from kicking. And I will deal with the police to find out who died on the property of R. DeVere." He kept a steady gaze at me. "Do prepare yourself to spend a few days in the Hudson Valley. And remember, dear Val, that I am my parents' trustee, and your name is also DeVere.

Chapter Three

A RED RIBBON TIED around a horse's tail warns that the horse kicks. I brought the scarlet sash from a silk robe and tied it around Comet's brushy black tail. I rubbed her nose and let her nuzzle me here in the stable. She was fed and watered, the groom assured me, and her stall was reliably clean.

"Well, done, ma'am. Best to flag her tail for your ride, just in case."

"Zachary," I asked the groom, "has she kicked?"

"Once yesterday, ma'am, and she cocked a hind foot this morning, but that was it." The young man stood aside. "She remembers who treats her good. No flies buzz a minute in this stable."

The groom guessed that Comet might have tried to kick flies away from her legs in the Carolina stable where she was boarded during the winter. Our coachman, Noland, agreed that her kicking probably began in a fly-blown, dirty barn. I told him the advertisements made the southern barn look ideal. "In a trustworthy magazine," I said, "all about country life."

Our coachman muttered, "Blarney," a word my papa used time and again. Noland mainly tended our carriage horses, while Zachary took charge of Roddy's Justice and my Comet. We shared this private stable with our good friends, Dudley and Cassie Forster, whose teams were cared for by their coachmen, while other grooms worked with their saddle horses, Dudley's Venture and Cassie's Bella.

"Zachary," I said, "there's a slim chance that Mr. DeVere and I might need to spend a few days outside of the city this month. If so, I'll count on you to work with Comet."

"Absolutely, ma'am."

"And you'll use my saddle?"

"Your Army saddle, yes, ma'am. I promise. Ready to mount?"

"Ready."

Zachary pushed a hank of dark red hair from his forehead and led my horse to the open stable door, where he handed me the reins and saw me raise my left boot to the stirrup, then push up and seat myself astride Comet on the saddle that was standard issue for the US Army Cavalry. Roddy had said that a western saddle from Nevada was too alien for the bridle paths in the city or the oceanside in Newport. I selected the saddle named for General George B. McClellan, which let me mount without a granite mounting block and straddle my horse—a sight which had caused a stir in Society when I rejected that unholy contrivance, the lady's sidesaddle.

Nudging my boot heels at Comet's sides, I heard Zachary call, "And you might catch up with Mrs. Forster, ma'am. She took Bella out just a bit ago…on the drive with friends."

"Thank you, Zachary."

I urged Comet to a trot, eager to see whether my friend might be in view on her American Saddlebred, Bella. The overcast day promised sunshine. Central Park's trees had leafed out, and bright yellow day lilies were in bloom. A few carriages moved at a good clip on the broad pathway, a cabriolet and a phaeton driven by grooms exercising the owners' horses.

Around a curve, three women on horseback rode single file just ahead, one of them my friend, Cassie, and in front of her the pleasant Felicia Ordway on a dark bay Morgan horse and the cool Paulina Bourne atop a gray Andalusian. "Ladies, good morning," I called, bringing up the rear to hear cordial greetings from Felicia, a wintry word from Paulina, and a warm welcome from my friend.

In moments, the two women abruptly turned around, waved at Cassie, eyed my saddle and Quarter Horse—and the red sash—and with fretful smiles sped off with the words, "garden" and "Hortie."

"Who is Hortie?" I asked, drawing Comet alongside Bella.

Cassie laughed. "You heard 'horticulture.' Felicia and Paulina remembered a planning meeting for the new

Horticultural Society. They refused to abandon me, so you came just in time." My friend shifted the reins in her kid-gloved hands.

"How is Comet faring?"

"Better, we think."

Cassie knew of the kicking and sympathized. The South Carolina stable should not appear in a magazine we counted on, she agreed, and said that advertising these days was a pitfall. Cassandra Van Schylar Fox Forster (Mrs. Dudley Forster) had become my closest friend in New York. Descended from the Old Knickerbocker elite, she was every inch the lady and welcomed this Wild West newcomer as a friend, even as Society regarded me as something of a separate species. We had met on a bicycling path in Newport when I helped Cassie with a blown back tire. Our friendship followed, and I learned that her scientist husband, Dudley, was at sea in quest of fossils on faraway islands that were thought to hold the secrets to the earth's origins. During Dudley's months-long expeditions, Cassie cared for their two young children, Charlie and Bea, and oversaw their household staff in New York and Newport. Roddy and I were the children's courtesy aunt and uncle, and my husband remembered Cassandra Fox from childhood when they both took formal dancing lessons, a necessity in their world.

By now, I could not recall whether my husband had first cautioned me about my friend's Second Sight, or whether it was Cassie who confided that otherworldly visions had filled her mind at intervals since childhood. Her "spells" were thought to be a nervous disorder, she said, but the famous Doctor Beard was stumped, as was her mother, a bitter, angry woman who blamed Cassie's nanny, Saffira, for infecting her daughter with "daydreams." Cassie loved the nanny who opened unseen worlds to her, and the child sobbed into her pillow when Saffira was banished to her native Islands. As time passed, playmates teased mercilessly, and adults settled on the word, "superstitious." I tried to understand when Cassie described the auras and visions that impacted her body and mind. At times I felt baffled, at others chilled to the bone when unfolding events proved Cassie's harrowing visions to be prophetic.

"Cassie," I asked, "have you and Dudley been houseguests in the Hudson Valley?"

"In the 'between' seasons?" She laughed. "Once for each of us. Dudley was in college and was convinced fossils could be found in the nearby limestone, so he took a rock hammer instead of a tennis racket and was not invited again. For myself, a weekend of teasing about trances was quite enough."

She shifted the reins, a woman so poised, even regal in the dark long skirt that swept along Bella's left side. Cassie's top hat concealed her glossy, auburn hair, and her jacket let a white scarf peek at the neck. The sidesaddle was meant for her.

The soft tattoo of our horses' hooves played against the bird calls from nearby oaks and maples. When fast hoofbeats approached from the rear, we curbed Comet and

Bella as two men cantered past, one tapping his forehead to salute our courtesy.

"The thing about country house parties, Val, in case Roderick hasn't said so...the guest list will be a scramble, the host and hostess and their family and close friends are on hand, of course. But other guests are distinctly younger, bachelors and single women, total strangers that the host and hostess have never met. Filling every guest room seems to be the goal. You two are invited this month?"

"We are. To Ulster County, to Alfred and Mercedes Kidds' place."

"Kiddwood, isn't it?"

"How do you know?"

She laughed again. "It was Kiddwood where I spent that one wretched weekend enduring taunts about spirits."

"Oh, awful."

We reined our horses to a stop at a scenic spot and gazed at the greening of the new season before us. Suppose I confided about the body found near Kiddwood? I hesitated. Cassie would share my concern, but my friend would ask questions, and Roddy and I knew so little about the situation. For sure, this peaceful moment would be shattered.

Cassie broke our silence. "The Hudson Valley has a history of seers, Val. They lectured and wrote books claiming spirits guided their every movement. They announced that disturbing the limestone riled up the spirits." She shrugged. "It's not for me to say. Right now, I must try my best to be... grounded. You understand."

I did. My friend had promised her husband to make every effort to foil the visions and auras for their children's sake. Dudley advised that a Swiss doctor could treat Cassie in Zurich if she found herself unable to thwart the supernatural events that came to her unbidden.

"So," Cassie said, "hope for good weather when you go."

"It's not a certainty, Cassie," I said. "We're not sure that we'll be going."

"But you will. I know you will." My friend's gloved hands tightened on the reins. She turned her head, but not before I saw the faraway look I knew all too well.

"Let's go, Val...." Cassie seemed to shiver. "Let's go to a trot and a canter. No racing. Let's just exercise these horses. And let's call it a day."

❧

At midmorning, I left Comet with the groom, letting him walk her, loosen the cinch, and all the rest. I hastened home to hear the butler say that Mr. DeVere wished to see me in his study without delay, so I flew upstairs, still in my riding boots and culottes skirt.

At his desk, my husband sat twiddling his thumbs instead of gripping a pen and poring over law books and papers or drinks recipes.

"Roddy, are you all right?"

"Sit down, Val," he said. "I am trying to piece together some very sketchy information...doubtful information." He turned to the desktop and snatched a yellow legal tablet. "These notes barely make sense. The Kingston telephone connection faded in and out, and the officer's voice was scratchy." Roddy cleared his throat. "I gather that an actual body turned up in a grove...or maybe in weeds...discovered late yesterday afternoon."

I had perched on a tufted chair. "But the telegram came at midnight. How many hours—?"

"—Val, let me finish, please." My husband glanced at the tablet. "Seems a delivery wagon driver saw something and reported it. The police looked into it when they could, and they found a body...female. They checked about missing persons, and that failed, so they tried to find out who owns the property. The Ulster County Clerk of Deeds was roused at night and told them the name...from memory."

"'DeVere' from memory," I said, "but not from records? And are they sure? Are they certain the body was on DeVere property?"

"They have convinced themselves."

"Who is 'they?'"

Roddy looked at the tablet. "I wrote the name, Clyde Fitch, Assistant Chief."

"And where is the body?"

"I don't know."

"You didn't ask?"

"Val, the line went dead. The chief said to meet him on Wall Street...then hung up."

Wall Street? Could there possibly be two Wall Streets in the state of New York? My husband and I faced each other, glanced to the side, and met one another's gaze once again. I wet my lips. "Roddy," I said, "what must we do?"

His tone became somber. "We must immediately accept Alfred and Mercedes Kidds' kind invitation to Kiddwood."

"No other way?"

He shook his head. "The social obligation is part of it, Val, and my parents need help with the management of the tract. But this muddle about a body and the police means we must go without delay."

"The train to Kingston, I suppose," I said.

"No," my husband replied, "we'll take a steamboat in the morning. There's another reason to go up the Hudson. The steamboat business is under threat by the Temperance crowd. We will ride to Kingston on the *Mary Powell*."

Chapter Four

HAWKERS ALONG THE LOWER Manhattan wharves were thrusting handbills at every passenger, nearly blocking our way to the gangplank of the *Mary Powell*, which looked more sedate than the other steamboats. Dark wisps from every smokestack signaled on-time departures when every giant sidewheel would churn the waters named for the Dutch explorer who sailed here nearly two centuries ago.

Roddy guided us firmly through the gauntlet. "Eyes front, Val," he said, as a bullish boy in a newsboy cap yammered, "The *Saratoga*, mister! You want the *Saratoga*."

A beetle-eyed fellow stepped in front of me. "The *William F. Romer* ...fanciest steamboat on the Hudson, lady. Nobody rides the old *Mary Powell*!" Roddy pushed away his handbill.

The steamboat that we approached boasted its own hawkers who bellowed about free cups of punch. "*Mary Powell* punch for every lady and gent! For all deck passengers, folks! Compliments of the captain! And lemon seltzer for the kiddos! No thirsty family on the Queen of the Hudson River! Free punch! Ride the Queen!"

We reached the top deck of the *Mary Powell*, which buzzed with small groups of women who circled with picnic baskets, along with families who found seats and relaxed in the mild air on a warm day, a contrast to men in dark business suits who toted valises and drummed fingers on the railing. We could pass as tourists on this open deck, Roddy in a sack suit and Equadoran straw hat that dovetailed with my sun bonnet and light blue skirt and Empire jacket.

Our luggage for the Kiddwood visit had been put aboard at dawn by our footmen, Chalmers and Bronson, two small trunks and carpet bags that held Roddy's clothing and my wardrobe that was hastily assembled by Calista. She was eager to accompany me, though I felt the short visit to the country house would not require my maid's help. (Roddy could fasten and undo my clothing hooks, and I would keep this "dishwater blonde" head of hair pinned up and back, as I did in Virginia City.)

Roddy eyed the crowd for the steamboat official who would discuss the Temperance threats. I pointed to the other boats. "The *Saratoga* and the *William F. Romer*...don't they serve alcoholic drinks?"

My husband nodded.

"But the Temperance bunch only threatens the *Powell*? Not the others?"

"It's the free punch, Val. The *Mary Powell* is nearing the end of her long life on the Hudson, and competition in recent years got fierce, so the owners decided to take action."

"With free punch?"

"Yes indeed. As soon as we leave the wharf, our fellow passengers will sip and smile. The owners are pleased. The *Mary Powell* Punch has done its job."

"Roddy," I whispered, "Is the punch your recipe?" I knew that my husband's secret consultations and recipes for signature drinks included hotels, resorts, railroads, and ocean liners, but I had never thought of steamboats. "Is it yours?"

Roddy winked as the steam whistle suddenly let loose a deep-throated blast to announce departure. The *Mary Powell* eased into the river. I gripped a railing.

"We could enjoy cruising the river...if the city of Kingston did not wait with questions about a corpse on the DeVere property."

"Allegedly found on the property," Roddy said. "We do not have the facts."

My lawyer husband's watchword, the facts. At the railing, I looked down at the eel-green water while Roddy scanned the crowd for the man who approached us not fifteen minutes later.

"Mister DeVere? I beg your pardon, but I believe you must be Mr. Roderick DeVere? I am Mr. Thomas Kelton, Vice-president representing owners of the *Mary Powell*. If you would please follow me...?"

The men suggested that I enjoy the promenade deck, but I joined them in the mid-deck saloon where ornate furniture, carpeting, framed murals, and chandeliers lent a subdued feeling—until we saw the mahogany bar that had been splintered, the large mirror behind it cracked, and the glass lamp globes at the sides shattered.

We stood in silence. "Worse than threatened," Roddy said, turning to the official. "You are certain a Temperance group did this?"

Mr. Kelton nodded, a thin man in a gray pinstriped suit who looked pained to see the damaged bar. "Three women," he said, "came in here as nice as you please, and our bartender picked up the ladle to offer them punch. They knelt down...looked like praying, as the bartender recalls. Then they jumped up and yelled about the Lord's work and fighting the Devil."

Mr. Kelton blinked. "One used a hatchet, and the other two threw rocks. They sped off at the Newburgh stop before the crew knew what happened. We are searching the passenger manifest and will take legal action. The owners will wish you to represent the company, Mr. DeVere. We have photographed the damage with a Kodak camera. At present, we rely on the forward saloon, which is smaller but serviceable. We are serving your punch, Mr. DeVere, and if you will excuse me...Mrs. DeVere."

"So, it *is* yours," I murmured when we returned to the promenade deck where passengers, as Roddy predicted, sipped and smiled. I heard a young woman say, "Anise...I taste anise." She wore a bright yellow cloak and matching shoes. Her companion, a man in a straw "skimmer," murmured, "Anise if you like licorice, my dear fiancée."

Roddy muttered something I could not make out. "Roddy," I asked, "is there anise in the punch?" We had stepped away. "Is there?"

My husband shook his head no and went for cups of punch for both of us. In moments, we stood at the railing overlooking the river and the skyline. Roddy said, "Salud, Val" and touched his glass cup to mine. We sipped, and I knew at once why my husband's recipe had garnered business for the *Mary Powell*.

Mary Powell Punch

Ingredients:

- Rinds of 24 lemons
- Rinds of 24 oranges
- 4 gallons brandy
- 12 pounds sugar
- 6 gallons water
- Juice of 24 oranges
- Juice of 12 lemons

Directions:

1. Macerate lemon and orange rinds with brandy (let stand for 24 hours).
2. Heat water near boiling point, add sugar and dissolve to make syrup.
3. Add orange and lemon juices to the warm syrup.
4. Add macerated rinds.
5. Combine and mix all ingredients.
6. Filter, cool punch, and serve.

"Delicious," I said, "but one cup is plenty." Nearby, the families unpacked sandwiches, while little boys and girls sipped seltzer through drinking straws. Were any of these passengers to be guests at Kiddwood? Perhaps the young woman who thought she tasted anise and her companion who sported his straw skimmer at a rakish angle? Doubtful that others were bound for the Kidds' country house, Roddy said, since the train was faster, and speed itself an attraction. It was predicted that railroads would bring down the curtain on the steamboat era, though the newer boats were faster. Ahead of us, the *William F. Romer* was nearly out of sight.

"See that mountain up ahead on the left, Val?" Roddy said. "The Dutch settlers called it 'Butter Hill,' but the English thought the clouds around it foretold bad weather. They named it Storm King Mountain."

"Storm King," I murmured, sensing bad weather ahead.

Kingston, I saw at once, was a sizable city with an industrial waterfront, railroad yards, commercial blocks, sturdy churches, and municipal buildings of stone and brick. The dock where we disembarked bordered a park with amusement rides and a hotel with a pagoda roof. The police station, Roddy was informed, would be found on the ground floor of the new jail building at number 284 Wall Street, a few blocks away.

We decided to walk. Our trunks and bags would be held for us at the railroad depot. The sidewalks were paved, but the four-story police station and jail squatted squarely on a lot that was yet to see a blade of grass. The stone building's oak door was opened as we approached, but before my eyes could adjust, a man's nasal voice demanded, "Dever? Are you Mr. Dever?"

"Mr. DeVere," Roddy said, "with Mrs. DeVere. We wish to see Chief Clyde Fitch."

"Assistant Chief," said the voice. "Chief Wicker is upstate for now. Sit down. I'll get him. He's been waiting for you."

Roddy pointed me to a round table with chairs behind a bulky front desk. A locked safe and file cabinet left little room for the table where we sat. A wall-mounted telephone box and coat hooks filled a corner of the room, and a brass cuspidor glowed in a shaft of sunlight from a barred window. The jail cells, I guessed, must occupy the upper floors. A wall clock read 4:32 p.m. The steamboat journey took up most of the day. Roddy put his hat on the table just as we heard, "DeVere? R. DeVere?"

The guttural voice announced the rangy figure in a dark blue uniform tunic that was unbuttoned to the navel. "I am Assistant Chief Fitch. We waited all day. Every train from the city, we had a man on the lookout for you."

The chief stuffed his hands in trouser pockets, and therefore no handshake with Roddy, who was on his feet and introduced me in a cool voice. The chief nodded in my direction, repeating, "Roderick...so, your name is Roderick.

The given name on the deed was smeared, but the county clerk looked up the surname this morning."

His trim goatee and shaven cheeks seemed at odds with the rumpled uniform. He turned his chair backward and straddled the seat. Roddy sat beside me. The chief looked up with steel-gray eyes. "The property in question is deeded free and clear to DeVere. That's Yours?"

"The DeVere property here in Ulster County," Roddy said, "belongs to my parents, Mr. and Mrs. Rufus DeVere. I represent them, and I am here with my wife in regard to your telegram and my conversation on the telephone with you, Chief Fitch. I regret the connection was poor."

"That makes two of us, but you are here now, so let us discuss the body we retrieved from the DeVere property."

His matter-of-fact tone sent waves of dread from my legs to my throat. The location was a fact. The body was a fact.

"A female, approximately twenty years of age, five feet in height, light brown hair...." He went to the front desk and returned with a notebook he opened to flip pages. "...first reported as seen in overgrown field. No visible marks or signs of injury. Time of death unknown. Clothing matted. Ring, possibly gold, on middle finger of left hand."

For the first time, he looked directly at me. "That would not be a wedding ring, Mrs. DeVere, am I right?"

"Probably not," I said.

"Engraved on the inside," he said, "and a red jewel in the middle." He looked from me to Roddy. "Do either of you have an idea about who the woman might be? Light brown hair, five foot tall...or why she would be found on your family property?"

We shook our heads.

The steel-gray eyes shifted back and forth. "Temporarily," he said, "the body is at the Leahy Funeral Home. They have ice...." He paused. "If you got here in time, you could see for yourself, but Joe Leahy has a funeral this evening, so we put it off for another day." He closed the notebook, laid it on the table beside Roddy's hat, and again straddled his chair.

My husband said, "One question, Chief Fitch.... Have the Kingston police considered that death perhaps occurred elsewhere? That the woman did not decease on the DeVere property?"

"First, she died, then the body was dumped in the over-grown field? Yes, of course, Mr. DeVere, and if that field was scythed now and again, the body might have been abandoned elsewhere. We would not trouble you on this matter."

Reproached for neglecting the tract, Roddy started to protest, but the chief raised his palms and said, "No offense. The fact is, we are short-handed on the force, and Chief Wicker is out of town...away for a few months for his health." He gripped the chair back. "If the chief was here, he might handle this another way, but the property is yours, so you ought to know a few more things before it all comes out in the *Kingston Weekly Freeman*.

Roddy said, "Very well," and I nodded.

"If you read the notes on this case," he said, "you would see a name that means nothing unless you know Kingston.

The *Freeman* will print the name Henry Boynt, known in the city and the Ulster Townships as Hank. It's roughnecks like him that got us to fix our nightsticks. Straight hickory didn't do the job, so we bored holes in the ends and filled them with lead. Order was restored."

I glanced at Roddy, whose face was impassive.

"At the present time, Boynt drives a delivery wagon, hauls lumber and groceries, coal in the winter. The truth is, we expect to see Hank upstairs before long."

The chief pointed at the ceiling. "The New York Prison Commission calls this building the most perfectly constructed jail in the state, four floors, sixteen cells on each floor, all completed this year."

His grin became a grimace. "Before he went upstate for his health, Chief Wicker predicted who will be upstairs enjoying the abundant light and Ulster County's free meals. A good bet is Hank Boynt."

Why was he telling us this?

"You want to know why I bring up a disturber of the peace, Mrs. DeVere? Isn't that how the ladies put the case, 'disturber of the peace?'"

I looked into his steel-gray eyes and said, "In the West where I grew up, Mr. Fitch, we said 'outlaw' or 'desperado.' If the man in question pertains to the woman found on the DeVere property, would you please say so?"

He drummed his fingers on the chair rail, and said, "It's Hank Boynt that reported the body."

A long minute passed. "How so?" Roddy asked.

"Off a roadway, coming back from a grocery delivery, he spotted something light colored in the field, and he stopped to see what it was. He claims he came directly back here to report the body."

"And your men investigated immediately?"

"Mr. DeVere, our officers went as soon as possible. We are short half a dozen men."

"So, there was a delay," Roddy said.

"I can tell you our men went out there soon as they could, and a police wagon brought in the body."

"And this man, Hank," Roddy said, "...do you believe his account?"

"You mean, did he disturb the body? Or is he connected to the young woman's death? If that is what you are asking, we do not have a definite answer."

He rubbed his cheek. "Boynt says he wants no more time behind bars, and that's what he told us when we questioned him."

"And your interrogation was thorough?"

"All we got out of him is that he saw something on the way back from a delivery, stopped the wagon, walked into the field, saw the body, and drove back as fast as the old nags from Webster's Livery Stable would move.

I had questions, but just then, a young uniformed officer came from a back room, begged our pardon, and handed the chief a note that he read and folded between his knuckles. "Tell them ten minutes," he said, then looked from Roddy to me. "Tomorrow will be time enough," he said. "And you will spend the night in Kingston? At Bauer's Hotel? Or the Oriental?"

"Actually, Roddy said, "we will be guests at a nearby country house."

The chief's jaw clamped. "Country houses," he huffed. "Good land that could be quarried for limestone, or else farmed...do some good in Ulster County. Instead, good land with houses left empty most of the year...folks with nothing better to do with themselves." He rapped knuckles on the chair rail. "And may I ask, which country house is it?"

I heard Roddy say in a mild voice, "Perhaps you know of Kiddwood?"

"Kiddwood...." The chief's eyes narrowed to a squint, and he stroked his chin. "Kiddwood, is it?" He started to speak, then held back. It felt as though he saw us through a different lens. The air got very still, and the chief's boot scraped the floor.

"So, it's Kiddwood. Well, I hope you dine good and sleep good too. There's an old iron mine...you'd best stay clear, both of you." His knuckles rapped again. "Tomorrow, you will come back here to see about the body that was found on your family property, Mr. DeVere. And we will talk about whatever else might be happening out there."

Chapter Five

THE KIDDS' LARGE BROUGHAM met us at the depot where their coachman seated us, loaded our baggage, and snapped the reins of a matched pair of ebony Fresian mares. The city streets soon yielded to a tar-and-gravel road into the countryside where a few token houses on either side gave way to woodlands and bird songs mixed with horses' hooves and carriage wheels. Fading sunlight and shadow followed the curving road, and the coachman told us the distance from the edge of Kingston to the Kidds' private road was about three miles.

The specter of a young woman's dead body on ice at a funeral home kept us quiet for long moments. The delay in her retrieval seemed unforgivable, and doubly so since the body was first seen and reported by a local roughneck.

"Roddy," I said quietly, "the chief reacted when you said 'Kiddwood.'"

"He obviously dislikes country houses."

"But Kiddwood made him edgy, almost startled. You saw him...his eyes."

"I did."

"You were not tempted to tell him that you have been a guest at Kiddwood many times?"

"And prolong that tense encounter? Not when I must see him tomorrow about the body at the funeral home." Roddy took my hand. "You need not go, Val. I will borrow a horse and ride into Kingston."

"Borrow what horse?"

"From the Kiddwood stable." Roddy saw my face and checked his smile. "I forgot...your first country house visit." He took my hand. "This carriage ride gives us a little time, Val. We will be at Kiddwood soon, and this long day will become longer. So, let me say a few things to help you feel a bit better...."

"Roddy," I said, "if you please...."

My husband cleared his throat, gazed from the Brougham window, and said, "I believe you will enjoy the Kidds, Val. Alf and Sadie...that's Alfred and Mercedes...they always want their guests to have a good time. I sometimes wondered why my folks were not more like them."

I knew better than to pursue that point.

"It is customary at country houses," Roddy said, "to offer guests the use of saddle horses for trail rides and to provide a tennis court, a croquet lawn, perhaps a space for badminton...and racquets and shuttlecocks, of course."

I wondered whether Cassie had enjoyed Kiddwood's recreation among the guests who taunted her about her trances. I had not told Roddy about my friend's recollection.

"In the evenings, there is sometimes an entertainment, musicians or a magician from the city. And about mealtimes, Val.... As I recall, breakfast and lunch were casual, but Sadie loves to see everyone dressed for dinner."

Dressed meant formal wear. Thanks to Calista, dinner gowns were packed in one of the trunks.

"Alf grew up on the property," Roddy went on. "Before the place became Kiddwood, it was his family home for generations, and he loves tramping around with guests to retrace the old days. I think Alf would happily live there all year round if Sadie would give up the winter social season and summer at Bar Harbor."

I felt the Brougham move into a turn. "Were the first Kidds farmers?" I asked.

Roddy smiled. "Maybe chickens and a few vegetables, but the enterprise at the start was an iron mine. Nowadays, the Kidds' major investment is cement, which is hugely valuable—and profitable. Alf supplied cement for the Brooklyn Bridge towers back in the 1880s."

"Impressive," I said.

"Indeed, but at the start it was iron, and Alf is nostalgic." He grinned. "He will invite you to tramp to the farthest marsh to see where his great grandfather dug the iron mine. Be prepared. Every guest is invited to visit the iron mine shrine."

"And must one go?"

Roddy cocked his head. "When Alf offers a pair of rubber Wellington boots and offers a tour, best to go."

"But the police chief warned us to keep clear of an old iron mine. How would he know?"

Roddy chuckled. "He might have played there when Kiddwood was vacated, after the 'between' seasons. Clarence and I played in the mine as boys...until his father called a halt, said it was too dangerous."

"So, you played elsewhere?"

"Val, we were boys. The danger made the mine irresistible. We sneaked in and dared each other to crawl in deep. The deepest would win, and I wanted to win...."

My husband's smile faded, and he paused, staring into space. "Later on, things changed, and I thought back to those days. Clarence and I went to different prep schools and colleges...rivals in sports, which is natural, but Clarence seemed different when we came to Kiddwood as young men. Or maybe I was different."

Roddy paused. "I think back to the mine, how he egged me on to go deeper and deeper. Maybe I missed his mean streak. His mother always liked practical jokes, and maybe Clarence took after her...too much."

"Roddy," I said, "you visited the Kidds from boyhood and...how long afterward?"

"My last visit was the first year of law school, my dear, just before the westward trek when I met Miss Valentine Mackle and showed off in the Silver Dollar Hotel and Saloon."

I leaned for a kiss, just as the carriage lurched onto a hard-packed roadway. "The Kiddwood road," Roddy said. "We are almost there."

The short private road took us through a colonnade of oaks and beeches to a long, low cream-colored house surrounded by verandas. Footmen sprang to help, and a portly man stood on the verandah, smiling and rubbing his palms as if ready to open up a holiday present.

"Roderick, my boy," he boomed, "and your bride too. Introductions, if you please...never mind, I shall welcome Missus Roderick DeVere myself... Valentine, is it not? A Valentine for our Roderick." We climbed the steps to the veranda, and our host bowed deeply and touched my fingertips. "I am Alfred Kidd...I kid you not."

He winked and took my arm to guide me inside, where a rosy-cheeked lady that the *Ladies' Home Journal* magazine might describe as "pleasantly plump" took my hands in both of hers. She intended warmth, though her gemstone rings gouged my fingers, and I flinched.

"Oh, my dear, these rings...I am so sorry." She looked closely at my hands and murmured, "No harm done, praises be...." She spread narrow fingers flashing with large stones gripped by prongs. "You see what happens when Mr. Kidd visits the jewelry emporium? He felt sorry for the young Frenchman at the Cartier reception room, and here you have it." She smiled. "Now, let me welcome you to our beloved Kiddwood, and please do call me Sadie. No one says Mercedes except third cousins."

One glance at my daywear, and she said, "Poor dear, you must rest and freshen up. Travel is exhausting, and I would expect Roderick to prefer the train over a pokey steamboat. Dinner is at eight on the dot at Kiddwood, and you will meet everyone, a jolly group. Your maid will be Willa, who probably has already unpacked your things." Sadie patted my arm, and a servant led me down hallways right and left to our two adjoining bedrooms with a bathroom between them.

A cheerful Willa curtsied as I entered my bedroom to find my trunk unpacked and dinner gown hung up. "And your bathroom, ma'am...." She pointed to a deep bathtub and sink, the chrome faucets gleaming. The maid hesitated before stepping out, "Beg your pardon, but I am to ask, please do not fill the bathtub way up ...and please do not let the faucets drip. The water at Kiddwood...we are asked to be careful."

"Thank you, Willa. Mr. DeVere and I will take care."

I waited for nearly half an hour before Roddy joined me with a drink in hand and a fretful face. "Brandy," he said.

"So, the valet assumes the gentleman traveler arrives parched?"

"It's from a flask...from Clarence. He stopped me to beg for a private word at the first possible minute. He's fiddling with a contraption to light cigars, a little brass tank with a flint wheel. He offered to show me how it works, but I said later. He looks haggard, maybe not enough sleep."

"Perhaps he needs water instead of brandy?"

"Water..." Roddy said slowly. "The valet warned me, no deep tub soaks."

"And no dripping faucets," I said. "The water situation sounds serious."

"And puzzling. Even though it's been a dry spring, the water ought to flow," Roddy said. "I will see about it right away...and learn what the tract manager has to say...Roland Keith, if I can find him."

I sat on the edge of my bed, and Roddy took a rocker by the window and put the drink on a table. "Roddy, shouldn't Mr. Kidd...Alf...cross into your folks' tract and look into the problem himself?"

I remembered how Papa got involved in Virginia City when bilge water from the mines made the food taste awful. Papa helped to plan the pipe that brought water down from Sierra mountain lakes.

"If Mr. Kidd likes to hike around his land," I said, "wouldn't he cross into the DeVere property to find out for himself what's gone wrong?"

"I could see him doing exactly that," Roddy said, "but he sent Clarence instead. I learned that much in the few minutes when he poured the brandy. I'll find out more, but Clarence swore me to secrecy. I almost laughed, thinking he was ribbing about our boyhood stunts. No, he was stone-faced."

Roddy tapped the drink glass. "He's haggard and pale, but Clarence is every inch a gentleman of leisure. He has joined the ultra-fashionable peerage of America."

"The what?"

"Never mind. When you meet him, you will understand. My guess is, Clarence would rather be yachting on the Mediterranean. For now, my dear, I suggest we rest a bit and dress for the evening. The Kidds' valet will cope with my shirt studs, and your maid...?"

"Willa," I said.

"If the hooks and snaps prove too much for Willa, then I am at your service. And remember, it will be dinner at eight. As Sadie likes to say, 'On the dot.'"

Chapter Six

AT 7:45, RODDY AND I joined guests who had gathered around a baby grand piano in the foyer. At the keyboard, a dark-haired young man played a popular tune, *Just Tell Them That You Saw Me*, and two young women in pastel dinner gowns sang along in shaky harmony. The vocalists, I guessed, were debutantes who signaled eligibility to the bachelors standing close by, perhaps the red-headed fellow whose sneer defied any female to browbeat him to the altar.

Leaning against a wall beside him, a tall, slim man seemed to isolate himself with half-lidded eyes and arms folded across his chest. No necktie, but a creamy silk scarf flowed from his collar, and his dark suit nearly glowed. His coiffed hair, silken moustache, and tiny triangle of a goatee seemed at odds with his red-rimmed eyes and his drawn cheeks. Other guests gave him uncertain smiles but kept their distance. The man looked haggard.

He must be Clarence Kidd.

We took our place midway between the piano and a couple who might be related to Mr. or Mrs. Kidd, perhaps here at every 'between' season. The piano grew insistent, but so did the vocalists. "...tell them that I was looking well.... Just whisper if you get a chance...."

"No whispering this evening, my dears," a woman's voice rang out. "And Jack Barrott, you must vacate the piano bench and take a lady's arm, for it is eight o'clock, meaning—"

"—meaning dinner at Kiddwood, dear Sadie." The dark-haired young man glided from the bench and escorted both pastel-gowns, one on each arm as he comically intoned, "We process at Queen Sadie's command...."

A spacious dining room with pearl-white beadboard walls and deep red velvet hangings surrounded a baronial table that gleamed with crystal and silver under two chandeliers. Place cards sent us searching for our names. As tonight's guests of honor, Roddy would be at Sadie's right side at the head of the table, while I would dine at the right side of our host at the other end near a fireplace.

Alf waved away a footman and held my chair. "Lady Valentine," he said, "I must learn all about your celebrated silver mines. I am something of an old miner myself. But first, a tradition my Sadie prizes, the Kiddwood toast."

Rising, our host appraised the guests with a delicious smile, his cheeks so florid he reminded me of St. Nicholas eyeing the elves in his workshop. In a manner of speaking, weren't houseguests like elves, obliged to make the season bright? I doubted that anyone at this table knew anything about a body found somewhere over the property line.

Not the guests.

Not the Kidds.

"Good friends and family, welcome to our humble table...."

The "humble table" followed etiquette's rules, men and women beside one another, the dark-haired debutante in pastel mint beside an older man whose lapels sagged with military medals. Her friend in peach silk sat between the red-headed bachelor and a square-jawed man who slightly resembled Sadie Kidd, perhaps a brother or cousin. The pianist, Jack Barrott, found himself beside an older woman with an angular jaw who seemed to be chaperoning the two debutantes. On his left sat a single woman I had not noticed, her gown a faded purple that cast her neck and face in a pallid gray. She might be twenty-five. Or fifty-five. To my right, belatedly taking his seat, was the bored bachelor with the neck scarf who gave a short nod just as Alfred Kidd welcomed one and all in a robust voice that introduced the day's newest newcomers.

"...and so, we raise a glass to Valentine and Roderick DeVere, who have spurned the railroad in favor of a Hudson River floating palace."

The glasses were raised, the wine sipped, and the footmen hastened with refills, though the water glasses were to remain only half filled throughout the dinner.

We might have been in the city or Newport, since the footmen's claret-colored coats and knee-length britches would be perfect livery for either place or season. So would their white stockings and patent leather pumps glittering with rhinestones on the silvery buckles. The forested woodland close to Kiddwood was not to enter anyone's mind. We might as well be on the moon.

"So, Roderick is an old-fashioned lad who shuns the railroad for a steamboat," Alf declared. "How quaint. Took the *Romer*, did you?"

"The *Mary Powell*," I said.

"The old queen of the Hudson," he chortled. "If you'd come a few days ago, you might have sailed with Clarence. Isn't that right, son?"

The haggard young man nodded his tonsured head, and said, "...do not believe I have had the pleasure, Mrs. DeVere, although Roderick and I have a very long friendship... you might call it fraternal. We might have been fraternity brothers." He sipped his wine.

I sipped mine. Roddy did not join a college fraternity, and the notion of brotherhood with Clarence Kidd was a stretch for me, so I changed the subject. "And you have come up the Hudson by yacht, Mr. Kidd?" I asked.

"A smaller vessel," he said, "until the Belfast shipyard workers complete my *Fly Away*. I expect the summer of 1900 will find me sailing to Piraeus, or perhaps Barcelona."

"No American resorts for you?"

Alf broke in. "Clarence indulges his parents in the 'between' seasons. We welcome him always, but once my son met the Prince of Wales, life on these shores became ...did you say 'dull,' son?"

Clarence touched his tiny goatee and said, "Perhaps somewhat stale." He dutifully murmured, "Present company excepted, of course."

A silent moment, and footmen arrived with split pea soup, which Roddy detests. Shortly afterward came hors d'oeuvres of olives and sardines, and we were soon on to braised scallops and different wines. The Kiddwood dinner pace was surprisingly brisk. Plates were removed before guests had rested their forks.

"I understand that Roderick has become something of an expert in wines," Alf said. "Or is it the new drinks, the cocktails?"

"Something like that," I said.

Clarence raised an eyebrow. "The very topic for our chat." He smiled wanly. "If you will kindly allow me a few words with Roderick after dinner, Mrs. DeVere?"

The man sounded forlorn. "Certainly, Mr. Kidd," I said. Clarence's hand trembled, agitating the water in his glass.

His father took offence. "Do not remind us at the dining table, Clarence. The water problem will soon be dealt with, and the ice-house wagon delivers what we need. You best have your word with Roderick. He expects to find out what the trouble might be. Since you could not, Roderick will deal with it."

Clarence fingered his scarf and gave another wan smile. "And so, Mrs. DeVere, thanks to your husband, my valet can soon draw a bath and turn the faucets without spraining a wrist?"

I said, "Let us hope so." Our plates were whisked away and others put before us. Light conversation rippled around the table during the roast beef, and the lady in the faded purple gown asked in a high voice, "Alf, dear fellow, what entertainment will amuse the young people this evening? The acrobats?"

"Heavens, Edna," he replied, "the acrobats are touring with the circus, so Jack will favor us with piano tunes tonight."

"You mean, he will tide us over," she replied in a voice at ease with Kiddwood ways. "But, Alf, what about the magicians? That couple calling themselves the Houdinis? Everybody liked them."

"Going to vaudeville," Alf said, "in great demand."

"Mercy," she said, "no acrobats, and no Houdinis." She lowered her voice to sound confidential. "At the very last, might you capture another vagabond from the woods?"

We were midway through the roast beef at this point. I was to remember the impression that his words apparently made on the Kidds, the father and the son. "Your woodland vagabond," she said again.

Not that the actual word was rude, nor the tone of voice other than pleasant, but the air felt different. The two men stirred, Alf thrusting his fork at the meat, and Clarence raising a manicured finger in request for wine. Other courses soon followed, the salad, cheese, and dessert. Coffee and liqueurs would also be served, and Jack Barrott obligingly play tunes from a new operetta, *The Fortune Teller*. The dinner and the evening would pass without incident, and Roddy and I were wished a very good night. Nothing out of the ordinary had happened, but to me, the air at Kiddwood had shifted.

Chapter Seven

BREAKFAST PASTRIES, MUFFINS, AND beverages lay untouched on a buffet table when Roddy and I entered the morning room at nine o'clock. Two guests were seated on the cushioned wicker furniture, the square-jawed fellow who might be Sadie Kidd's relative and the elderly man pinned with military medals at dinner. With a "good morning," they resumed intense talk about Napoleon Bonaparte. Neither Sadie nor Alf was present, so I guessed morning appearances were not the hosts' duty. Nor guests' obligation.

Roddy was eager to ride to Kingston to see Chief Fitch, so he sipped a quick cup of tea and went to the stable to borrow a horse. A footman offered a full breakfast, but I took a hint from his waspish tone and declined, feeling extra cautious because of the strange tale Clarence related to my husband when the two slipped off to the veranda last night while Jack Barrott played piano tunes. It seems that Clarence was dispatched by his father to see about the water problem on the DeVere property and came upon a campground deep in the woods. He told Roddy of tents and adult campers and turmoil because a young woman masseuse had gone missing from the camp. Clarence reported none of this to his father, who reproached him for negligence, though Roddy did not learn the particulars.

"Try the scones," said a voice behind me in a stage whisper. "Take two...hold us until luncheon."

I turned to see the woman who had asked about the acrobats and took a dim view of last evening's piano tunes. Her green-print day dress accented her pallor, but high cheekbones in a narrow face gave her full mouth the suggestion of playful mischief heightened by darting blue eyes. Her French forehead bangs with upswept dark hair lent her a stylish air. Close up, she remained a woman of uncertain age.

"I am Edna Rossiter," she said, "and proud to be Sadie's oldest friend. We went to school together, made our debuts the same spring. Sadie loves practical jokes, and so do I." She smiled coyly. "And you are Roderick DeVere's bride ...Valerie, is it?"

"Valentine," I said, extending my hand to her graceful fingers with nails trimmed surprisingly short. She eyed my buttercup yellow day dress, and I saw that she wore no wedding band.

"Join me on the veranda. The Kiddwood mornings are subline." She beckoned the footman. "Fallowes, my usual, please, and for Mrs. DeVere...."

In moments, the footman placed a Royal Worcester plate of scones and two very small cups of coffee on a rattan table between two wicker chairs on the veranda facing a grove of trees, a lawn, a distant stable, and, farther still, the DeVere tract.

"Warblers," Edna said as we sat down. "They are serenading us in the maple trees."

"So pleasant," I said.

We nibbled the scones and sipped coffee from fragile cups. "This china," Edna said, "was in storage for years, but Sadie's butler retrieved the tiny cups when the water ran low."

She leaned across the table toward me. "I can tell you that Sadie and Alf both pray that your husband can get the taps flowing. And the household staff are on their knees every day. Can you imagine warning every guest not to bathe properly? Or how desperate the kitchen preparing each day's meals?"

I shook my head. She need not know about chuck wagon grub in a mining camp. Or icy creek water for a wash-up.

"We were promised that your husband would fix the water and mix us fabulous cocktails. Tell me, do cocktail drinks require water?"

"Sometimes, for simple syrup."

"Nothing is simple at Kiddwood in this 'between' season," Edna said, "and I would know because I am here every spring and every fall without fail. Sadie calls me the mortar that fills the awkward chinks in house parties."

"The mortar?"

She laughed. "So to speak. For instance, an old bachelor like General Coleman…? I volunteer to be his dinner partner, swoon at his Army medals, and appear raptured when he drones on about Napoleon."

She buttered a scone. "He's harmless, but favorite guests can overstep, and I give fair warning to them. Jack Barrott can light up the room at the keyboard, but he joked to Alf that Kiddwood might as well be the Gobi Desert. Alf did not take it well, and Sadie called me to patch things up. Jack is a dear, but he was left penniless and counts on invitations for long stays. I believe he will go on to Newport this summer. You go to Newport, yes? To the DeVere cottage? Drumtaps?"

"Drumcliffe," I said, feeling foolish to call Roddy's parents' seaside mansion a cottage and in no mood to field questions about Newport when my horse and the calendar were at odds, each day closer to our departure deadline. I said, "The Kidds prefer summers in Bar Harbor, Maine, I believe… And do you—?"

"—summer in that foggy outpost? Absolutely not. You will find me at Saratoga Springs, which is serene and lively. At the Springs, I plough through my stack of the newest novels and speed my reviews to *Town and Country* or *Ladies World*." She spread butter on her scone. "Similar to Kiddwood, serene and lively until this springtime. Sadie and Alf have found it necessary to trim the guestlist."

"Because of the water?"

"Precisely. And fewer the guests, the fewer evening entertainers, which is why the 'vagabond' evening was a novel surprise."

The footman refilled our coffee cups. "The 'vagabond,'" I said, "sounds intriguing...a person who suddenly appeared from my husband's parents' property? A trespasser?"

She sighed. "For certain, it's a mystery, whatever goes on in such wild, neglected places...oh, apologies for that indiscretion. Sadie tells me plans are underway for a DeVere country house in the next year or two, which should take care of any problem. Meanwhile, my dear friend decided that 'vagabond' sounds better than 'tramp' or 'hobo.' I completely agree."

"But a vagabond entertained you here?"

She nibbled her scone. "Strangest thing...one single man came from a path that leads to the next property, the woods. Disheveled appearance to the contrary, he delighted us by juggling."

I said, "A trespassing juggler?"

"Curious, isn't it? We asked about the circus, but he told us nothing, only showed the most agile juggling...saucers, caps, badminton shuttlecocks. Whatever was presented, he could juggle. Finally, we all had enough, and he asked permission to spend the night on the grounds. Alf offered him the stable, but he wanted to sleep by the roadway entrance. Sadie found him a blanket, and by morning he was gone. We think a delivery wagon might have given a ride into Kingston."

"And that was...this week?"

"Two nights ago...no, three. I remember because the moon was full that night, and Clarence accused us of lunacy.

He complained about the juggling and made rude comments until Sadie asked him to keep his views to himself."

"So…" I said, "on that evening, you were not called upon to be the 'mortar?'"

"With Clarence? Never…especially since that cigar lighting gadget has mesmerized him. That and the new yacht."

Edna set her jaw as if to stop herself from uttering another word about the Kidds' visiting son. A breeze crossed the veranda and riffled our skirts. She asked, was Roderick sleeping late this morning?

"He went into Kingston to attend to business," I said. Edna Rossiter need not know that a woman's body was found on the property that gave Kiddwood a juggler in a full moon. If Cassie were here, she would know how to move into light conversation.

I put down my cup and said, "It is so pleasant to hear these birds of the Hudson Valley, which are new to me. If we were in the Colorado Rockies where I grew up, I could identify the cedar waxwing. And in Virginia City, Nevada, where I moved with my papa, the house finch was my favorite."

Edna peered briefly into her empty cup. "Ah, the far West," she said. "Word did spread fast that Roderick found his bride in the gold fields."

"Silver mines," I said.

"…and broke hearts along the East Coast, debutantes from New York to Baltimore."

"Oh?"

"And has he not spoken of Miss Mandy Sterling? Amanda Gosslinger Sterling?"

"I...I'm not sure I recall."

"Debutante of the year, a great beauty and a favorite everywhere."

"Here? At Kiddwood?"

"Kiddwood and other country houses in the spring and fall, then the city, Newport...Paris and London. Everyone expected a certain proposal of marriage, but you must ask your Roderick. I shall say no more."

Did I want to hear more? Did Roddy ever speak of Amanda Sterling? My bid at politeness somehow curdled.

Edna pointed to the table. "When the morning light crosses here, it's like a sun dial telling me to find out what Sadie has in store for the day. So, Valentine, enjoy the veranda. We will see one another again at luncheon, at dinner, and perhaps on opposite sides of the badminton net."

She was gone. I squinted in the hot sun but did not budge when the footman removed the cups and plates. I stayed on the veranda as household clatter began to echo from the breakfast area and indistinct voices, along with Sadie's "Oh, my goodness" and Alf's jolly laughter, plus a few piano chords.

I ought to join them, gear up and do my part, but I kept watch on the stable and peered at the mass of trees in the farther distance—the DeVere tract where a juggling "vagabond" had appeared and a woman's dead body had lain in the weeds. And where Clarence saw a campground and heard of a masseuse who was missing.

It made no sense.

The sun had risen higher when Sadie's "There you are!" and scolding finger broke into these thoughts. "Why, Valentine, just as Edna feared, you are at risk of a sun burn. And the day is young, and so, my dear, you must join in and enjoy yourself. We have no house rule except for dinner at eight, but no one dawdles at Kiddwood."

"Sadie," I said, "I was about to fetch a sun bonnet, and I'm sure Willa has put it in the best spot in our guest room. Count on me to make the most of this amazing visit to your country house."

❧

Roddy found me in the rocking chair in our room. He looked as flustered as I felt. "Val, my dear, are you feeling unwell? You're not ill…?"

"No," I said, "but I did not feel sociable this morning." Impatient to demand answers about Amanda, the debutante, I would try my best to wait for Roddy's morning report. His face was flushed, his hair mussed. "And you, sir," I said, "do not appear eager to join the party."

"True enough." Roddy rubbed his neck and perched on the edge of my bed. "I came back as soon as I could, Val. Chief Fitch kept me cooling my heels for nearly an hour. The man resents country houses, and Kiddwood most of all."

"Why?"

Roddy lowered his voice. "Fitch told me the Kingston police have been called twice to pull guests out of Alf's iron mine."

"What?"

"Val, shh...." Roddy nearly whispered, "Kiddwood is beyond their jurisdiction, but the Kingston cops came twice last autumn to rescue guests who got stuck in the old mine."

"The mine where you and Clarence—"

"—played as boys, yes. The second time, Chief Fitch told Alf that his guests better go to Coney Island for thrills. He would not send his men to Kiddwood again. Alf offered a donation to the police, but Fitch refused it. Anyway, I believe the chief and I came to an understanding."

"About the body? You saw the body?"

"No, the body is being buried in the Kingston public cemetery...a sort of potters' field where indigents are interred. The city pays the Leahy Funeral Director a nominal sum for the burials and certificates of death. Leahy is also the coroner for Kingston and Ulster County. But indigents' bodies are photographed if they are not too...I mean, if they are recognizable."

I shuddered, my fingers suddenly cold. "The young woman's body has been photographed?"

"It has been, yes, and the photograph will be filed with the police when the film is developed and made available at a later date by parties with a legitimate interest."

"Like the next of kin," I said. "And was the young woman reported missing? A flyer posted? Some effort to find her family?" My throat had tightened, and Roddy reached for my hand. The debutante matter would have to wait. "Her family...?"

"Not to our knowledge, Val. Chief Fitch said some families do try to locate missing relatives. He showed me last week's *Kingston Weekly Freeman*, the pitiful descriptions."

"But none a match for—"

"—the young woman on the DeVere tract? The wording could fit any number of young women, Val. Whoever she is...was...Chief Fitch doubts that we will ever know. Or that her family will learn where she went, and perhaps not care."

Roddy rolled his shoulders. "According to Fitch, Kingston is plagued by transients, men and women both. Some are immigrants, some trying for a new start, and others on the loose from trouble. Until a few years ago, the main work was at the rail yards and stone cutting, but nowadays workers show up to quarry limestone for the cement works...mostly single men, but young women come too. Fitch said that when Kingston was smaller, the police could keep better tabs on things. The city has two breweries, saloons, and what the chief calls sporting houses."

"Brothels," I said. "And he thinks the deceased young woman was a prostitute?"

"He did not say...would not say. He worries about single young women who turn up, walk the downtown streets, and then disappear."

"Into the brothels?"

"Sometimes factory work."

"But Clarence told you about a young woman who was missing from a camp of some sort...on your parents' tract."

"I brought it up, but the chief scratched his head. He knows nothing about such a 'camp,' and I was no help. My parents' tract is beyond his jurisdiction."

"Just like Kiddwood."

"Like Kiddwood." Roddy sounded rueful. "The road leading outside the city limits...we were on it last evening in the brougham, a tar-and-gravel roadway. It's a county road and passes Kiddwood and my parents' tract. This month, the police have noticed small groups of strangers that come and go every now and then on that road. They are keeping an eye out, but it is beyond their—"

"—jurisdiction...?"

There is one possible clue, Val...the ring she wore. The funeral director turned it over to the police, and Fitch showed it to me in case I recognized jewelry belonging to our family. It is yellow gold with a red stone, engraved on the inside, 'Fiona from Papa.'"

"Oh...." I nearly gasped. My papa once told me that if I had not been born on St. Valentine's Day, I would have been named Fiona. He sometimes surprised me with a "bauble" from San Francisco, and the idea that the young woman's father had given her a piece of jewelry struck like a blow. "Roddy," I said in a tremulous voice, "a father and daughter... perhaps a present for her coming of age birthday?"

"I thought so, Val, but the chief laughed it off. He thinks she was an older gent's floozy. He invites you to inspect the ring. You will?"

"Of course."

"And he thinks that Hank Boynt might have taken other jewelry when he found the body, perhaps a necklace or bracelet. He plans to question Boynt again and visit the local pawn shop in case the man was foolish enough to pawn stolen jewelry here in Kingston."

"And the police will hold the ring for safekeeping? And the photograph? "

Roddy nodded and crossed his legs. "There's something else, Val."

I waited. My husband uncrossed his legs and planted both feet on the floor. "The chef said the funeral director, Leahy, found something in the dead woman's mouth...like seaweed or pond grass."

"As if she drowned?"

"Perhaps...and under her clothing, he saw dark marks near her neck ...bruises."

"Oh...." I clutched my own neck. "Strangled?"

"Or held under water until she drowned. We don't know."

"Don't know..." I echoed.

Roddy drew out his pocket watch. "We know this is the Kiddwood luncheon time," he said. "And we know the hour has come to explore the DeVere tract."

"You won't go alone," I said.

Roddy gripped my hand. "A gentleman might insist that his lady take her afternoon's ease," he said, "but this gentleman counts on his lady's western eye for the sharpest sight in the very dark woods."

Chapter Eight

AFTER LUNCH, RODDY TOLD the Kidds we would take an afternoon trek into the DeVere property to see about the water problem. The guests had settled for the afternoon, Sadie at a foursome for bridge and Jack Barrott taking requests for new tunes. Clarence sat across a chessboard from General Coleman and cringed when Alf cautioned the general not to be "rooked" by his son. Roddy urged Clarence to go with us, since he knew the path, but backed down when Clarence swore that one bout of poison ivy from the DeVere woods was quite enough. He advised us to wear close-fitting clothing and started to tell Roddy more about the mysterious camp and 'vagabond,' but Alf interrupted with a blustery demand that his son pay attention to the debutantes.

I suggested that we borrow a shotgun, but Alf said a Kingston gunsmith was cleaning every firearm, including the .22 rifles that Clarence and Roderick had fired as boys. The guns would be back at Kiddwood for the autumn 'between' season when guests hunted pheasants and deer. He and Sadie counted on seeing us then, along with Rufus and Eleanor. We thanked him.

Setting off by one o'clock, we walked swiftly past the badminton court and the stable on the way to the wood fence at the property line where Roddy remembered a short cut where a board collapsed years ago.

"Just as I remember it, Val." My husband and I stared at a mossy fallen board at the fence.

Why didn't the Kidds repair the fence, I wondered. Did they cherish memories of Clarence skipping over the same board with Roddy for frolics in the DeVeres' creeks and falls?

"Step carefully, Val. The board will be slick. It was always slick." Somehow, my husband sounded sad.

Across the fallen board and through the opening, we entered the DeVeres' tract, where the air felt suddenly close and moist. Fallen logs sprouted thick brown mushrooms—or were they poisonous toadstools? The tract allowed little sunlight, and Roddy named the black locust, the chokeberry and sumacs along the overgrown path. Dappled spots of light disappeared when wind stirred the canopy. We talked quietly.

"It feels moist, Roddy...damp."

"You'll like the waterfalls," my husband replied. "There's been plenty of rain this spring. Even though it's been dry, the water should be plentiful."

Roddy had guessed the water shortage began when an early spring storm sent a major creek flowing in a new direction over the limestone, or perhaps a beaver dam interfered with the flow. In either case, a crew of workmen manning picks and shovels ought to correct the problem shortly.

We had asked ourselves why Alf failed to act when Kiddwood's water shortage was first evident. Why did he wait until Clarence arrived for a visit and then send his son to inspect the tract?

Roddy thought perhaps the seasonal entertainment troubled a host who felt his dear boyhood home was to be overrun once again with strangers devouring his food and alcohol without a care. Alf might secretly want to turn off the spigots, Roddy guessed, and sent Clarence to the tract to guarantee the dry spell would continue. A gentleman son who socialized with the Prince of Wales was not about to re-route creeks and waterfalls in Ulster County.

To my mind, Clarence Kidd seemed both foppish and somehow fragile.

"This path," I said, "you're sure you remember?"

"With my eyes closed...almost," Roddy said, stumbling on a tree root. "I admit the path is overgrown. But the distance would be greater if we took the roadway, so this saves time."

We walked single file in silence, my husband in the lead. Dark ferns competed for space with bulging tree roots, and the mossy rocks felt slippery underfoot. I could not remember whether poison ivy had three leaves, or four, but the ivy brushed my stockings at the ankle. Finally, a trickling sound. "Roddy, I think it's water. I hear water."

"I hear it too." We paused to listen, but the first hint of something foreign with an acrid scent. The ferns, moss, and wood had blended, but the new odor smelled like vegetables …vegetables cooking."

"Roddy, do you smell something?"

"Like asparagus? …wild asparagus?"

"More like cabbage," I said.

We continued on, but then a hollow, echoing sound, like a gong. "Roddy, did you hear that?"

We stopped. Insects buzzed, and the trickling became insistent, like a flowing brook. I stifled a sneeze from the foul vegetable odor.

Then, the gong sounded once again.

"No animal makes that sound," I said softly.

Roddy put a finger to his lips to signal, silence. My neck prickled, and I wished my papa's Colt .44. were strapped at my side. We stood as still as statues.

"Crouch down," Roddy whispered, "and let's tiptoe."

"Should we go back?" I crouched, and we frog-walked on the path, through the ferns…and then…."

"Stop. Who are you?"

The voice should strike fear, but it sounded musical. "Who…?

Roddy and I found ourselves face to face with a tall man with dark hang-dog eyes and a lantern jaw. He wore an undershirt, balloon-like trousers, and slippers...no, sandals. His hair looked wet-slicked.

A hobo?

Dangerous?

Roddy rose to full height. "Sir," he said, "this is private property."

"Indeed, it is," the man said, "Won't you join us?" As if he were the host. "Join us in the grove?"

"Grove?" Roddy's voice rasped. "What grove?"

"The Health-to-Wealth grove, of course."

"The what?" Roddy's exasperation flared.

The stranger smiled. "If you please..." As if extending an invitation, he pushed back a branch and ushered us forward. The sound of rushing water grew louder and the vegetable scent stronger. I sneezed.

"Gesundheit," he said softly.

I had read of soldiers taken prisoner, forced to march long distances. The war between the North and the South was not that long ago. We were being marched, but where? This hundred-acre tract was not so large, but could we run away in these thickets?

Could we overpower this man?

Could we?

As he suggested, Roddy and I walked single file just ahead of him. "We will pass by this next stand of trees, and you will see...."

"See what?"

Roddy got no answer as we walked toward the trees, passed them—and then stopped at the sight before us all of a sudden, like a mirage.

"What is that?" I blurted.

"Behold," said this strange man, "The Health-to-Wealth grove."

Dumbfounded, both of us. What did we see but tents? Camping tents in a clearing, a tent village clustered around a raised wood platform. I counted eight of them...no, eleven, all the same size except for one that was larger. Every one, a canvas tent.

Whose were they? At one side, an outdoor cook stove was tended by a woman who stirred the contents of a huge kettle. The foul vegetables? Two wheelbarrows stood by the cook stove. Farther still, a makeshift corral with one gray draft horse and a cart.

Who arranged all this? I saw two young women in white robes skip from one tent to another. A pottery bell hung from a nearby branch. Was that the gong? Roddy and I came to a halt with the strange man at the edge of the clearing. Or was it supposed to be a grove?

"Allow me to introduce myself," he said. "I am Cedric Ferris, the executive director."

Director of tents? Grotesque.

Roddy said, "So, Mr. Ferris, you are in charge of...of all this?"

"Absolutely not," he said in a rich voice that sounded like a cello. "The person in charge is, of course, Vanessa."

"And who is Vanessa?" I asked, trying to sound sociable, as if making acquaintance at teatime. "I don't believe we have met...." My voice trailed when a man wrapped in a towel came out of a tent, jogged toward the trees, and disappeared.

"To go bathing," Cedric Ferris said. "For restoration, Vanessa insists that a part of each day be portioned for our bathing hour."

"Who is Van...?" But Roddy touched my wrist.

"Mr. Ferris," my husband said in the firm voice of a trained attorney, "I believe a serious misunderstanding has occurred. I am Mr. Roderick DeVere, and I have come with Mrs. DeVere to investigate present conditions in regard to water on this private property. I believe a visitor from an adjoining property was very recently here?"

"Mr. Kidd? Mr. Clarence Kidd?" Roddy nodded. "Ah, yes, but I regret that we made little time for acquaintance. You see, one of our young women masseuses had departed unexpectedly, and we were rather in a bind. The Kellogg massage technique is fundamental to Health-to-Wealth, and we were pressed to adjust the schedule with just two sets of massaging hands."

"Because one masseuse departed?" I asked. "A sudden dis—"

"—disappearance, Mrs. DeVere? We prefer 'unexpected departure.'" He smiled sadly. "At times, an employee becomes homesick and slips away without giving notice. We are inconvenienced, but undeterred. No masseuse is required to remain at Health-to-Wealth property without a bit of free time. Each enjoys a day of leisure in the interval when one group departs and another arrives. Perhaps you noticed the amusement park rides at Kingston Point? Our young women masseuses have already found the rides and other amusements to be a joy."

His smile deepened. "We are a center for life's restoration, not confinement. It happens that one of our clients left his tent and disappeared into the woodland a few nights ago, a fellow whose juggling skills might have made him a forefront entrepreneur in the art so prized for entertainment."

Roddy said, "Mr. Ferris, whatever your purposes here—"

"—a single purpose, Mr. DeVere, the one-and-only purpose is to restore health to those who seek a greater life with wealth. The poor may pretend that poverty is a blessing, but we know better."

"Mr. Ferris," Roddy said impatiently, "the sound of rushing water is audible. We insist on an inspection."

"Of course...if you will follow me."

Cedric Ferris led us around the back of the tents and cook stove and wheelbarrows, past the horse and cart, and then through a screen of trees at the opposite side of the clearing, where, once again, Roddy and I stood agog at the sight before us. A dozen or more bathers were up to their necks in a pool that looked as though a creek had been widened and deepened.

The bathers were bobbing their heads sideways in rhythm, both men and women as far as I could tell. All wore bathing caps. Their loose clothing and towels were spread across nearby bushes.

"Vanessa was so pleased to see the beaver dam at this location," Cedric said. "We always seek campgrounds near mineral springs or a shallow river wherever we plan Health-to-Wealth programs. But the beavers did us a favor here in...Ulster County, is it?"

"It is."

"As you can see," Ferris said, "the beavers took down a good many nearby trees, and a few workmen hired from the city of Kingston shoveled out the dammed area. In a day or so, the pool widened and filled nicely. The beavers have gone to another creek, and we have the benefit of the waterfall flowing from out there...." He pointed about twenty yards from the pool. "You see the falls?"

"We do," said Roddy. We squinted at the sunlight sparkling on streams and rivulets that cascaded down limestone ledges to flow into the creek below.

"That waterfall, as you see, nicely refreshes the bathing pool, Mr. and Mrs. DeVere. Before wealth, one must regain health."

"Mr. Ferris," said Roddy, "I must speak frankly to you. All of this...." My husband swept an arm to indicate the tents, the stove, the bathers, their clothing. "All of this must be removed without delay. The penalties for trespassing on private property are severe. Perhaps you mistakenly thought this to be unclaimed land, but—"

"—but nothing of the kind, Mr. DeVere." The cello voice deepened. "Be assured, Vanessa would never in the world conduct a Health-to-Wealth program beyond the bounds of the law. Whatever one may think property ownership, our program operates within the legal system." He smoothed his hair. "We have a contract for occupation of this property for the months of June, July, and August."

"Not possible," Roddy said.

"Allow me, sir...."

In the next moments, we trudged in silence to the larger tent where Cedric Ferris retrieved a leather satchel and produced documents with official seals. I stood by while Roddy read, reread, and returned the papers without comment.

"Mr. Ferris," my husband said in a terse voice, "I assume that all your equipment came in through a roadway?"

"By hired teamsters and carts on the first of June, Mr. DeVere. And our lumber was purchased locally. Your property manager helped a great deal, and both Vanessa and I appreciate his assistance."

His voice rose into the treble cleft. "Now, I suggest that you return by the roadway. Let me lead you to the entrance."

The sun began to dip west. Roddy and I were about to begin our long walk along a hacked-out road of packed clay. It would lead, Cedric Ferris promised, to the tar-and-gravel road to take us wherever we might be going. We did not say where, and he did not ask. On behalf of Vanessa and the Health-to-Wealth program, he sent his warmest wishes to our property manager.

"Roddy," I said, as we fell into step together, out of earshot of Cedric Ferris. "The masseuse who 'departed,' isn't it possible that she was...? I swallowed. "The woman whose ring...? The woman in the field?"

Roddy said, "F. P...Fiona."

"And that property manager...that man your father hired?"

"We must get hold of him, Val. The man issued a contract to that camp, a contract signed, sealed, and delivered by Roland Keith. It's a contract as tight as a tick."

Chapter Nine

"WE THOUGHT YOU WERE lost," Sadie trilled as we climbed the stairs to the veranda, every step weary and footsore from the long walk.

"We were getting up a search party," Alf chortled as he opened the front door.

Roddy said, "Good to be back." I only nodded.

We had not spoken as we measured the miles from the "grove" to the tar-and-gravel road and back to Kiddwood. Each of us, however, cast furtive glances at the place where the body had lain in the DeVere field in sight of the road, the 'Fiona' of the gold ring with a red stone. Her name could have been Scottish, but probably Gaelic, Irish, meaning the Fair One. Papa sometimes called me his "Fair One." Passing the place where Fiona lay, I felt for a moment as though a sister had died, and I imagined crushed foliage where nothing would ever grow in that place again, as if the young woman's death made it barren.

If Cassie were with us, could she sense something about Fiona? Would her 'vision' be helpful? If I mentioned this to Roddy, he would dismiss the very thought as wild superstition.

"And did you spy any vagabonds?" Sadie asked.

"Vagabonds?" Roddy shot me a warning glance.

"No vagabonds," I said.

"Never mind," Sadie went on, "you are here...here for the cocktail hour." She clasped Roddy's hand and winked at me as we entered the hall. "Poor things," she said, "mustn't let the woods get you down. The ice wagon came this afternoon, and we have set aside a full hour before dinner for cocktails. Isn't that the new name, Roderick? The cocktail hour?"

She did not wait for an answer, nor notice our fatigue. "Each and every Kiddwood guest," she trilled on, "is thrilled that Roderick DeVere will mix these new drinks. Alf dares you to know of Clarence's favorite, and Jack asks whether he can rest his cocktail glass on top of the piano. I told him Mr. Steinway would be upset."

"Sadie," I said pleasantly, "Roderick and I would appreciate a little time to refresh ourselves."

She blinked, for the first time seeing our rumpled clothing, our dusty faces. "Why, of course, poor dears. We are so pleased to have you back. As you wish...."

With that, we made our way down the hallways to our rooms. Doors closed, we undressed, donned robes, and took turns washing up in water that trickled from the bathroom faucets.

"Shall we talk in your room, Val? Or mine?"

We sat side by side on a small settee in Roddy's bedroom and faced a wall with framed lithographs of hunters with a pack of dogs and horses at a steeplechase. I thought of our dear French bulldog, Velvet. I thought of Comet and wished we were in the city. In an hour, Roddie would mix cocktails, and he would be asked about the water situation. What would he say?

"What can we make of all this, Roddy? That 'grove'—"

"—clearing, Val. The DeVere tract has a large clearing, an important distinction. Our task is to retrieve the clearing space, to rescue it from the 'grove.'" He bit his lip. "Above all, to resolve the matter of the young woman who was found...."

"Fiona...." I gripped my husband's hand. "Fiona comes first."

"Val...." My husband gently put his hand on my cheek and softly said, "The name has taken hold of you, and I understand because it sometimes occurs in court when Jane Doe becomes someone with a first name."

He paused, gazing into my eyes. "But the ring does not, in and of itself, mean that the deceased woman was 'Fiona.' The ring might have belonged to someone else. The deceased might have been a Millie or Sally or Annie, or—"

"—stop, please stop." I nudged Roddy's hand away and blinked back tears. Roddy was right on both counts, but I could not dismiss the name that could have been mine. "Could we talk about the grove...the clearing?"

"Yes."

"Those tents, Roddy, who owns them?"

"A private concern called Health-to-Wealth. The contract names Cedric Ferris as its legal representative."

"But who is he, really? And who is Vanessa? We should have insisted on meeting her."

"Perhaps she was not on the grounds."

"Where else could she be, Roddy? I think she was in the pool, leading the bathers in their exercise. You saw those heads bob side-to-side all together?"

"No, I didn't. I was watching Cedric, who seemed to be counting the heads. I'd guess each one of those bathers is a paying customer. Each one thinks a jackpot is just beyond a cash payment for a quota of nights in a tent, bathing in a cold pool in the woods, and some sort of a dietary plan."

"That vegetable concoction, I said. "It smelled terrible."

"And something else, Val. One of the tent flaps was open as we passed, and I looked inside. Someone lay on a bed."

"Napping?"

"No, lying supine."

"Supine," I repeated, remembering the word meant lying on one's back. "On the bed," I said, "was it a woman?"

"A rather corpulent man," Roddy replied tartly, "being kneaded by a young woman."

"Oh," I said, "a masseuse?"

"If that is the right word for what I saw."

"What do you mean?"

"You know what I mean, Val. Don't be prissy."

"I am not prissy. What did you see?"

"Only a glimpse, Val. The young woman closed the flap when she saw me stare."

I rolled my shoulders and tightened my sash. "Who are those people, Roddy? One of them came out of the woods a few nights ago and juggled for the Kiddwood guests. That 'vagabond' escaped, didn't he?"

Roddy shrugged. "So it seems."

"But where did he go in the morning? Did someone come for him? And what are those people up to in their secret campground? Whatever goes on inside the tents, Roddy, the property belongs to your parents...and you, the trustee."

My husband's fretful gaze met mine. "You needn't remind me."

"And the young woman—'Fiona'—with pond weed in her mouth and bruises near her neck." I wailed. "Suppose she is the masseuse who 'departed?' Departed this life, lying in the field...we both peered at the field."

"Val...not now."

"Dead in the field...buried in the Kingston public cemetery."

"My dear...." Roddy held me tight. "Take hold, Val. We must take hold. Before we go to dinner, I will tell Alf that Kiddwood's water problems are probably caused by a beaver dam that we saw on the DeVere tract this afternoon. I will ask for a dogcart to drive into Kingston tomorrow morning. Alf will hear of my plan to see about see about workers to deal with the dam. Actually, I will stop at Wall Street to have a word with Chief Fitch about the 'vagabond,' and I will visit a telephone exchange to make calls to find out where to find the property manager as soon as possible. We must find Roland Keith. And we will take it from there."

Roddy put his cheek next to mine, his voice low as he spoke words that I already understood. "So many questions, but nothing will not be solved this evening. We have just begun...."

❧

"Presenting Mister Roderick DeVere, who is Kiddwood's very own Sultan of Cocktails!" Alf thundered. The guests had assembled in the parlor space, already dressed for dinner, as were we, Roddy in his tuxedo and I wearing an amethyst off-the-shoulder gown. Sadie had let it be known that the six o'clock cocktail hour would precede dinner, and the Kiddwood assemblage obediently appeared as she demanded, "on the dot." The piano was moved to make room for a table with glasses, bottles, huge blocks of ice resting on platters—and kitchen implements.

Seeing the impromptu barware, Roddy smiled pleasantly, though I saw annoyance in his blue eyes.

Alf boomed on, "On this rare occasion, the Kiddwood house of champagnes and wine is transformed into a café, where Sultan Roderick DeVere will prove his mettle with tools on loan from the kitchen." Alf chuckled and pointed to the table. "Your workstation, sir."

My husband's fixed smile measured the insult to a man whose *bon-vivant* sideline was a serious endeavor. For Roddy, cocktails were no trifling matter, and his barware at home was custom forged from Sheffield steel. He stepped forward to eye the spatula, the paring knife, the ladle, and an egg turner. No ice pick was to be found, but a chisel and hammer were hastily supplied.

So, Roddy was expected to improvise on the spot. Somehow, the "vagabond" juggler came to mind.

Alf called out like a field coach, "Jack...Jack Barrott, do play us café cocktail music. Go to it, man."

The reluctant pianist agreed when Roddy promised him the first cocktail, and the melody of *Daisy Bell* began to ripple as my husband surveyed the bottles, set a number of glasses in a row, and asked, "Who would like to try a version of the Alabazam?"

"Ala-whatever it is, for General Coleman and myself," the square-jawed man piped up.

"And does this Ali Baba contain spirits?" Edna asked. Roddy held up a bottle, and she proclaimed, "Brandy? Well, in this private home, we ladies may indulge, and nobody the wiser."

Edna tapped the dark-haired debutante on the shoulder of her vermillion gown. "Young lady," she said, "the cocktail hour is yours to enjoy...in secret."

The young woman spoke shyly. "Then, Miss Edna," she whispered, "I do wish to try the...Alabama, is it?" She hugged herself, alarmed by her own bold move.

The debutante, like everyone here, knew that all women who surrendered to the adjective, "lady," were forbidden by the rules of etiquette to imbibe beverages stronger than wines in a public place and in most of the "better" homes as well. Ladies' after-dinner liqueurs were permissible, probably because the glassware was the size of a thimble. Otherwise, the cocktails were solely reserved for men in this day and time.

I intended to break this ridiculous rule, but not just yet. My in-laws were still mortified that their son-and-heir had married a Wild West "gal" and would torment Roddy no end if I ordered a gin martini at Sherry's or a rye Old-Fashioned at Delmonico's. Or another liquor drink at the Waldorf-Astoria dining room.

But when the time does come, count on me. And count on the weekly scandal sheet, *Town Topics*, to slather my breach of decorum across its first page. Though I plan to beat the publisher to the punch by announcing my intention ahead of time. As an ancient saying goes, "the skillful warrior's energy is all about timing."

Roddy bowed gracefully, and I watched him measure brandy into the glasses, add a pinch of sugar to each glass, then the dashes of curacao and chunks of ice he hammered away with the chisel. He stirred each drink with the handle of the spatula. "For the ladies and gentlemen," Roddy said, "although this first Alabazam is to be presented to our music-maker, Monsieur Barrott!"

"And I will hold his glass for him between sips," Sadie chimed in, "lest Mr. Steinway be offended."

Laughter followed, and all pronounced themselves delighted. Roddy later told me the drink was a knocked-down version of a perfectly sound cocktail, which he detailed for my notebook:

The Alabazam

Ingredients

- Juice of ½ lemon
- Teaspoon of sugar
- Dash of seltzer
- 2 dashes of curacao
- 1 ounce brandy
- Ice (finely chipped)

Directions:

7. In large bar glass, add lemon juice, sugar, and seltzer.
8. Mix well.
9. Fill glass 2/3 full with ice.
10. Add curacao and brandy.
11. Stir well and serve. (Strain to remove ice if desired)

"Who would like another?" Roddy asked when ice began to rattle in empty glasses. "Another Alabazam?" he asked again, and the guests raised their glasses like eager school-children. General Coleman saluted, and the debutante in vermillion held her glass aloft with her eyes closed.

"Not just yet, Roderick DeVere," called Alf. "I have a request on behalf of my son." He sounded taunting. "By any slim chance, Roderick, is the Bottle Cocktail in your repertoire? If so, please mix a Bottle Cocktail for Clarence Kidd."

The request sounded like a challenge, and guests turned to see Clarence in the shadows against a back wall.

"Dear sir," Roddy called to Clarence, "do you prefer your Bottle Cocktail with brandy, or whiskey? Or must it be gin?"

Heads turned back and forth as if a lawn tennis match began. Clarence finally murmured, "Gin."

"And are you aware, Alfred," Roddy asked, "that your son's cocktail requires water by the ounce?"

"Water?" cried Sadie.

The room suddenly quieted, the atmosphere chilled at the very word. A moment passed, and relief was palpable with Alf's rousing, "Footman, a pitcher of water for the Sultan, if you please."

Guests soon merrily clustered at the table, watching my husband pour water from a pitcher as if working magic. He added clear-as-water gin, plied several bottles, and finally chiseled ice chunks to announce, "One Bottle Cocktail for Clarence Kidd."

Clarence did not budge from the back wall. Once again, it was Alf's voice that rang out. "Madam DeVere, If you please, would you do Clarence the honor?"

He meant, would I deliver the drink, a request verging on insult. Did my western youth somehow make me Alf's saloon girlie? Roddy's chin thrust forward, but I took the cocktail before he could object, smiled, and made way among guests who parted like the seas.

Clarence received the drink with a surly thanks, and I curtsied, a deep and lingering curtsy that prompted light applause from the guests but gave me a close, unexpected look at the man's bare ankles, which were red and blistered, doubtless from poison ivy when he went to the "grove."

Rising, I met his uneasy glance. "No matter," he said, apropos of nothing. A metal gadget in his empty hand must be the cigar lighter Roddy mentioned, "No matter at all." He elbowed me away as he sipped his drink.

I hastened back to the table as Roddy called, "Cheers, Clarence." Jack Barrott again launched into *Daisy Bell*, and Roddy mixed Alabazam cocktails for Edna and General Coleman, whose medals dinged against his glass.

Guests began to sing, *"Daisy, Daisy, give me your answer true...."*

Roddy beckoned me close.

"I'm half crazy, all for the love of you....

"It won't be a stylish marriage, I can't afford a carriage...."

"Roddy," I said, "please fix me a drink. I want something sweet, something pleasant. Not too strong, Roddy. Just strong enough."

Chapter Ten

THE DAY DAWNED OVERCAST and humid. Dressed in a light woolen skirt and cotton shirtwaist, I joined Roddy as he sat for a full breakfast before setting off to Kingston in a dogcart.

Roddy told Alf that he would bring back a few liquor selections from Kingston and wanted a dogcart. Our host was "pleased as punch" to order the cart and agreed that a Western Union wire must inform Rufus DeVere about plans to dig out the beaver dam. He offered to send a limestone mining crew to blast the dam because dynamite was quicker.

To me, *dynamite* recalled one terrible explosion in a silver mine and my papa's close call. Four men were "blown to atoms," according to the newspaper. Chilled at the thought, I nonetheless kept quiet when Roddy recounted the offer.

Alf insisted that the dogcart be pulled by Sweetie, a Cleveland Bay horse. Nothing to do with Ohio, he had said, but a Yorkshire breed born to drive.

Roddy set off by nine o'clock, leaving me to the muffins and pastries and wondering how much time remained before the beaver dam falsehood would be exposed here at Kiddwood. Any day, the "vagabond" trespasser would be traced to the "Health-to-Wealth camp—and possibly involved in death on the DeVere property...Fiona's death. The stranger's sudden appearance from the woods was as startling as his juggling was amusing, but the tent camp, the mysterious Vanessa, the smooth-talking Cedric Ferris, and all the rest would have to be accounted for. Clarence had seen it all, but how much did he tell his father? His mother? He was evasive when Roddy tried to pin him down. I caught glimpses of him fiddling with the cigar lighter, a brass gadget like a tiny lantern. The Kidds' son was a mystery, somehow pitiable but wily too.

Alone in the morning room, I chose a muffin and asked the footman to bring my tray to the veranda, imagining a few minutes to myself. Instead....

"Valentine DeVere, the veranda is ours once again."

"Good morning, Edna."

"Just getting a start on reviewing this dreadful book, *The Awakening*. I tell you, if readers take it to heart, the American family is doomed. The book is an assault on respectable husbands and fathers. The main woman character is a slut. Fortunately, she drowns herself and so teaches a lesson to one and all. The irony is, her name is Edna."

"Then your review must vindicate every Edna," I said, wishing I stayed indoors. I sat down.

"And tell me, Valentine, is Roderick resting from his labors at the bar?"

"He is on his way into Kingston," I said, "for errands and cocktail hour supplies."

She closed her book and put down her pencil and note-book. A mischievous smile played at her lips. "So, Valentine," she said, "does your Roderick have a sense of humor?"

I assured her Roddy enjoyed jokes and a good laugh.

"Then, Valentine, why did your husband not appreciate Sadie and Alf's cocktail bar joke last evening?"

"What joke?"

"My dear, did neither of you catch the joke?"

I took a bite of muffin, shook my head, and waited for the likely barb.

"The kitchen implements," she said. "The spatula, the egg turner, and the rest."

"They were a joke?"

"Well, of course they were. We expected Roderick to take one look and burst out laughing. When he set to work, we all thought he got the joke and joked right back."

"So, the utensils were—"

"—a practical joke. I told you, Sadie is a practical joker, and Alf is not one to veto a good prank."

The muffin tasted like sawdust, and the footman came just in time for the Royal Worcester two-ounce coffee refills? Three?

"I believe," I said, "that my husband feared offending the Kidds by objecting to the...the barware."

Sadie asked the footman to bring her a scone. "Well, my dear," she said, "you need to know that amusements at Kiddwood run the gamut. These late spring days go on for hours, and outdoor games only take us so far. Croquet or badminton, an hour in the saddle on these trails...." She waved at the distant trails. "People like to enjoy surprises," she said, "and Sadie and Alf keep it lively. They have a knack, even when it rains."

"I'll tell Roderick about the joke," I said.

"Oh, you must." She leaned across the small table. "And did you have a chance to ask him about Mandy? Amanda Sterling?"

"Not just yet, Edna...so much going on."

"When you do," she replied, "you must remind him of what he said about her hair."

I lifted my cup and pretended to sip.

"He praised her 'tresses of spun gold.'"

My ear tips burned. "I'll try to remember."

"You must." She took a long look at my dishwater blonde hair and thanked the footman for the scone.

I would have fled, but Alf appeared, waving a pair of rubber Wellington boots.

"Ladies, good morning...and a special greeting to you, Lady Valentine DeVere." He dropped the boots at my feet. "Not Cinderella's footwear, but these Wellies ought to do. I hereby invite you to tramp with me to the old Iron Mine Number One. Are you game?"

Were the two guests pulled from the mine by police last autumn "game?" Could I plead a sudden headache?

"The former Valentine Mackle ought to have mines and mining in her bloodstream," Alf said, "and so, we will make haste before the heat drives us indoors, but first, a short visit to the library, which is really my private office here at Kiddwood. I have something special to show you."

He eyed the book on the table. "Edna, we leave you to the author being guillotined by your pen, as per usual?"

"Truth be told, Alfred," she replied.

He pretended to cringe, then said, "Fifteen minutes until rendezvous at the library. We will then depart from the rear service entrance. No dawdling, Lady Valentine."

I changed into a culottes skirt, and Willa found me a wide-brimmed hat. "The sun can burn you on a cloudy day, ma'am," she said, "and Mr. Kidd's mine is a good ways off."

She pinned on the hat. "And those boots? Do they fit you? Many a lady guest comes limping back from that mine. The young lady yesterday? She took dinner in her room last night, if you get my meaning?"

I vowed not to limp, asked a footman the directions to the library, and walked stiffly through hallways in the rubber boots to enter a high-ceilinged room with clerestory windows, books, a fireplace, a long table, a globe, and a glass-front cabinet where Alf stood grinning ear to ear.

"Come over here, Valentine. Something you ought to recognize on these shelves."

I approached warily, as if he might pose a test that I would fail and give him fodder for jokes at my expense, then laughed because the objects displayed behind glass were a museum of my youth. "A miner's hammer," I said, pointing, "and there's the drill."

"Hammer and drill," Alf repeated, "from the old iron mine. The basics of hard work that pays off, as your Old Man found out in the silver mines." He put his fingers against the glass. "Sadie wanted to put knick-knacks in this cabinet, but I said, absolutely not. A miner's hammer and drill are worth their weight in gold." He beamed. "And now, Lady Valentine, to the mine...."

We stepped in silence to the rear service entrance, where crates and bushel baskets of produce were being pulled from a grocery wagon by a muscled deliveryman. I stood by Alf on the little porch while footmen took the load inside to the kitchen.

Leaping onto the wagon, the driver took the reins, touched his cap, and called, "Morning, Mr. Kidd,"

"Morning, Hank."

Hank? Hank Boynt?

"First delivery of the day?"

"Pretty near, sir." He whistled to the team and drove off before I got a good look at the man who might have found the body on the DeVere tract.

And might have driven the "vagabond" from Kiddwood on that early morning days ago.

Unnerved. I was unnerved. Kiddwood threw me off balance. I squinted at the dull silver sky and pledged caution.

From now on, I would pay close attention until we said goodbye to this country house. For good.

Alf handed me one of two stout walking sticks, and we stepped off the porch. "Hardwood ash," he said, "both sticks come from an ash tree on Rufus and Eleanor's property when they first got the option on it. What do you think of that?"

"Very nice," I said. My stick felt clumsy and thick.

We circled around the house and set out past the croquet and badminton grounds, then struck out in the opposite direction from the stable and the fence at the property line. The earth felt soft underfoot, my boots awkward. Alf's footwear looked snug. His walking stick looked thinner, easier to manage. He wore a sun helmet, like the explorers.

Like my friend Cassie's husband, Dudley, who spent weeks in jungles in search of fossils and at times used his hat as a wash basin, a hat with a double purpose.

"Iron mining," Alf said, "has been important here since colonial times, and could still be so today." He pounded his stick at the earth. "But in Minnesota the Mesabi range put us out of business...biggest iron deposits up there, and ore boats to ship it across the Great Lakes. You've seen the Lakes?"

"Lake Michigan in Chicago," I said, and left it at that. A recent, distressing visit to the "City by the Lake" need not be detailed.

We tramped on, and Alf grew more animated as the house receded. "You'll see the old works," he said, "the mine and the furnaces too, and bee-hive kilns. In the old days, charcoal fired the smelting furnaces, and the rock crusher doubled the output." He added, "Hats off to Queen Victoria. In her heyday, iron was in demand for balconies, for fences, railings, and all sorts of decorations. I say, when Victoria really ruled, iron ruled too!"

He jammed down his walking stick. "Then, before we knew what hit us, Carnegie took over with steel mills. But no matter, we moved on to cement. So much good limestone to mine around here, so the crushers do the job, and the powdered stone 'cooks' in the big kilns. Long as we have the limestone, life is good."

He gazed ahead as if to see the limestone kilns. "They tried to make concrete without cement, and they came crawling back...tail between their legs, you might say." He stopped and turned to me. "Just imagine if your old man tried to work raw ore without quicksilver."

He meant mercury, which seemed to make the men sick. Papa tried every which way to find a substitute, but he never could.

"Where would the Mackle company be? Where would your old man be?"

"Alf," I said quietly, "my papa passed away a few years ago."

His neck and cheeks reddened. "I didn't mean...I wasn't sure."

I did not point out that Papa's obituaries filled newspaper columns coast-to-coast.

"Maybe I didn't keep up," Alf said. "No offense. Anyway, it's a new day for Kidd & Company. Our outlook is shiny bright as long as the limestone holds up. Supply, that's the long and short of it."

Was "Kidd & Company," I wondered, solely Alfred Kidd's enterprise? It seemed farfetched to think the stylish Clarence took any active part in the family business of cement. His fixation appeared to be his yacht and cigar lighter.

I stayed silent as we entered a broad marshy field. With each step, the mud sucked at my boot. I could easily fall, and my calves and thighs cried out as the useless walking stick sank down every time Alf urged me to trust it and high-step my way through the marsh. "Not much farther," he said. "Sadie tells me I ought to drain all this, thinks mosquitos will set up shop."

We crossed onto firm ground at last. "Catch your breath," Alf said. "Sadie calls the marsh a swamp."

"Not a walk in the park," I said.

"Everybody gets winded, but you, Valentine, did pretty well, better than Sadie's cousin, and he played football."

I gave him a tight little smile.

We approached two beehive-like domes of stone and a brick structure like a fort that had partly crumbled. Beside it, a dark, cavernous opening was covered with a grillwork of bars, like a jail.

Alf propped his walking stick against the brick building, and I propped mine.

"To have you here…what can I say? The daughter of the famous Mackle silver mines right here at the old Kidd Iron Mine Number One."

He stepped toward the barred entrance to the mine. "Come over here, Lady Valentine. I don't do this for everybody... Let's have a look."

He pulled hard at the grillwork, which groaned but yielded, exposing the pitch-black opening of the old mine shaft.

"Look familiar?"

What was I expected to say? My papa always said that a mine meant wealth—and death. Men's hard work brought riches from the earth but always cost lives. A mine, Papa said, was a vault of wealth and a tomb. He had his share of near misses, and he prayed for the miners. And did his utmost for safety.

What was I expected to say to Alfred Kidd? As it turned out, he wanted me to step into the shaft.

"See if it feels like a silver mine, Lady Valentine. You toured your old man's mines, didn't you?"

More than toured, I had accompanied Papa on inspections countless times. I simply said, "The Nevada silver mines attracted visitors, Alf. And yes, I took tours."

"Then step in and see how it feels."

Was this an invitation? Or a dare? The Kingston police rescued two of the Kidds' guests from this mine shaft last autumn. Was I to be number three?

Or would it be too late for a rescue, my body retrieved?

"Go right ahead."

"I'd rather not."

He shrugged nonchalantly but squinted, eagle-eyed. I squinted back at him. In days to come, I would question whether Alf meant to shove me into the mine shaft. His touch on my shoulder hardened into a grip that steadily pushed me forward as the black shaft yawed closer. The grip released only at the last second, when I thrust my left knee just behind his right knee, which tripped him.

Another lesson I learned from Papa, just in case.

Without another word, Alf regained his footing and slowly pulled the grillwork over the shaft. The day was hot, but cold sweat ran up my spine. "Shall we return?" I said brightly, reaching for the thinner walking stick. I smiled. "Shall we...?"

I turned to start the trek back, and Alf fell into step several feet away from me, but subdued. The rubber boots chafed my feet, and the marsh loomed in front....

I paused briefly, no more than a minute, to remind myself of the Irish bogs that Papa described crossing as a boy. For my papa, I would march forward and keep my balance. And I would not be seen limping back to Kiddwood.

"Roddy...." On the bed, my husband lay on his back, his hands cupped behind his head, his eyes closed.

"Roddy, are you...?"

"Asleep? Far from it." He sat up. "I've been back for a little while. It's lunch time, Val, and I've waited for you." He leaned for a kiss and peered closely at my face. "Are you feeling all right?"

In my husband's blue eyes, a shadow of distress. "And are you?" I asked.

"Quite a morning," he said, "starting with the dogcart horse."

"Sweetie?" I sat down at the foot of Roddy's bed. "Tell me."

"I should have listened to the groom. He warned me the Cleveland horse was balky, especially in harness. But Alf's orders...." Roddy rubbed his eyes.

"And so?"

"And so, I thought the groom was mistaken because Sweetie trotted nicely into Kingston. I visited Western Union and the telephone exchange, then purchased a few bottles from Bauer's Hotel bar. I also had a word with Chief Fitch. When I started back, Sweetie had other ideas."

"Meaning what?"

"She became a different animal, indifferent to the reins and the whip. We narrowly missed a deep ditch, which is now christened with scotch and rye whiskey. And vermouth. And maraschino cherries."

"The bottles broke?"

"Smashed. The package tumbled off the dog-cart into the rocky ditch. A few bottles are small price to pay."

Roddy reached for my hand. "It was close, Val. The cart would have been destroyed, and Sweetie probably put down."

"And you?" I clasped his hand tightly.

"I like to think I would have jumped clear."

My husband's horsemanship met the gentlemanly standard, which was quite high. "Like locoweed," I said.

"What?"

"Different wild plants in the West. The livestock graze on them and go crazy. Maybe Alf is Mister Locoweed, Roddy...I'll tell you all about the walk to the iron mine. But first, what about the property manager? Did you—"

"—track him down? I think so. The secretary in his New York office says he has appointments in Poughkeepsie tomorrow morning at a hotel."

"So, we will go to Poughkeepsie?"

"By train, we must. And something else, Val."

"Which is...?"

"Which is...." My husband hesitated, then spoke fast. "Chief Fitch talked to a man who came from Newark, New Jersey, in search of his daughter. He thinks she might have come to Kingston. He filed a report, and the chief suggested he put her description in the newspaper. He brought it to my attention because of her name."

"Her name is...?"

Roddy took both my hands in his. "Fiona Peebles."

I swallowed but my mouth was dry. "The engraving," I said, "the engraving on the deceased woman's ring...*'Fiona from Papa.'* It's her father, Roddy. It has to be her father. What should we do now?"

"We should go into lunch. We should applaud when Jack Barrott plays the piano. We should keep our heads down and never once let our eyes close."

Chapter Eleven

THE KIDDS AGREED THAT a talk in Poughkeepsie with the manager of the DeVere tract was necessary, and their groom drove us to the depot. Our standing at Kiddwood, however, seemed up in the air. It was noticed that the DeVeres spent a bit too much time by themselves, when guests were expected to be good sports, including Roddy who was to remedy the water shortage.

Yesterday afternoon, Sadie circulated with "pointers." Roderick must enjoy croquet, and Valentine must take her chances at badminton with Kiddwood's fiercest competitor. Roddy won his match against General Coleman, but I lost badly to Edna Rossiter. ("Edna's racquet is her badminton guillotine," Alf chortled, seeming to enjoy beheading as a favorite quip.)

Indoors after the games, Jack Barrott was dispatched to time-honored favorites when no one proved able to sing along to the new syncopated rag-time. So, strains of *The Band Played On* and *Ta-ra-ra Boom-de-ay* filled the indoor space. By the cocktail hour, Roddy handled proper barware but joked with a straight face that he would miss stirring drinks with the spatula. He improvised the ingredients but did not mention the episode with Sweetie. Nor did Alf inquire about the Cleveland Bay horse. Nor did our host hark back to our morning at the iron mine. Clarence did not appear for cocktails, and Roddy and I turned in shortly after dinner at my husband's insistence that we must be alert for the Poughkeepsie meeting.

The train was a local "milk run" that stopped at every hamlet but let us talk in private. "Roddy," I said as we rounded a curve, "you're sure about the contract your father signed with Roland Keith?"

"While my father paced and cursed his bad knee? The answer is, yes."

"And the contract that Cedric Ferris showed you at the tent camp. It was legally binding?"

"To the letter."

"Then, what can we say? What remains for a discussion?"

Roddy glanced at the window, doubtless thinking of how to explain the contracts so I could grasp key points.

"There are terms of 'consideration' in a contract," my husband said at last. "Both parties bring something of value to the contract, but if one party is found not to have the 'something,' then the contract is terminated."

"So," I said, "your parents provided the property, and Roland Keith offered experience as a manager."

"They did, and he did, yes."

"But you learned that Keith had defaulted on mortgages and got sued," I said. "And the tenement he managed caught fire, and children died. And...and he would be in jail if the tenement's insurance company had not gone bankrupt."

Roddy's side-eye look meant that he had just heard a wish for justice.

"Maybe not jail," I said. "Maybe fined?" Roddy nodded. "But the contract on the DeVere tract would be canceled."

"If that were the case."

The train car was stuffy with cigar smoke. "So," I said, "Roland Keith is free to conduct business as a property manager."

"He is."

"But the second contract, Roddy...for the Health-to-Wealth tent camp?"

My husband bit his lip. "The contract with Health-to-Wealth is not the problem, Val. The obstacle is the agreement my father signed with Roland Keith...Keith Property Management."

Roddy's jaw tightened. "It allows the manager to subcontract at will for the benefit of both parties. A clause forbids the exploitation of timber on the property and prohibits the operation of petroleum-fueled machinery. Otherwise, Keith can authorize activity on the tract for financial gain that is deemed mutually beneficial to both parties."

"Meaning that Keith and your father both profit from the tent camp?"

Roddy nodded. "Ten percent to Keith, the rest to 'R. DeVere.'"

Through the trees, the Hudson River glistened on the left side of the train, then disappeared behind the trees, then shone again. "Roddy," I said, "surely your father did not mention earning additional income from the tents?"

"Of course not. My father knew nothing about the Health-to-Wealth scheme, Val. He would never go along with such a freakish idea, and Mother would be horrified."

My husband glanced at the river. "The language of law is precise, Val, but the terms are deliberately wide...general. The courts are filled with cases involving specific applications. In this instance, a suit would be filed alleging that the subcontract violates the initial contract...that Keith Property Management is in violation because Health-to-Wealth breeches the contract with R. DeVere."

"But does it?"

Just then, an infant in the car wailed in decibels that silenced everyone, but the clouded expression in Roddy's eyes said he was far from certain. The train slowed, the conductor called, "Poughkeepsie...next stop," and we braced ourselves for the property manager who let children die in a fire.

The Nelson House hotel, a few blocks from the rail depot, looked long overdue for a refit. Roddy's pocket watch said 10:51 a.m. as we entered the lobby to look for Roland Keith and faced furniture in faded maroon with tassels the color of dead leaves. By a rear window, a grizzled man in a wing chair rattled newspapers, and a young man with a sample case circled the threadbare Brussels carpet, muttering to himself.

"Drummer," Roddy whispered, "...drygoods man rehearsing his sales talk."

"Can't be him," I said.

Roddy motioned to a back corner, where a wiry man perched on a straight-back chair and tapped one foot as he leaned toward his companion whose back was turned to us. A head of well-tonsured dark hair and the shoulders of a contoured coat came into view, along with a snowy French cuff at arm's length when the man gestured to his companion.

"So, evict them," said a robust baritone voice to the wiry man. "Do your job, evict them all."

The foot tapped faster, and the wiry man said something inaudible until the baritone voice repeated, "Evict them without delay, and let me know at once."

The man stopped tapping, jumped up, and brushed past us as he left the lobby.

Arm-in-arm, we went to the chair where the head-and-shoulders became a man who rose at once and bowed. Roddy said, "Mr. Roland Keith?"

"Mr. Roderick DeVere, I believe?" Neither man spoke as each appraised the other.

My husband had a quick, early morning shave, but Roland Keith might have stepped from a tonsorial parlor that trimmed his velvety black moustache and long side-burns and toned his skin to a ruddy glow. His navy-blue cheviot suit with a gold watch chain across the vest was a contrast to the sad furniture. His light brown eyes offered a cagey welcome.

Roddy introduced me, and Keith motioned at a sofa while he settled into an armchair and put his soft, creamy wide-brimmed hat on a table.

I noticed for the first time that Roland Keith's left coat sleeve was pinned up at the elbow. The man had lost his arm.

"My office alerted me that a Mr. Roderick DeVere was likely to call here at the Nelson House," Keith said in a pleasant voice, "but my secretary failed to say that I would have the pleasure of meeting you, Mrs. DeVere."

He smoothed a sideburn. "The Nelson House owes guests and visitors a worthy interior, but their new work won't begin for a few months. Our timing appears regrettable."

"The timing is necessary, Mr. Keith," Roddy said. "I believe you know that we are here in regard to your contract with my father, Mr. Rufus DeVere."

"And compliments to your father," he said, "a property owner who understands the wisdom of economic management."

Roddy sat forward. "Mr. Keith, let us discuss the issues that have prompted this meeting. Mrs. DeVere and I have inspected the DeVere property that you manage in Ulster County. The egregious problems that we find are twofold. First, the water flow on the property has been seriously disrupted. Second, the property is now occupied by persons who have not been authorized for tenancy.

Roland Keith's glinting gaze followed a solemn nod. "By contract, sir, the Health-to-Wealth organization is entitled to occupy the DeVere property for three months, beginning—"

"—the first of June," Roddy nearly growled. "I am aware of the agreement you signed without consulting my father."

"Mr. DeVere," Roland Keith said slowly, "if you are familiar with the law, you must know that Keith Property Management can enter into a separate agreement under two conditions. The trees are not to be sacrificed, and no petroleum product can fuel machinery."

"I believe," I said, "that Mr. DeVere and I saw a cookstove in use."

"Fired by charcoal, if I am not mistaken, Mrs. DeVere."

Roland Keith crossed his legs. "Touring the property," he said, "you met Mr. Cedric Ferris?" We nodded. "And Vanessa? Surely you met Vanessa."

"We did not," I said.

He seemed to relax but also to take command. "This explains a good deal about this meeting. If you had met Vanessa, I daresay we would be sipping champagne to celebrate the Health-to-Wealth summer in Ulster County...a nationally renowned program."

"Exactly how is it renowned, Mr. Keith?" Roddy asked for both of us.

"Why, the newspapers of course, the handbills...the coast-to-coast success that everybody admires."

The property manager gave us an arch gaze. "Forgive me," he said, "for assuming too much. In my line of work, you see, we keep an ear to the ground. We pay attention to folks' day-to-day scuffles, their energy, their ambition, their rise and fall...who is revered and who is disgraced. And why."

He ran a finger along his hat brim. "Frankly, most of us do not breathe the rarified air of those who dwell on the Upper East Side and spend summers by the sea."

Insulted, we were accused of ignorance by way of privilege, but this meeting would not work if pique got the better of us. If only Roddy stayed calm, as he must do in the courtroom.

"Mr. Keith," my husband said in an earnest voice, "won't you enlighten us?"

The manager plucked a gold time piece from his watch pocket and held it within our sight. "My schedule, I regret to say, does not permit the time needed for the story of Health-to-Wealth and its founder."

"Vanessa?" I asked.

"Vanessa Zee," he said, "from California, where her program began...near the City of the Angels."

"Los Angeles," Roddy said.

"On a beach at sunrise, the newspapers say, she stood on a chair and began to teach."

"Teach?" I said.

"Some say 'preach,' but Vanessa says that her gift is teaching that the golden key to wealth is...is...?" He looked to me to fill in the word.

"Health," I said dutifully.

"Exactly. Word spread, and men and women sought her out and followed her teachings. Some came as far away as Indiana...Pennsylvania too, and also New Jersey."

New Jersey.... Fiona's father had come from New Jersey. Probably a coincidence, but the name so raw in mind.

Roland Keith checked his watch again and spoke faster. "The story has been in all the papers. They say Vanessa was inspired to take her message across the country because she worried that seekers...she called her followers the seekers... could not journey all the way to California. Then Cedric Ferris came into the picture. He organized the business side of Health-to-Wealth. He made arrangements and talked to reporters. The tents were his idea. Cedric mapped out the year, and the travel started up."

Keith reached for his hat. "I tell you, the competition for this Northeast season was fierce. A Connecticut outfit bid for Health-to-Wealth, and Rhode Island too. Vanessa was tempted. She wanted to teach by the sea, as in California."

He began to rise. "I take credit. Connecticut was good, but the Hudson Valley won out. I gave it my undivided attention, and Cedric understood the advantage. If you have a question, let Cedric know, and he will be in touch with me. You must meet Vanessa, Mr. and Mrs. DeVere. You've never met anybody like her." He looked at Roddy. "Regards to your father. A bank cheque will be cut, and I predict everybody will be very happy."

Chapter Twelve

ROLAND KEITH WAS OFF with a nod to the train schedule. "Busy Saturday in the Hudson Valley...next train to Beacon." He left us on the sofa as a grandfather clock struck the noon hour.

"Let's look for a luncheon place, Val, where we can talk."

With the hotel clerk's tip, we walked to a restaurant with a long dining room, white tablecloths, and bentwood chairs. The Smith Brothers Restaurant also had a soda fountain and a candy counter.

Seated beneath a framed print of the Hudson River, Roddy ordered oyster stew and an omelet for me. On the center of the table, a pink carnation bloomed in a little vase. "Pleasant," I said. "And out of range of Kingston and Kiddwood too."

I nonetheless looked around and kept my voice down. "Roddy, the nervous man in the lobby handles Roland Keith's dirty work here in Poughkeepsie, doesn't he? And on your parents' tract, it's Cedric Ferris?"

"So it seems." Roddy poured us water from a carafe. "Val, are we thinking the same thoughts?"

"About the body?"

My husband nodded. "We would have expected Keith to say something, especially because of the contract terms."

"If he knows," I said. "And if Cedric knows...or Vanessa. Or anyone in the tents. So far, nobody knows a thing, and it's 'mum's the word'...and what about the 'vagabond?' How many of them are lying?"

"Val, let's slow down."

But I could not. "Or else the wagon driver who found the body...maybe he knows something. He could be the same Hank who delivered produce to Kiddwood yesterday. He said good morning, and Alf called him by name."

"He did? Why didn't you tell me?"

"Why?" My shoulders scrunched. "Because I tramped through a marsh and learned that Sweetie nearly pulled you into a ditch, Roddy. I meant to tell you. I forgot."

I sipped my water. I had not told my husband that our host seemed ready to shove me into the mine shaft. Roddy did not need that extra worry. I said, "If the vegetable driver is Hank...Boyd?"

"Boynt, I believe."

"Don't ask me for details, Roddy. I did not get a good look at him. But if he's the driver who found the body, his route might be the country houses and the tract too."

"The police chief planned to question Boynt again," Roddy said. "I will speak with Chief Fitch."

"Or we both will...both of us."

Roddy merely nodded at my forceful tone that came from guilt. I had not told about the vegetable wagon at Kiddwood's back porch, which was a mistake. This morning with Roland Keith had proved eye-opening but frustrating.

"Health-to-Wealth, Roddy," I said, "what is it? If it's that popular, how did we miss it? Roland Keith treated us as though we are deaf and blind to...what did he say, people's hopes and dreams?"

"Ambition, Val," Roddy said slowly. "I think the word is ambition." He added, "For material wealth."

"So, the tents on your parents' tract are supposed to make people rich?" I toyed with the little vase. "Can you guess how many nights I slept in a tent in mining camps when Papa dug at the rocks near the timberline...wind howling, sleet and snow and sometimes hail?"

"But Val...." Roddy leaned across the table and spoke slowly. "Wasn't it ambition for wealth that drove your father? The Mackle mines...the Mackle Mining Company...?"

I started to repeat what Roddy had heard from me countless times, that Patrick Mackle immigrated from Ireland to save himself from starving during the potato famine. I added that Kathleen Louise O'Hara reached these shores in a "coffin ship," then met and married Patrick in Brooklyn and went west with him to seek a better life. "Roddy," I said, "are you accusing my father and my mother of indecent ambition?"

"Nothing of the sort, Val. I am pointing out that your father's smart hard work paid off. He seized the opportunity, and your late mother joined to be his partner."

My husband took my hand across the table as I fought sudden tears at the thought of Kathleen Louise, the mother who died before I knew her. "So, then...where are we?" I asked, my voice near choking.

Roddy sat back, glanced at a family at a nearby table, and said, "Suppose you father had not gone west, Val. Suppose he toiled year after year in the Brooklyn shipyard, doing good work timbering the ships, earning hourly wages...as factory workers do to this day?"

"Why 'suppose' Roddy?"

My husband stroked his chin. His brows narrowed in a familiar lawyerly look. "I am thinking," he said, "about the Health-to-Wealth tents...about who is free to take the time to occupy them...and to listen to Vanessa."

I glanced up at the painting of the river. "No wage worker could do it," I said, "because every hour on the job must count."

"Precisely."

"So," I said, "you are thinking about ambitious people who already have the means to become Vanessa's 'followers?'"

"Exactly so...I'd guess that most already own small businesses and dream of expansion and huge profits. We saw them here on the way to this restaurant. A stationary store, a drygoods merchant, a druggist—"

"—a milliner, a tobacconist. Roddy, I see your point. Ambitious small business owners who are thinking...bigger.

They have the help to keep things going while the owner takes time out for Health-to-Wealth." I looked around the dining room. "Maybe this Smith Brothers Restaurant too. One brother could take the time."

"But only if Brother Smith or the druggist or milliner is wide-eyed enough to believe in a scheme that promises sure-fire wealth," Roddy said. "It's like a Wall Street stock scheme, but instead of scraping every last dollar to buy stocks—"

"—that dollar goes to Health-to-Wealth, doesn't it?" I said. "To Cedric Ferris...and Vanessa." I laughed sharply. "Easier to lose it all on Wall Street."

"Not necessarily, Val. There's a twist. Consider the harsh winters you and your father endured."

"And blazing summer sun at times. But what's the point?"

"Simply this...rigor can feel like a necessary step toward the great prize. The tents, the special diet, bathing in ice-cold water, and whatever Vanessa preaches ...they're the groundwork. The difference is, your parents did not subject themselves to a flim-flam scheme before they went west."

Our lunches arrived. I peppered my omelet, and Roddy floated oyster crackers in his stew. For the next several min-utes, we enjoyed the Smith Brothers' midday offerings. When the meal drew to a close, we ordered coffee and listened to the cheerful hum in the dining room.

I nearly held back intrusive thoughts as we sipped our coffee. Nearly, but not quite. "Roddy, on your parents' tract...

Fiona. What if she was the daughter of the man from New Jersey? The man who talked to Chief Fitch? Fiona...."

"Peebles," Roddy said. "Fiona Peebles."

"A father in search of his lost daughter...heartbreaking."

"A runaway, Val. Probably a runaway, like other young women who show up in Kingston. The chief said so."

We both approached and avoided this terrible topic. "But suppose the body was Fiona Peebles, Roddy? What if her death did not occur far away from your parents' tract? What if she was killed in connection to the tent camp and the strange Vanessa?"

My husband did not answer and could not answer. He paid our check, and I reached for my gloves. We would shortly board an afternoon train to Kingston. Facing the Kidds, we would sink into the mire of the DeVeres' tract, the excuses and lies about the water.

"Roddy," I said at last, "we must meet Vanessa, but what can we tell the Kidds? Alf might want peace and quiet, but Sadie is frantic for water so she can invite more guests."

I pulled on my gloves. "You told them about a beaver dam to be shoveled out, and that buys a little time. But if the water does not start to flow at Kiddwood, what then?

Roddy pocketed his billfold and gave me a grim smile. "The beavers, Val...the beavers can buy us time."

"What do you mean?"

"Fur. I mean fur...the coats in ladies' wardrobes, the lapels on gentlemen's better overcoats? If not sable or seal...."

"Beaver."

Roddy nodded. "Valuable beaver fur is the reason to delay the destruction of the dam. We will remind the Kidds that John Jacob Astor's fortune came from the fur trade. We will suggest that my parents could be interested in trapping at the opportune moment when the lodge is jammed with beavers. We will anticipate that the Kidds' splendid 'between' season will resume in the Fall. And to compensate for the inconvenience this spring, the Kidds can expect to benefit from the sale of the pelts. If the Kidds agree, we will have an interlude."

"An interlude," I said, "but what can we do? What must we do?" My strident voice began to attract attention in the restaurant. People stared, and Roddy took my arm. I would recall this to be one more "between" moment in a deathly 'between' season.

Chapter Thirteen

AT KINGSTON BY LATE afternoon, we took a hansom cab to Kiddwood, which stirred with farewells and greetings on the veranda. The dour bachelor was departing while new guests arrived, including a young woman in a bright yellow traveling suit with a gentleman companion who doffed his straw skimmer hat.

"Roddy," I murmured, "it's the couple from the steamboat...the young woman who tasted anise in your punch."

"So it is. Where have they been for the last three days?"

"Wherever they went," I said, "we're likely to find out. The elderly woman in a black cloak with them is doubtless their chaperone."

The young woman's high, reedy voice objected to the handling of her hat box as the footman hauled the couple's luggage to separate guest rooms. Alf chortled a welcome but winked to telegraph his wish for a private word with

Roddy. Sadie accepted the gift box of candy I had brought from Smith Brothers Restaurant.

"Hopefully not cough lozenges," Edna jibed. "The Smith brothers are selling lozenges they call cough drops."

"No Kiddwood guest dares to cough," Sadie said. "Our Ulster County air guarantees health for one and all. We will raise a toast to our pure air, will we not, Roderick…at the cocktail hour?"

"But first," Alf said, "let me handcuff our Roderick for a quiet word."

My husband disappeared with Alf, and I went to my room, where Willa "refreshed" last night's dinner gown with lace and ribbons.

"Willa," I said, "you mentioned a young woman who took dinner in her room, someone who returned rather lame from a long walk with Mr. Kidd?"

"I meant nothing by it, ma'am. No offence."

"No worries, Willa," I said. "But I might enjoy a word with her this evening."

"Too late, ma'am. She left this afternoon."

"I see." Pausing while the maid threaded a needle, I asked, "Were you in service at Kiddwood this past autumn, Willa?"

"All the year round, ma'am. The Kidds employ a few of us all through the year. We are fortunate in that regard. Jobs can be scarce."

I nodded and perched at the foot of the bed. "Last autumn," I said, "it seems that guests had mishaps while touring Mr. Kidd's iron mine, and the police were called for help?"

The needle stopped at mid-stitch, and the maid's eyelids fluttered. "You'd best ask Mr. Kidd about that," she said. "Now then, let me see about the lace." She hastened her work, hooked me into the undergarments and gown, touched up my hair, picked up her sewing basket, and fled.

I listened for Roddy in the adjoining bedroom and tapped softly. When the door opened, I leaned for a quick kiss from my handsome husband in his silk tuxedo.

Roddy gave me a peck on the cheek and spoke quietly. "We have a few minutes before I mix cocktails, Val, so let me tell you...tomorrow morning, the Kidds and their guests will be driven to church in Kingston, but you and I will take a dogcart to the DeVere tract to see about the beaver dam and the beaver lodge...or lodges."

"Alf agreed?"

"Not without cajoling. The fur idea surprised him, and he warned that Sadie will need convincing. I told him that we would go to the DeVere tract in the morning and take stock of the beaver lodges so that he can persuade 'the missus.' He told me to look out for "vagabonds" and be ready to report them to the police."

"Seriously?"

Roddy nodded. "Alf suspects that tramps or hobos have camped on my parents' property, but Clarence reported no such thing when he went to see about the water."

"Then he lied...lied to his father and mother about the actual camp. Why would he do that?"

"I don't know, except his mother is obsessed with entertaining, and Alf frets that it's late to invite guests for this 'between' season. The Kidds' favorites have made other plans, and Sadie is scraping bottom, as we might have noticed this afternoon, Alf said."

"The couple with the chaperone? The young lady in yellow and her 'gent' in the skimmer hat?"

"Most likely. I think Alf and Sadie are mainly worried about their son. They fear that Clarence will go abroad and cease his visits. They are terrified that he will go into permanent exile."

"Roddy," I said, "you talked with Clarence. What does he say?"

My husband frowned. "He hardly says anything. He'll talk about cocktails and ask if he can patent his cigar lighting gadget. He'll joke about the time we climbed up a sycamore tree until the high limbs cracked. He admits he saw the Health-to-Wealth camp and met Cedric, but he won't tell his parents and swore me to secrecy."

"You agreed?"

Roddy flushed, hesitated, and silently pushed back his shirt cuff to point to the tiniest scar near his wrist, the "memento" of a long-ago scratch, as I thought. He now told me that, at nine or ten years of age, he and Clarence were fixated on Cheyenne Indians, so they drew a steak knife across their arms, put them together, and declared themselves to be "blood brothers."

"Ridiculous," I said.

"Nowadays, of course. But Clarence brought it up last Thursday and asked me for the same loyalty we shared as boys. He said something needs to get worked out with his father, but until then, he will rely on me for 'old times sake.' Meanwhile, he likes to be in the shadows."

"Standing against the back walls," I said, "or is he lurking? It sounds lame to me, Roddy, and I'm surprised that you agreed to protect him."

"I am protecting our interests, Val. To expose Clarence's dishonesty would not help us one bit, not now. We are complicit in the lie as well, and we know far too little." Roddy took my arm. "Now, my dear, do you hear the tinkling keys of the piano?"

"I do."

"Jack Barrott at the keyboard, and Roderick DeVere at the bar. Smile, my dear...smile and sparkle. The evening has just begun."

Sunday morning saw the Kiddwood entourage depart for church in Kingston, while the groom hitched a sorrel horse named Granny to a dogcart. Alf had urged us to take Sweetie, but the stableman rejected the Cleveland Bay in favor of the sorrel. "Steady as a rock," he promised. "Nothing like Sweetie."

Cautious, we set off on this sunny morning, Roddy in a lightweight coat and trousers, while I chose a gored skirt, shirtwaist and gray jacket. We both laced up ankle-high boots.

The tar-and-gravel county road would take us less than an hour with Granny's steady pull and the light dogcart, but tension rode with us in the sunlight. What could we learn about the Fiona whose body was found on the DeVere property? And would Vanessa offer a hint? Or Cedric? Or someone in the tents? What about the 'vagabond' escapee?

When would the matter finally be settled, so we could go back to the city in peace?

"Roddy," I asked, "what about your parents? They know nothing of this beaver scheme."

My husband shifted the reins. "We might need to take a flying trip to the city, so I can talk to Father."

"And to your mother?"

"And Mother, yes."

A flying trip meant to go in-and-out fast. It meant we would merely pause at our home and return to Kiddwood in a day or two.

"But what will you say to them? What will you say?"

"I'll tell them that the water repair will take time. To mother, the promise of fur, and father will appreciate no further loss of timber."

"Isn't protecting the timber Roland Keith's job?"

"Beavers are wildlife, Val, and legally not considered to be poachers."

"So, the contract does not specify damage by beavers. I give up, Roddy." I fell silent. The horse's soft clop-clop failed to soothe, and the sorrel's reddish coat reminded me of Comet, somehow doubly depressing in this place. Would a flying trip permit time to visit our stable? Ride my horse?

Crossing into the DeVere property, I shut my eyes tight while we passed the weedy field where the body of Fiona Peebles had been discovered.

"A blessing that she was taken to the mortuary," Roddy said softly.

So, both of us burdened with similar thoughts while the horse plodded past the field. My breath had stopped. In my mind's eye, buzzards circled overhead, and the earth below now blackened.

We finally entered the woodland where the crude roadway had been hacked open just wide enough for the dogcart or a narrow wagon. Birds twittered, and snapping sounds echoed from deep in the brush. Squirrels? Mice? Please, no bears. Memories of grizzlies in the West could still haunt me if I let them.

The first sign of the Health-to-Wealth camp was, once again, the wretched odor of overcooked vegetables.

Roddy flicked Granny's reins as we entered the back edge of the "grove" just as the pottery bell sounded its dull, flat gong.

"We're here, my dear."

"Here," I whispered, stepping down to the ground while my husband tied the horse to a sapling. Unseen so far, we walked softly toward the clustered tents and the wood platform, seeing people emerge from the tents, each person carrying a camp stool toward the platform area. I counted eleven men and two women, each wearing a long, buff-colored caftan. None of them saw us as they unfolded the stools and took their places in front of the raised platform, where two figures stood on either side of a small table. A very tall man to the left wore the same buff caftan, though his sleeves were extremely wide. It was Cedric. On the right stood an athletic woman in a white dress and the dark blue cape of a nurse. On her head, a nurse's cap.

"Vanessa," I whispered. "It must be...."

"And Cedric," Roddy said. "What's on that table between them? It looks like a melon...."

At that moment, Cedric Ferris raised an arm to point in our direction. "Hello, visitors," he called in his musical cello notes, whereupon the assembled figures turned to gawk at us.

"Welcome to our visitors," Cedric repeated, "and we extend our warmest Health-to-Wealth greeting. Do we not, Vanessa?"

"Indeed we do!" she countered in a rich contralto. "Let us welcome our guests!"

Applause crackled, and the nurse held her arms wide as if to summon us from afar. I noticed two young women in white robes standing by the tents. Helpers? Maids?

"What should we do, Roddy?"

"Follow the leader."

I had not felt so utterly on display since my first ball as Mrs. Roderick DeVere in New York City. A glimpse at

Roddy's jawline meant he felt as awkward as I when we walked arm-in-arm toward the platform.

"Friends...new friends, we do welcome you! A fresh breeze...a view unparalleled in the woodland sublime! Join us! Join with us!" Vanesa's rich, warm contralto commanded the scene with a voice from the concert stage. She flashed a broad smile. Why did she dress as a nurse? Was she a nurse?

"You might desire to be seated in upholstered comfort," she continued, "but we have learned that nature is health's best friend. And so...." Her arms seemed to float like wings toward the platform planks. "...won't you join us here?"

Roddy and I sat on the bare wood platform edge and faced the assembly on the stools, the men who were variously bearded, clean shaven, bald, or hirsute, but all with wolfish eyes that glittered. They looked to be in their mid-thirties to early forties, as did the two women whose eyes also looked fierce, despite hair that was wound high and garments snugged close. Short or tall, the bodies before us were mostly concealed in the buff caftans that looked like burlap.

The boards that Roddy and I sat on reminded me that a Kingston lumberyard had delivered this wood at the beginning of the month. Who built this platform? Who drove the nails? The two white-robed women at the tents? They did not seem to participate with the others.

"Our favorite Sunday prelude," Vanessa said. "And Cedric, if you will, please...."

Her arms swept wide as if to conduct an orchestra, and Cedric Ferris took a knife from the table and split open a watermelon.

"For the season of mellow fruitfulness," Vanessa chanted, "the very melon that explorers of the New World discovered and called sweet 'Pink Snow.' And now for one and all, summer's Pink Snow for health…and may we be the good hosts who present the first offerings to our new guests.…"

Roddy and I were handed chunks of watermelon, after which Cedric and Vanessa invited the assembly to form a line to receive their fruit. The two white-robed young women stayed by the tents, but each man and woman in line took a piece of melon cut by Cedric and handed to them by Vanessa.

"Communion by watermelon…" Roddy murmured. "Blasphemy." He gathered seeds in his palm. Juice dribbled down my wrist.

When everyone had returned to the camp stools, Vanessa announced that "Reverend Cedric" would deliver his Sunday words while she took these precious moments to introduce the new visitors to Health-to-Wealth. She glided off the platform and crooked her finger to summon Roddy and me to the same large tent where Cedric had kept the contract with Roland Keith.

"Do sit down, please." Vanessa pointed to the folding chairs often found on steamship decks. She perched on a blanket-covered cot, removed her cap, introduced herself, and loosed a cascade of red-gold hair. My husband's intro-duction brought no sign that that the name, DeVere, was linked to this property in Vanessa's mind.

She smiled at Roddy and asked, "Are you a Libra?"

"I beg your pardon?"

"Your sign, Mr. DeVere?" She said, "your astrological sign? I am a Libra, a water sign."

Roddy said he did not know his sign. She asked about his birthday and offered to reveal his sign and its meaning.

I broke in. "Are we to understand that Health-to-Wealth is a religious organization? Or astrological?"

"Why, no...how droll." Vanessa's buttery laughter melted slowly. She winked at Roddy and said," Cedric offers a short homily each Sunday because so many of our clients are church goers. We thought he ought to get himself ordained."

"In what church?" I asked.

"I should remember...the certificate was by mail. He bases his homily on the prayer of Jabez." Vanessa steepled her palms and spoke in low, slow tones. "'Oh, that thou wouldst bless me indeed, and enlarge my coast.'"

"That's it?" I said.

"The Book of Chronicles, somewhere," she said. "It's not too wordy and follows up with pleas to be guarded against evil and so forth. The key is the enlarged 'coast,' meaning territory, meaning wealth. The Jabez prayer fits our program, you see, and Cedric talks about it each Sunday."

"With watermelon?" My short tone drew a sharp glance from my husband. "Watermelon is not in season," I said.

"Not in New York," she answered in fluid tones, "but Florida's ripe melons are shipped here and delivered to us."

Delivered by Hank Boynt, I started to ask?

But Vanessa held up both palms to signal quiet. She closed her eyes and murmured, "...please, guidance in this moment." Eyes open, she gazed at Roddy. "May I ease your inquisitive mind?"

"You may, indeed," Roddy said with a charming smile.

I wanted to pinch him. "Both of our minds," I said.

She held her gaze on my husband. "Mine is a story of health imperiled and regained," she said. "A child of California's orchards and groves, I took the earth's bounty for granted until illness struck and death drew near."

She unbuttoned her cape and ran a hand through her coppery hair. "My family despaired, but a good-hearted gentleman, a total stranger, heard of my plight and came to me with a bitter vegetable cure, which no sooner crossed my lips than recovery began...slowly but steadily. I learned that in years past, the gentleman's own life had been jeopardized, but he had recovered and amassed great wealth. It was he who joined the idea of health to wealth, and his inspiration became my life's purpose. I began to speak on the public beaches of southern California near my home. I stood upon a chair on the sand and spoke my piece."

I said, "So, you do preach."

"Absolutely not, Mrs. DeVere. I teach the principles of health. Perhaps you know the work of Sylvester Graham? Or John Harvey Kellogg?"

"Graham crackers," I said. "Kellogg's corn flakes?"

"You speak dismissively, Mrs. DeVere, but the quest for health in our country is vital and urgent...like the quest for wealth."

She threw back her cape. "We do not promise gold nuggets plucked from creek beds. Today's wealth triumphs with a mighty effort that begins with health. We offer a diet that removes all excitement from food. And we follow John Harvey Kellogg's *The Art of Massage*. Do you know it?"

She did not wait for an answer. "A manual this thick," she said, "with detailed instruction for manipulations for all constitutional conditions." She looked from Roddy to me. "The applicants for our massage program are required to study Kellogg before laying one finger on our clients."

"Your clients," Roddy asked, "are they with you all summerlong?"

She laughed. "Dear sir, our clients run businesses. Their time is at a premium, and they come to us for ten days. Each Health-to-Wealth program continues for ten days."

"Turnover," I said.

"Rotation," she countered. "We run the program all year round by rail and wagon...the tents, the chairs, the cook stove. From California to Arizona and Texas...winter in Florida. Surely you have seen our announcements in magazines...*Demorest's Monthly, Harper's Weekly*?"

Roddy nodded, but I knew he lied. She smiled at him, the face of an angel and a fox.

"Miss Zee..." I began.

"Oh please, it's Vanessa. My family name...so many syllables, and Zee is simplest. Do call me Vanessa."

"Mr. DeVere and I," I said, pushing on, "are guests at a neighboring country house called Kiddwood."

She seemed not to recognize the name.

"And it has come to our attention," I continued, "that a young woman might have passed away on this property."

She pulled her cape closer, frowned, and sucked her lip. "A most distressing rumor," she said. "And when did such a thing supposedly occur?"

"A week or so ago," Roddy said.

"And you know nothing about it?" I asked.

"Absolutely nothing," she said. "And I speak for Cedric too. If a mere wisp of such a rumor reached us, we would at once seek advice from Mr. Roland Keith. Mr. Keith is our manager, and he would be informed immediately, without hesitation. The reputation of Health-to-Wealth depends on honesty—and our results. Let me give you Mr. Keith's card...just in case."

She reached for the satchel that held the contract, and Roddy took the card with thanks but no comment.

Should we have told her that we already met Keith—told her right then and there?

Would our silence hurt us in days to come?

Roddy slipped the card into a pocket, and Vanessa cocked an ear. "Cedric," she said, "is concluding his Sunday message, and this Health-to-Wealth afternoon schedule means the bathing pool, so if you will excuse me...?"

She reached for the nurse's cap, and we stood, ushered from the large tent, ready to find our horse and dogcart at the edge of the "grove." The "clients," as Vanessa called the paying customers, were folding their camp stools and returning to their tents. One white-robed young woman walked toward a wheelbarrow, but the matching robed figure was not in sight.

That is, not until we reached the dogcart and Granny at the edge of the clearing, where the other young woman held a bucket and stammered, "Your horse...your horse... water, before you go."

Her dark eyes in a taut, narrow face darted from Roddy to me, and the tremor in her large hands caught my eye as she held the bucket up to the sorrel's muzzle, spilling more than the horse drank. "Thoughtful of you..." Roddy began, but she leaned close to me, pressed something wet into my palm, and muttered, "...people, peoples" then backed off and ran, her white robe flapping.

"What did she say?" I asked. "So nervous...could you hear?"

Roddy pressed his lips together until he untied the reins and sat hip-to-hip beside me. "Val," he said slowly as the horse pulled us into the woods, "I think the young woman tried to say a name. I think we heard her try to say the name, Peebles."

Chapter Fourteen

WE SPOKE NOT A word until the dogcart had reached the tar-and-gravel county road. The sorrel kept a steady pace, and our wheels bit the gravel to carry us from the bizarre encounter. Within an hour, Kiddwood would engulf us once more, and what would we say? What could we say?

Roddy asked, "What did she give you?"

"Vanessa?"

"That young woman with the water bucket." Roddy looked at my hands, both balled into fists as if to strike blows. The air felt tight in my bosom.

Slowly, I opened my fingers to see a small wad in my right palm.

"What is that?"

"I don't know." I looked closely. "She pressed it into my hand. It's...a scrap of fabric...wet." I squeezed, then smoothed it on my lap. "Black marks on it, Roddy...like writing, but I can't make out the word...words."

"Could it be the name? Fiona Peebles? Do you see an 'F' or a 'P?'"

"Roddy, you really think she might have meant Fiona—"

"—Peebles? I thought so. She seemed upset."

"Very." I leaned closer. "Definitely an 'F' but otherwise smeared...." I lifted the cloth scrap and laughed despite myself. "Maybe I need eyeglasses, Roddy. The letters seem to spell 'S-a-n-t-a'...and...would you believe 'Santa Claus.'"

My husband shot me a look. "Let it dry, and we'll see." He rolled his shoulders. "Did you get a good look at her?"

"Only her hands," I said. "...large hands for a slender woman. And nervous eyes. The water for the horse...was it an excuse to give me this little rag?"

"Maybe Cedric sent her to us, Val...or to you?"

"Or did Vanessa Zee? She took charge of us this morning, didn't she? The life story specific and farfetched too. Is Health-to-Wealth hers? Or is she under Cedric's thumb.... Or they are partners?"

"Collaborators," Roddy said.

My husband stayed stoic, but I blamed the senior DeVeres. Why their itch for a country house? It was late in the day for a big undertaking in the Hudson Valley. So far, their son and daughter-in-law were tasked with the Ulster County dealings. Eleanor and Rufus had not lifted a hand. A young woman was found dead on their property, and they were blithely unconcerned.

"Would you like to take the reins, Val?"

Without a word, I let the leather lace easily in my fingers, and the tactile feeling brought up memories of Virginia City when I drove wagons and buckboards. Since coming East, I had let myself be a passenger too often. At times, I felt as harnessed as Granny, the horse. Annoyance at my in-laws mixed with nostalgia, and I warned myself to keep quiet.

My final thought at the moment? That this wagon road smelled of softened tar, and the body of Fiona Peebles had lain in the field we were passing.

The Kiddwood Sunday dinner was nearing dessert when we arrived, and our host narrowed his gaze at Roddy and looked closely at me. Places were quickly set for us on either side of Alf, who raised a bushy white eyebrow to inquire about our morning. We agreed to say nothing about Vanessa but would weave our tale of beavers and timber.

How long could this story hold up?

"This one day of the week," Sadie announced, "we dine at midday after church. And we expected you to be back here, you truant DeVeres. Will you now begin with dessert and dine backwards? We are having *Bombe Nero*."

A bomb? The word jolted me, and Alf laughed. Our host announced that Roderick and the lovely Valentine DeVere would be introduced presently to the newest guests, meaning the couple from the steamboat, their chaperone, and a new bachelor with slicked-back hair and eager eyes. The others were now familiar from Edna to Jack Barrott, the dark-haired debutante, General Coleman in his dress uniform with gold braid and epaulettes, the square-jawed man and the others. Clarence managed a civil how-do-you-do. The Sunday sermon and the dinner had done their work. Smug rectitude showed on every face.

Suppose that Alf now probed us for details of the morning? Or gleaned information from slips of the tongue... probably mine. Or ventured into the tract himself to lord it over his son, though the old Kidd iron mine had its grip on the man. How had it happened that guests needed rescue by police last autumn? Were they enthusiasts, or did they try to placate Alf?

The next prospect to be offered the Wellington boots? Odds on, the young woman from the steamboat.

"Presenting..." Sadie announced, and we all looked up to see a dome of meringue borne aloft on a silver platter by a footman in full livery. Behind him, a second footman brandished silver servers, which he thrust like sabers to slice and serve. The mousse *bombe*, Sadie promised, was filled with "delights," but the *Nero* missed its flaming rum, she regretted. "Escoffier promises hot rum set alight, but our Roderick 'stayed too long at the fair.'"

"Is a fair nearby? the steamboat young lady called out. "I love a county fair."

"For godsake, it's a line from a ridiculous nursey rhyme," Clarence blurted. The table hushed. Alf and Sadie's son scraped back his chair and stomped out. Sunday dinner at Kiddwood had come to an end.

ex9

New York City felt like an oasis, if not an island in a fiery river. I dreamed exactly that scenario last night before today's flying trip to the city. In the dream, Roddy and I were swimming in a blazing river, but the island receded as we swam, and I feared we would drown.

At dawn, we prepared to catch the early train for the city. The Kidds agreed last evening that the senior DeVeres must hear the plans for their property without delay and directly from their son. Roddy added that my presence would help, so the Kidds did not press me to stay while my husband did his filial duty. Sadie seemed pacified that prize fur pelts were in the offing and that next autumn's between season would find Kiddwood water brimming for the household and every guestroom occupied.

Our train from Kingston ran on time, the ride smooth and swift. Roddy said we ought be at our front steps by noon.

We were. Our butler, Sands, welcomed us at the door, as did footmen Bronson and Chalmers, who sprinted to retrieve our luggage at the curbside hansom. Our forbidding housekeeper, Mrs. Thwaite, managed a terse greeting and, for once, the woman was a welcome sight at 620 Fifth Avenue.

But where was Velvet? We counted on our French bulldog to wriggle a furry welcome. She would roll over for a tummy rub and sniff for goodies. "Sands," I asked, "where is the dog?"

"Out for a walk?" Roddy asked.

Our butler, a figure of dignity and irreproachable con-duct, tapped his fingers against his trouser leg and cleared his throat. "Velvet..." he said, "has been a bit under the weather the last few days."

"Under what 'weather?'" Roddy asked. "Why were we not informed? Why were we not wired?"

Both footmen froze with our bags in hand and looked to the butler for response, as did Mrs. Thwaite. None of the four moved. Nor did we.

"Sir...and ma'am," the butler began, "we believe that Velvet might have eaten...."

"Something that disagreed with her?" I asked, alarmed.

"On the contrary, ma'am..." the butler said. "We found almost everything agreeing with her...too much."

"Overfed," Roddy snapped. "Are you saying the dog ate herself sick?"

They all looked sheepish except Mrs. Thwaite, for whom Velvet's purpose was shedding dog hair to be banished from every room.

"I take full responsibility for indulging Velvet," Sands said, "but as of yesterday evening, ma'am, your personal maid has taken charge."

"Calista," I said.

The butler gazed up at the frieze. "I believe that Velvet is to be found in your maid's apartment...or perhaps in your boudoir, ma'am."

"Thank you, Sands." I sprang upstairs to find Calista at work by my dressing table. Lying beside her on a down-filled cushion with her head between her paws, our Velvet.

My maid's "so good to see you, ma'am" saw Velvet stagger off the cushion to lick my hand, her little pink tongue hot to the touch.

"She's on the mend, ma'am," Calista said. "I sat up with her most of the night." The dark circles under my maid's eyes told of wakeful hours. "She's like the passengers' dogs on the coastal steamers," Calista said. "The friendlier the dog, the more the treats, and by and by, the poor dogs suffered ill effects."

My maid folded her hands. "I hope Mr. Sands won't take it amiss, but I took over, for everybody's sake. The household loves Velvet...almost everybody...but all that feasting did her no good. I said, enough."

"Enough," I echoed as we watched the dog approach a water bowl beside my dressing table and drink heartily.

Once again, I murmured, "Enough."

"Ma'am?" Calista smiled, pleased to see the dog sniff a shoe, as was I. "May I help in some particular way?"

The guidebooks warned against mistress-to-servant confidence for the sake of employers, but they got it backwards. In all sorts of ways I relied on Calista, but more than once drew the line.

For her sake.

"Shall I unpack your things, ma'am? And is this all, just one valise?"

"Because Mr. DeVere and I will return to the Hudson Valley in a day or two," I said.

"The country up the river seems quite enjoyable, ma'am."

"Not a dull moment, Calista."

Whispered words at the door called my maid away for a moment, and then she turned to say, "Mr. Sands wishes you to know that Mr. DeVere has been invited to lunch with his parents. He expects to return in the later afternoon and apologizes for any inconvenience."

To my mind, the phrase meant definite inconvenience.

Calista unclasped the valise and began unpacking the few toiletries, bottles and jars...and a small shred of fabric, which she held up. "Torn cloth, ma'am...."

"Oh, that..." I said.

Trash?" Pincering the cloth between thumb and forefinger, the maid stood ready to move toward the rubbish basket. "Trash, would you say?"

"I would say, Calista... if I could." My mouth had gone bone dry. "I would like nothing better. But for now, put the cloth on top of my dressing table. I better keep it in sight for the days ahead."

Chapter Fifteen

RODDY'S LUNCH WITH HIS parents freed me for an afternoon on the bridle path. Calista must have a nap, and Velvet could lounge on the cushion. I changed into my culottes skirt, jacket, hat, and boots, then dashed off a note to Cassie and sent a footman to the Forster home on Madison Avenue. If you are free this afternoon, I wrote, please join me for a horseback ride. I then approved our evening meal without a glance and snatched an apple and handful of walnuts to speed me on my way—with an extra apple for my horse.

On the spur of the moment, I also tucked the cloth scrap into my jacket pocket. The cloth from the camp might stir Cassie's otherworldly feelings if I put it into her hands. Perhaps she could decipher the blurry dark writing that looked like "Santa."

If Roddy were here, he would warn me not to encourage our friend's superstitions, especially as Cassie tried to tamp down the auras that consumed her. I would tell my husband that honoring friendship was uppermost in mind. Even if Cassie caught up to me on the Central Park drive, I would stand on principle.

Surely I would.

The aromas of leather and hay, of saddle soap and horses beat out the perfumes of Paris. The shuffling and stomping hooves, the nickering and neighing were music to my ears. Roddy's Justice paid no attention when I passed his stall, but Comet turned her head and nickered as I approached.

"Comet...girl...." I patted her nose, fed her the apple, and heard footsteps.

"Who is it...why, Mrs. DeVere...."

"Zachary."

"Gave me a turn, ma'am. I was not on the lookout for you."

"Sorry, Zachary," I said to our groom. "Mr. DeVere and I are in the city for a flying trip."

"Flying, ma'am?"

"It means a short time," I said. "A few days." The young man nodded to fix the term in mind, as I once had to do. In Nevada and the Colorado mining camps, we did not speak of flying trips.

"So, just a couple of days," I said, stroking Comet's neck. "She looks good. The new feed is working. What can you tell me about her kicking?"

He flashed a broad smile. "Ma'am, she cocked a hind foot on Thursday, and that was the last of it. Elsewise, she took to the park like she owns the place. Let me tack her up for you , ma'am." The young groom went for the blanket and saddle, the bridle, the reins—and my red sash.

"Her tail was flagged every time I took her out, ma'am, but Comet had no need of it. Would you want her tail tied today? She'd likely not need it."

I hesitated. The scarlet sash from my silk robe was a reminder of Comet's fatal kick that saved my life. Otherwise, the kicking was a menace. I said yes for safety's sake and watched Zachary work with the skill of a man whose hands moved in harmony with his work.

"Good thing you came along before I took her out, ma'am. She's happy it's you this afternoon."

I smiled at the sort of compliment my papa called blarney. "Zachary," I said as he tightened the cinch, "Mrs. Forster might join me this afternoon. If she comes for Bella, please tell her groom that I will be on the park drive closest to Fifth Avenue."

"Yes, ma'am. Count on me."

"I will." And I did. Neither of us spoke of our shared, harrowing experience in this stable just weeks ago. Zachary held the reins for me at the stable entrance, and in seconds I vaulted onto the U.S. Cavalry saddle that took me along the bridle paths of the East Coast. A nudge at her sides sent Comet into the bright sunshine and into Central Park. What could be better?

Better, actually, would be Cassie or another companion, since etiquette forbade a lady in Society to ride alone. But I could not care less today, even if gossips caught a glimpse and gave the senior DeVeres and their social set this tidbit about the Wild West woman who straddles a horse and rides by herself. The freedom from Kiddwood and escape from the Hudson Valley felt like a jail break.

Is this what the "vagabond" might feel? The juggler who fled the Health-to-Wealth campground, entertained at Kiddwood, and vanished by morning? Or did the "vagabond" flee his crime? Was he mixed up in Fiona Peebles's death? Did he kill her?

The sunshine, the blossoming flowers and the leafed-out trees darkened with these thoughts, and I looked about to catch a glance at a juggler in a buff caftan, though he would shed the camp garment. He would wear street clothes and could be anybody on a city sidewalk. I urged Comet to a trot to outpace these thoughts.

Cassie would join me if she could, but for now, I put Comet through her paces. On a straightaway, we slowed to a walk as a carriage approached from the rear and passed on our left side. The coachman frowned at Comet, and the twosome in the carriage turned their heads and whispered to each other until they were out of sight. I did not care.

At the stable just before four o'clock, my cool-down walk with Comet was done when a phaeton pulled up to the stable. The coachman tipped his hat. "O'Boyle," I said, recognizing the Forsters' coachman.

It had to be Cassie inside the closed carriage. Sure enough, O'Boyle carefully sidestepped my red-sashed horse and said to me, "Mrs. Forster invites you to join her when you are ready, Mrs. DeVere. She wishes to drive you home."

"In a minute, O'Boyle," I said, calling to the groom. "Zachary, let's untie the sash. I will take the chance that she no longer needs it."

Seated in the phaeton that turned and moved ahead, I wound the scarlet silk in my lap, pocketed it, and greeted my friend as if months had passed. "Cassie, I missed you this afternoon. Did you plan to ride with me?"

"I did," she said, "until Charlie and Bea raised a fuss about their dinner." My friend smiled ruefully. "First, my son complained that green peas invaded his mashed potatoes and 'ruined' his meal. His sister decided her potatoes were likewise ruined, and their nanny was beside herself, so I stepped in. By the time a truce was declared, it was too late for the saddle, but O'Boyle suggested the phaeton to drive you home. He took us around a few blocks to warm up, and here you were with Comet."

"Timing," I said.

"But you rode by yourself, Val." Cassie frowned, a tiny crease between her beautiful eyebrows. "Alone on your Army saddle, you know how people will talk."

"Cassie, I don't give a fig. I need to catch a breath in my own way. The Hudson Valley is a...a sinkhole. It's like a mine shaft giving way...a collapse. That's what I feel about Ulster

County. About the Kiddwood country house and property that Roddy's parents own. All of it."

"Roderick's parents own property in Ulster County?"

"Right beside Kiddwood."

Cassie put her hand lightly on my wrist, a touch she doubtless gave her children when needed. "Val, we can ride quietly, but if you wish to talk, I am right here."

Where to start? How much to say? Would the Kidds' water shortage be enough? Cassie recalled taunts about her "trances" at the Kiddwood weekend years ago." I could imagine Edna's jibes, Sadie's brickbats.

Suppose I also told my friend about the Health-to-Wealth tents, Cedric and Vanessa? The Poughkeepsie meeting with Roland Keith? Would all this be enough? I would be unburdened, and Cassie informed.

To a point.

The phaeton moved slowly but steadily as I began to recount the visit. "And the ridiculous Health-to-Wealth maneuver in the woods," I said, "supposedly a favorite all over the country, but neither Roddy nor I ever heard of it."

My friend's smile reminded me of the muses in oil paintings, all timeless and wise. "Val," she said, "if your magazines in the West included *Physical Culture* or *Health Reformer*, you would know about such things. If your papa was not busy mining silver, maybe he would have read *The Wilderness Cure*. And maybe Roderick's parents would have believed in Horace Fletcher's theory that every bite of food ought to be chewed at least one hundred times."

"Not really."

My friend dabbed at her moist eyes. "Val," she said softly, "my parents stopped short of the 'Wilderness Cure,' but they put me through much of the rest to stop my 'superstitions.' I told you about Doctor Beard."

I vaguely remembered.

"The famous Doctor Beard," Cassie went on, "who said our machine age makes everybody nervous. My father bought his book, *Eating and Drinking,* to learn how to calm me down, stop my 'dreaminess.' I think Father still has his copy."

I nodded in sympathy. I had not known about the health systems my friend endured to stop her "superstitions" though I knew firsthand about Cassie's parents' turbulent divorce, the ever-angry Rowena and her husband, Robert, a kindly, sensitive and loving father.

I glanced out the tiny side window of the phaeton, the model supposedly originated by queen Victoria for privacy. We were turning onto Fifth Avenue, and I would soon be home. I slipped two fingers into my jacket pocket and felt the silk sash... and the cloth scrap too. To ask Cassie about special feelings from the cloth...this was the moment, my need to know against the care for my friend. If I took out the cloth and asked what she felt, would my principle of care hold? Or was it merely a feint and dodge? I fingered the fabrics in my jacket pocket, the sash and the scrap. The phaeton moved. I hesitated.

Cassie sighed just then, a sigh that sounded like a gust of breath. I turned to see her swallow hard and clasp her hands together. "Cassie," I asked, "are you feeling all right?"

"Trying, Val...."

"What is it?"

My friend's eyes slowly squeezed shut, and her lips trembled. "Val," she said, "I am trying."

"Trying what?" I asked softly.

Eyes open, she gazed at me with that faraway look I had seen before. "I promised Dudley...no visions."

"Cassie," I whispered, "what visions? What have you seen? What do you see?"

She turned away, her voice sounding as though it came from a deep well. "These last days, Val, since you and Roderick went up the river...I tried to push them off, but just now again...so much."

"Push what, Cassie?"

"...high grass," she said, "and water. I see water and high grass too...and a person lying still."

"Sleeping?" I asked. "Is the person sleeping?"

I held my breath in dread and hope, but my friend's words were already being spoken.

"The person..." she said, "does not awaken. The person in the grass cannot move...and those too close become like...like stone."

❧

I had not changed out of the cullottes when I joined Roddy in our upstairs Green drawing room, where he was straightening bottles on the tea wagon refitted as a portable bar.

He turned for a quick kiss and smiled at my outfit. "A ride in the park?" he said. "And Comet behaved herself?"

"She did."

"And Cassie went with you?"

"All the way home," I said, too upset to talk about Cassie's "spell" in the phaeton. The cloth scrap never left my pocket, but her vision silenced us both. She struggled for composure and apologized before we arrived here, though she looked pale and shaken. My own fast, shallow breaths barely let me say goodbye, and my hand trembled at our farewell clasp.

Roddy fingered the bottles as if counting them, or perhaps counting on them for reassurance. His afternoon with Rufus and Eleanor was surely a trial. They still suspected their son was captive to whiskey despite all evidence to the contrary. Roddy's law practice defending cafés and saloons from the Temperance crowd only confirmed their doubts. I also thought my husband's law practice embarrassed his parents. Gentlemen attorneys were not to be found in gritty city courtrooms.

So, here we were, both unsettled. At this moment, I would not bring up the episode in the phaeton. Nor my breech of etiquette riding solo, knowing Roddy would be dismayed. Instead, let him mix us cocktails, as he often did in the early evening hour, and let us go to our favorite Bergere chairs to sit and sip.

"My dear," Roddy said, "I propose a cocktail called the Fourth Degree." The glint in Roddy's eye meant irony in the offing. "The 'Third Degree,'" he said, "is the latest slang for an intense police interrogation, but an afternoon with my parents calls for the Fourth Degree."

Nodding, I watched my husband reach for ice tongs, lift the ice bucket lid, and in moments uncork bottles, measure liquids, and present the drinks. As always, I would record the recipe.

The Fourth Degree Cocktail

Ingredients:

- One ounce Italian (sweet) vermouth
- Two ounces Plymouth gin
- Dash of absinthe

Directions:

1. Put 4-6 clear, hard ice chunks in mixing glass.
2. And vermouth and gin.
3. Add absinthe.
4. Stir well, strain into stemware cocktail glass, and serve.

"Salud, Val. To us." Roddy touched his glass to mine, and we sat side by side in the dark green velvet Bergere chairs. "How do you like the Fourth Degree?"

I had promised to be frank when tasting a new libation. "Nice to have," I said, "but not a favorite. So," I said, "your father and mother raised questions, and you needed all your courtroom skills, but seriously, what did you tell them?"

I asked casually to circle the core issue, the body on their property...Fiona Peebles. "You told them...what?"

"That the beaver pelts would be well worth the effort and the timber spared." Roddy took a sip. "I also said the contract with Keith Property Management includes a provision for subcontracting, and that Mr. Roland Keith had acted on his own initiative."

My husband put his glass down. "Father wanted to know what 'his own initiative' meant, and Mother asked for 'plain language.'"

"And you told them exactly...what?"

"That Keith authorized a 'health' camp for adults on the property for the summer months under an air-tight agreement. Mother connected the camp to the 'vagabond' in Sadie's note, and she fanned herself against the 'vapors.'"

Society ladies, I learned, caught the "vapors" from unwelcome news. I wanted to know, were Rufus and Eleanor told that a body was discovered on their property.

"How specific?" I asked.

My husband picked up his glass, sipped, and leaned sideways in his chair. If our dog were here instead of snoozing with Calista, he would have petted her as a distraction from me, a familiar gambit.

"Specifically," he said, "I repeated Roland Keith's outlook for a handsome rental fee, minus ten percent for Keith Property Management." Roddy finished his drink. "I should have asked Keith more questions about the rental. That was a mistake."

"Roddy," I said slowly, "you did not tell your parents about the body, did you?"

"What good would come of it, Val? My father stomped around with dining room with his cane and overturned the chicken salad. Mother wept. They have hired an architect to draw up plans for their country house, and they feel younger for it. If they heard of a dead body on the site of their country house, there would be pandemonium."

A mantel clock chimed six p.m., and the light was waning. With reluctance in every syllable, I said, "Start with this...Cassie already knows."

"Cassandra...but how....? Roddy's voice suddenly turned plaintive. "Those daydreams...her superstitions, am I right?"

"Roddy, I can't account for Cassie's 'spells.' She is trying to avoid them. I did not tell you that she was once a guest at Kiddwood and taunted for her 'trances.' You don't remember seeing her there, do you?"

"No. I'm sure I would recall."

"Maybe the place haunts her in some way. She had a vision of someone in high grass...I did not tell her about Fiona."

"Just as well."

"But Roddy, Cassie also 'saw' that those who are too close are...like stone."

"Probably gems, Val. A ladylike superstition."

"I doubt that. More like...statues."

Quietly Roddy said, "I will not play this guessing game, and I will not demean Cassandra with rubbish about ghosts.

But we need information, We need facts, and fast. There is one man in New York City who might help. The man I want to see is S. S. McClure."

Chapter Sixteen

"S. S. MCCLURE? WHO is this S. S. McClure?"

I asked when Sands withdrew, having announced that dinner would be served within the hour. On principle, my husband would dress formally, but the butler frowned at my culottes. (Heaven forbid that Mrs. Roderick DeVere dine in her horseback riding outfit.)

"Let us dress, Val. We'll talk at dinner."

"Just a hint? A few words?"

He repeated, "Dinner," and I flounced off for the lilac dinner gown with Roddy's grandmother's freshwater pearls I liked for their nubbly contours.

I felt "nubbly" for saying yes to tonight's dishes without a glance at the menu.

"Val, what have we here?"

I motioned a footman to identify the pale pink slabs set before us. He announced, "If you please, tonight's appetizer is...eel with white wine and paprika."

We poked at the eel, and what followed drove us to bread and butter. After the eels came a chicken liver soup, then Scotch turnip-tops, after that beef with red currant jelly and then lamb kidneys "Piedmontaise" and a collapsed lettuce salad.

A dessert had yet to appear, and I apologized for the careless approval of the meal. Roddy understood my eagerness to see about Comet. We carefully avoided discussion of Cassie and her vision while sipping wines chosen by the butler as my husband tried to explain why the mysterious Mr. S. S. McClure could be critically important during this flying trip.

"If he is in town," Roddy said, "and not speeding all over the country to recruit reporters."

"Reporters?" New York's newspapers overflowed with reporters, as we both knew. The papers had feasted on the strange death of Cassie's cousin and the murders in Central Park last fall. "What reporters, Roddy? New York breeds them like...like...." I stopped because we were, after all, at the dinner table.

"Val, these are a select few, men and women too. They work for S. S. McClure's magazine, *McClure's.* He's a scrappy fellow, something of a hustler. He hails from Ireland, I believe, an immigrant who got himself through college, then ran a bicycling monthly in Boston and learned the ropes about magazines."

Roddy sipped his wine. "The difference is, Samuel McClure gives his writers all the time they need to find the facts and report them clearly. The man has a nose for issues that need a serious probe—and an instinct for the reporters who can do the job. He sends them all over the country. If anyone can unearth the facts about a Health-to-Wealth scheme, it would be a *McClure's* reporter. Our best chance to find out what happened to the young woman on the DeVere tract is to start at the *McClure's* office. Get ready to go first thing in the morning to Lexington Avenue between 25th and 26th Streets."

I did not argue. To me, the Kingston police seemed like a much better bet than a magazine man based in Manhattan, but I agreed to meet Mr. McClure, if he was not scouring the country.

In our foyer the next morning at 8:30 a.m., I saw something off kilter when Roddy bit his lip. "It's mother, Val. She made an early appointment with her doctor and begs me to go with her. She believes the news of the camp on DeVere property has brought on a nervous attack."

Eleanor DeVere's "attacks" were a frequent joke, but I took my cue. "Roderick DeVere," I said, "you're a dutiful son. You'll take a hansom with your mother, and we'll postpone the McClure—"

"—absolutely not. Noland will drive you downtown. If McClure is in town, you must ask the right questions, and I'll hear his answers…unvarnished."

"Unvarnished."

By 9:45, I arrived at the seven-story, Italian Renaissance *Lexington* Building, where a short, round man patrolled the lobby and frowned at my request to see Mr. McClure.

"A very busy man," he said. "You a girl writer? He hired a girl for the book on Lincoln. Is that you?"

I dodged men jostling in the lobby, their neckties loosened as phrases floated..."inside ring...politicians...beats the devil."

"Book on Lincoln...is that you?"

I looked him in the eye. "I am that writer," I said, and the elevator took me to the top floor where black lettering on a frosted glass door panel read, McClure, Phillips, & Co. The door was not locked. I walked in.

A bank of rolltop desks cluttered with papers crowded the office where a woman in a black sweater sat at a typewriter by a window that overlooked 25th Street. She looked up from typing and said, "You're early, Miss."

She eyed my light brown walking suit with a turquoise brooch on the lapel and said, "Mr. Phillips only cares about speed. Can you type fifty words a minute? Any less, it won't matter what you wear." She pointed to a typewriter on a nearby table. "If you want to practice...."

"No, thank you," I said.

"Then take a seat. You'll have quite a wait."

Her typewriter clacked in rapid fire, and I sat on an oak chair, irritated at Roddy and at myself. Mistaken identity got me here. Now what?

Never mind the imposture, I could be in the saddle on Comet this morning, then answering mail that stacked up at home. Sitting here was a big, fat waste of time, this flying trip foolish. It got me out of the Hudson valley but did not take me home.

I crossed my legs (at the ankle, as ladies must) when a postman brought a sack of mail the typist promptly sorted, piling letters on the cluttered rolltop desks. "If you get the job," she said to me, "you'll be responsible for the mail on Tuesdays."

"Tuesdays," I said.

A mustached man in a business suit arrived. "Morning, Mr. Phillips," she said, "As you see, your candidate...."

"I'm afraid," I said, "there's been a mistake...."

He glanced at me and nodded. "Then, you are here to see Sam...Mr. McClure."

"That is correct."

He looked at his pocket watch. "...he'll be here any minute. Get ready to describe your librarian skills, and fast. Mr. McClure has a train to catch. You'll need to make it snappy. Now, Mildred, let me see...."

"Snappy...." I murmured, fuming at this comedy of errors when a second business suit burst through the door, another mustached man, this one bristling with energy as he glowered "Good morning" to the office and fixed piercing eyes under thick brows on me. "This way," he said without a pause and led me to a far corner niche of a semi-private space with a desk piled high with papers, books, and a stack of magazines—*McClure's*.

"Sit down, Miss, and remind me...you work at which Carnegie library? Pittsburgh, isn't it? Miss Tarbell needs to know her assistant can handle documents, So...." He put his pocket watch on the desk.

"Mr. McClure," I said, "I am not a librarian. My name is Valentine Mackle DeVere. I am not a job-seeker." I paused. My only card to play with this man, my ancestry. "My parents," I said, "both immigrated from Ireland."

"What county?"

"County Donegal."

"County Antrim," he cracked, and my heart sank. "The Scots-Irish North," I said, "but the same island, the same seas...the same hard times."

He eyed me as if the lady before him might possibly be worth a few minutes in his jampacked day. "My parents went West to try their luck prospecting," I said. "My mother died, but Papa did well in the silver mines in Colorado and Nevada. My maiden name is Mackle."

He crossed his legs and folded his hands. "Patrick Mackle," he said quietly. "Your father was one of the Silver Kings...the honest one."

How would he know this?

"So, Mrs. DeVere, you are also an immigrant to New York. In a manner of speaking."

"I met my husband in Nevada," I said. "He is a fifth-generation New Yorker."

He rocked his chair forward. "Do you know that 'Old New York' owns the tenement slums, Mrs. DeVere? Fifth Avenue names, such as Astor." His voice dropped in quiet intensity. "The gentlemen of the social Four Hundred skim rents from tenants that fester in slums that would shame Calcutta. Airless firetraps!"

"Mr. McClure," I said, "the DeVere family does not own tenement property in the city, but I am here to inquire about a tenement property manager, a man named Roland Keith."

He rubbed his eyes. "Hearst exposed him, didn't he? Pulitzer too? Not every crook goes to jail, Mrs. DeVere. Right now, *McClure's* is after the biggest fish. Rockefeller's oil monopoly? Kickbacks and claw backs, and our own Ida M. Tarbell lays it out for *McClure's*. The big city grafters? Lincoln Steffens goes to Minneapolis, to Philadelphia...to dig deep and tell the story of grand larceny by elected officials. They call it muck-raking."

He fingered his bowtie. "*McClure's* goes for the big fish, which the American public devours with every issue." He pointed to the magazine stack. "Which you would know if...."

If Roddy were here instead of looking after his hypochondriac mother. "Mr. McClure, my husband planned to speak with you but was detained. There is a problem in Ulster County in the Hudson Valley...a summer woodland camp called Health-to-Wealth."

He waved a dismissive hand. "Bilking hard-earned money with health schemes? A ripe topic, and maybe *McClure's* will tackle it one of these days."

"There's been a death there," I said, "and foul-play is suspected."

He looked at his watch. "Mrs. DeVere, such deaths are a dime a dozen, every single one a newspaper headline, but not for us." He reached for his watch. "I have trains to catch...North Dakota." He started to rise.

"Wait...let me say two names, Mr. McClure, and I will be off. The names are...." I wet my lips and spelled them. "Cedric F-e-r-r-i-s and Vanessa Z-e-e. I believe that 'Zee' is shortened."

He blinked, paused, blinked again. "...hold on."

I had gathered my skirt, ready to exit the Lexington Building, but he cocked his head as if a new sound came to mind.

"Wait a minute."

He sprang from the chair, dashed to the front of the office, and rushed back waving a sheaf of typed papers. "Ferris..." he said, "and Zelonski...the two of them." He shuffled the pages and read from a page. "'...trained animal acts... stage and circus... conscious and deliberate cruelty and torture...cruelty as a fine art has attained its perfect flower in the trained animal world...to prevent the perpetuation of cruelties on animals.'" He glanced up. "A *McClure's* article on animal acts and the need for prevention of cruelty to dogs, monkeys, elephants.... It will be a big story, lots of culprits by name. The piece will be edited and published in a few months. I see these two right here, Vanessa Zelonski and Cedric Ferris. Now I have got to get going."

Chapter Seventeen

I TIPTOED PAST THE typist and Mr. Phillips, who hovered over a young woman seated at the second typewriter. At the open office door, the typist's words drilled on: "Fifty words at a minimum, and we will time you to the second, so, ready or not...."

Finally, the elevator, the lobby, and the street where Noland waited to drive me home, some forty blocks of frustration and delay amid countess carriages and wagons. Traffic in the street matched the traffic in my mind.

Roddy waited in our *Empire* reception room, whose recent renovation caused a rift between us. He sat on a lemon-yellow settee, clearly eager to learn whether I had seen Mr. McClure.

I sat opposite my husband. The revelation of Cedric and Vanessa's vile past pressed hard, but so did the impossible morning. "Roddy," I said, "you left me in the lurch. *McClure and his* magazine, hadn't a clue."

"Then, you saw him?"

"I felt blindfolded," I said. "Or was it blindsided? You should have been at the *Lexington* Building to talk sense to the man. How do you know the magazine, and I do not?"

My husband looked flustered.

We subscribed to the *Atlantic* and *Scribner's*, and my *Overland Monthly* because it features writers from the West. And I dutifully took *Vogue*. "How do you know about *McClure's*, Roddy?"

I should have predicted the answer. "The Union Club subscribes," he said, "and the Century Club too. Their reading rooms have magazines...for members."

He said this softly because the men's clubs were a powder keg between us. The gentlemen of New York and other big cities had clubs for socializing, exercising, joining in fellowship over cocktails and dinner.

The ladies? So far, not one club.

"So," I said, "you spend leisure hours reading *McClure's* at your clubs, and I sat squirming across from the publisher in full view of a stack of his magazines, which I never heard of...so humiliating. And who is Mr. Phillips?"

"A partner. They say he runs the office while McClure hunts talent wherever he finds it."

He's off to North Dakota," I said, as if it mattered. "And you probably know the names of reporters that I heard for the first time. Who is Ida Tarbell? I was mistaken for someone seeking a job as her assistant. Who is she?"

Roddy sounded like a reciting student. "Ida Tarbell," he said, "is investigating crimes in the Standard oil Company.

Her facts are rock-solid, and so is her prose. It's a multi-year project."

"And Lincoln somebody...?"

"Lincoln Steffens," he said, "was a Wall Street reporter, and now he travels for *McClure's* and unearths the crimes committed by mayors and cronies who rob their cities blind."

"And how does he do this?"

Roddy answered with bare facts. "Steffens chums with workers, bartenders, liverymen...anyone who can tip him to the graft of the 'commercial politicians.'"

Roddy reached for my hand, but nothing doing. "Val," he said, "please try to understand two things. First, taking mother to the doctor when Father's knee kept him at home.... It was meant to calm them both down. My parents are on tenterhooks about the tract."

Roddy put his hands on his knees. "And second, I trusted that if McClure was in his office, you would talk to him. You would find a way. If *McClure's* magazine is tracking health schemes or similar frauds, you would learn of it. Anything to do with Health-to-Wealth...."

"Not the health scheme, Roddy," I said, "but animal acts...savage animal acts."

"Acts? What acts?"

"Circuses, stage acts...animals trained to perform, but treated like baggage...and tortured. Probably cast off if they get sick or hurt. *McClure's* is planning an exposé. The names, Roddy...two names we know. Vanessa and Cedric were involved in training animal acts. Vanessa's last name is Zelonski."

"And Cedric?"

I nodded. "Cedric Ferris."

My husband grew quiet. "Was this in California?"

"I don't know."

"Did McClure say when the article will be published... this year?"

"I don't think the article is finished, Roddy. Mr. McClure was late for his train, but I managed to ask about Cedric and Vanessa at the last minute. He remembered the names from the animal article, and he shuffled a bunch of papers and read their names from a page."

"Who's the author? Which reporter?"

"I have no idea."

"Did they work for a circus?"

"I don't know. It's a miracle I got their names. They brutalized animals. That's enough, isn't it?"

Our dog came in at that moment, looked at us and sniffed the new draperies, which seemed to float. "Here, Velvet," Roddy said. The dog ignored my husband when he called her a second time. French bulldogs were notoriously quirky, alternately charming or irksome, depending on owners' moods. Velvet had never been trained to offer her paw or roll over. She walked on a leash and went outdoors as needed. Aside from Mrs. Thwaite, our household indulged her from affection.

"She's a little love," I said.

Roddy nodded as our dog trotted his way, licked his hand, and was lifted onto the settee beside him. At this moment, the thought of sweet dogs like Velvet being caged and whipped silenced us both. Other animals came to mind, even the draft horses on city streets that were called "living machines" and cursed when they collapsed.

"What should we do?" I asked.

"For the moment," Roddy said at last, "I see no direct course of action. It helps to know those two are frauds, that Health-to-Wealth is simply their current money-maker. Two charlatans, and the country seems full of them…grist for courtrooms and novels… séances too."

In minutes, my husband would probably bring up the spiritual medium that Cassie relied upon, Madame Riva, a manicurist who promoted evening séances to swell her income, all the while pretending to be a Romanian princess. Roddy and I agreed the woman is a fake, but Cassie had not cut ties despite my persuasion, though she temporarily avoided the medium, promising Dudley to curb her visions.

"You're thinking about Madame Riva?" I asked.

"Actually," my husband replied, "I was about to ask whether you raised Roland Keith's name this morning."

"I did. Mr. McClure remembered the tenement scandal in the newspapers but had nothing to add. Why?"

"Because it is possible that Keith is somehow involved with Cedric and Vanessa."

"The Health-to-Wealth contract is bogus?"

Roddy shook his head. "No, the contract is standard boilerplate, but perhaps Keith has other dealings with them, though we have no way to know."

"Unless..." I began."

He looked up.

"Unless, his secretary...." I was thinking out loud. "Roddy, I plan a brief stop at the United Charities Building before we go back to the Hudson Valley, and something has just occurred to me...." I shifted on the settee. "When must we go?"

"Tomorrow evening, Val." Roddy's sigh could have been mine. "We can take a late-afternoon train to Kingston. I wish it were otherwise, but another day or two at Kiddwood ought to be quite sufficient."

"Sufficient for the beavers and the timber," I said, "but what about Fiona Peebles? What if the man who came looking for his daughter is her father?"

"My dear," Roddy said, "her sad death must remain a matter for the Kingston police. Our small part in this matter has concluded."

He paused as a lapis lazuli clock on the mantel struck the hour. "So, Val, let us enjoy the rest of this day and make the most of tomorrow until train time. We each have errands and duties, but let's also make time for us." He stood, stepped close and kissed me. "Time," he said, "for the two of us, alone."

To shut away dark thoughts and feelings as easily as stepping from one room to enter another? Perhaps the need was greatest when time pressed, and the opportunity so short-lived. Time enough tomorrow to rethink the young woman lying in the weedy tract. For now, let there be a ***now*** with my Roddy. Let him be close to me.

He took my hand as we left the *Empire* Room, and the afternoon and evening became a holiday starting with a walk in the park with Velvet, a late afternoon glass of wine in the conservatory, and my dressing for dinner in an ivory and emerald satin gown that Roddy especially liked, though it was two years old, the embroidery passé according to *Vogue*.

Dinner was lovely, from the *Marguerite* Consommé through the sole *Orientale* to the strawberries with cream. Roddy shooed the butler and footmen away to pour the wines himself.

"Riesling, my dear? A highly recommended dessert wine."

"Recommended by...?"

At my ear, he whispered, "By your lover."

"And after dessert," I whispered, "where next...?" We had promised to make love in every room in the house.

Our suggested drawing rooms came and went in husky teasing, and a murmur about the billiard table made us both laugh. Roddy vowed he had a cue stick to win everywhere in the house. I giggled.

We lingered in the flickering candlelight and finally decided that Roddy had best call upon me in my boudoir and fulfill his vow to free me of "every single stitch of clothing, bar none."

Holding hands, we took our time climbing the stairs. I whispered in his ear that Calista had the night off, and the boudoir was ours to enjoy. The moon cast soft light through the sheer curtains as we entered the space, and soon every freed hook counted down as Roddy's hands nimbly, then urgently released the gown, the underthings, my shoes and stockings. He had flung off his coat, and I faced him, stripped his tie, and clawed at the shirt front but gave up and opened his trousers.

We tried for the bed, then for a feathery *chaise longue* but dropped to the thick carpet and lost ourselves in rolling tides that surged and surged again until we lay together without words, our breath mingling, our eyes softest in the pale moonlight. And so we lay until somewhere the clocks chimed, and my lover whispered, "It rings for you and me," and I said, "us...for us." And still we lay together, each of us shying away from the closure of the night until a distant, single chime announced a new day.

☙

We breakfasted as appropriate to the lady and master of the house, both served by a footman who brought the coffee and tea, the eggs, the toast, the extra butter and jam.

Last night's wondrous finale was now a weekday with a dreaded train ride looming in the late afternoon. I hoped for a midday horseback ride with Cassie, but she was committed to a lecture on "Feathered Hats and Sacrificial Birds." My plan to ride Comet also foundered when our butler telephoned the stable, only to learn that the groom was already exercising Comet in the park.

Over scrambled eggs, Roddy explained that he had court cases to prepare and an upcoming hearing in the

Mary Powell affair. The steamboat's owners had identified the Temperance women who vandalized the saloon and would appear before a magistrate here in the city later this month. Roddy would represent the steamboat company, and he was also asked to consult about a signature cocktail for a birthday event to be held at the Century Club.

"Busy day, Val," he said. "And you?"

"I'll stop for an errand at the United Charities Building. I have an idea...."

Roddy asked nothing further, which was just as well. He reminded me of our Kingston train at 5:15 p.m. One final sip of tea, and he was off.

A hansom cab took me to 22nd Street at Fourth Avenue, the United Charities Building. I had purposely not told my husband that the charity I planned to visit inside the renovated old stone church building was the headquarters of The National Consumers League, which Roddy suspected to be a coven of socialists, no matter how many times I told him otherwise.

The second floor headquarters was actually two tiny offices partitioned by a curtain no thicker than a bedsheet. I was here for a talk with the League's secretary, Miss Annie Flowers, whose name would also raise Roddy's ire. The staccato typing echoing from the second floor told me that Miss Flowers was hard at work. Whether she would spare time in her schedule for a conversation was another question.

My doorframe tap went unanswered, and I peered at the slender figure in a high-necked shirtwaist as her fingers flew at the keys until she cranked a rubber roller, freed the typewritten page, and quickly glanced at the watch that dangled on a neck chain.

"Fifty-five words," she said aloud to herself. "Fifty-five a minute, and soon to be sixty. See if I don't."

She turned to face me, her voice flat as a pancake. "Hello, Mrs. DeVere."

"Hello, Miss Flowers."

"Do you have a few minutes?" I asked. "I am here to ask a favor."

She fastened a hairpin and offered me ten minutes. "I hope, Mrs. DeVere," she said, "that you have not come to request that my group cease our efforts to promote Votes for Women, which we do on our own free time."

"Nothing of the kind," I said.

Annie Flowers knew that my eagerness to vote matched hers, but her suffrage hijinks fit a carnival. Weeks ago, her group demonstrated with a hurdy-gurdy, banners, and a pounding bass drum along the parade route of the New York Coaching Club. The hullaballoo infuriated Roddy, who adored the annual parade. My acquaintance with the secretary, however, reached back months earlier, which took me here today.

"Miss Flowers," I said, "your typewriting course last autumn—"

"—at the Fowler Secretarial College," she said. "I am certified to operate the Remington and Underwood machines. I earned a diploma."

"Excellent," I said, "and may I ask whether you socialize with other secretaries? Perhaps other graduates? Perhaps a circle of office workers who get together from time to time...?"

"Why do you ask, Mrs. DeVere?"

"There is an office in the city," I said, "an office with one secretary, and perhaps you might be acquainted with her."

"And who would she be?"

My cheeks felt hot. "I do not know the secretary's name," I said, "but Mr. DeVere has spoken with her on the telephone. The business is Keith Property Management."

Annie Flowers's dark eyes narrowed. "Mrs. DeVere," she said, "clerical work is conducted in strict confidence. The Fowler College teaches those who are privileged to operate the office typewriter must adhere to...." She stopped. "Are you here to suggest that I ask another secretary to divulge information that is privy to her office? That I spy for you? Mrs. DeVere, if that is the case, I am surprised. Perhaps you are not quite yourself today. I have headache powders at my desk. Before you go, would a headache powder be of help?"

Chapter Eighteen

THE NORTHBOUND WEST SHORE Railroad departed one minute late at 5:16 p.m., but we had been seated in the car for twenty minutes, both fidgety. We were expected at Kiddwood for dinner but not for the "cocktail hour," a relief for both of us. I gazed at the broad Hudson River, dotted with steam yachts and bright sailboats that seemed to beckon us from the shore to the summer season.

"Roddy," I said, "let's get a small boat and go sailing this summer. I'd like to learn to sail. You took lessons, didn't you? Can you teach me?"

He chuckled. "I could teach you how to capsize without intending to, Val. In the junior regattas, my nickname was Pearl Diver."

"Oops."

"But we'll get a boat and a teacher. Good idea."

The plan cheered us both. Earlier, I answered vaguely when Roddy asked about my errand at the Charities Building. His day's duties were met, and his delight was a birthday cocktail devised for a man named Thomas, who would be toasted with the "Tom Gin Fête." Across the aisle, a woman knitted from a giant ball of blue yarn, while I imagined hoisting a sail.

The Kidds' coachman met us at the busy Kingston depot, and so did a police officer, though not before I snatched *The Kingston Weekly Freeman*, the headline blaring, "WOMAN ARRESTED FOR WOODLAND MURDER." I quickly scanned the small-print. A Miss Ella Conklin was arrested and charged with the recent murder of co-worker Fiona Peebles in a wooded area and was now jailed. "Charged with ghastly killing...."

"Oh, Roddy...Fiona." I barely caught my breath before the policeman stepped up to verify that the gentleman just off the train was Mr. Roderick DeVere. He said that Chief Fitch would like Mr. DeVere's immediate attention at headquarters.

"Immediate?"

"The Wall Street station, sir. I can offer you a ride."

"In that paddy wagon? Officer, my wife and I will go on foot."

As it played out, we were driven to the police station in the Kidds' brougham with the police wagon in the lead. Our modest baggage was held in the brougham, and the coachman waited.

I jammed the newspaper under my arm and declined to sit on a bench in the station lobby. Roddy took my arm, and we were ushered into the same police office with the bulky desk, file cabinets, telephone box, and the round table with chairs. I took a seat farthest from the brass cuspidor, and Chief Fitch came in immediately, his uniform tunic buttoned tight to the neck. His shadowed cheeks hinted the start of a beard. His steel-gray eyes flashed.

"Mr. DeVere...Mrs... appreciate your time." He pulled back a chair and faced us across the table.

The silence felt awkward. "Chief Fitch," Roddy said, "my wife and I did not anticipate a police escort. We are expected at the Kiddwood country house, as you might guess."

"No need to guess, Mr. DeVere. We have talked to Mr. Alfred Kidd, who gave us your arrival time on the West Shore line."

How and why did Alf and the police talk about our train?

"We understand that you and Mrs. DeVere have not been in the Ulster County vicinity since the nineteenth of this month, and today is the...."

"Twenty-first," I piped up. Which was foolish. The man set the pace in his own shop.

Another silence, and then the chief pointed to the newspaper I had tucked under my arm. "Today's *Freeman*," he said, "printed extra copies. You saw that headline?"

"I did," I said, laying the newspaper on the table in front of Roddy, who merely blinked, though I felt his short breath.

"So," the chief continued, "there's lots that went on between June nineteenth and today." He crossed his legs.

"The woman that was found dead on your property? Her case has gotten clear...and maybe cloudy too."

"Chief Fitch," Roddy said, "if you would help us understand—"

"—right off, Mr. DeVere." The chief pushed forward. "I told you Kingston puts up with transients, men and women, and mostly they come and go. But some are wanted for crimes in other cities, other states. Warrants are out. Sheriffs and police know the score. We keep a lookout. Last winter, two brothers showed up here, both wanted for a holdup in Delaware. Chief Wicker personally supervised the handcuffs and shackles all the way down to Delaware."

He paused for respectful nods as the wall clock edged toward 6:15 p.m. Roddy eyed the newspaper. I folded my hands.

"Now and again," the chief continued, "somebody that's wanted for a crime disappears into the area. They change their name and go about their business. But sometimes we get a local lead, which happened on June twentieth, Tuesday morning, yesterday. That's when Mr. Ferris came to see me."

Roddy's eyebrow arched. "Mr. Cedric Ferris?"

"From that health camp on your property, Mr. DeVere."

Roddy said, "I see," but of course he did not see. Neither did I.

"The women that work at that camp, Mr. DeVere.... How much do you know about any of them?"

"Chief Fitch, the camp is managed under a contract."

"So be it, sir, but we have learned from Mr. Cedric Ferris that a young woman employed to give massages to the campers came under suspicion by Mr. Ferris. Her name is Ella Conklin, and Mr. Ferris came in to report his suspicion that she is responsible for the death of her coworker, who disappeared from the camp and was found on your property with the engraved ring on her finger...Fiona.

Roddy asked, "Chief Fitch, did Mr. Ferris detail the manner of death?"

"Drowning, Mr. DeVere." The chief put a notebook on the table. "Mr. Ferris alleges that Fiona Peebles was pushed and held under the water of a pool used by the camp for an exercise program. He believes the assailant, Ella Conklin, lured her victim into the pool and overpowered her, and did so deliberately and with the intention to commit homicide."

"At what time of day, Chief Fitch?"

"Nighttime, Mr. DeVere."

"And Mr. Ferris saw this heinous act?"

"He did not, sir. I asked him, first thing. He explained the camp shuts for the night when the tent flaps close and the workers complete their tasks, including the massage women who have a tent of their own. Mr. Ferris makes the final rounds and calls it a night. He believes Ella Conklin waited for everyone to bed down, then persuaded the intended victim to sneak off for nighttime bathing, intending to kill her.

"But Chief Fitch," I broke in, "why would she do this?"

"Jealousy, Mrs. DeVere, and greed. Mr. Ferris observed a 'great ill will' between the two women and regrets he did not intervene earlier in the month. The women are paid by the number of massages, Mr. Ferris said, and those two became enemy rivals, like California mountain lions, he said...seems he worked in California a while ago."

"But the body was found in a field a good distance from the camp," Roddy cut in. "So, how—"

"—how was the body moved? The very question I put to Mr. Ferris, who told me he debated that same question, especially because Ella Conklin is a physically slight woman. It seemed impossible to him that the Conklin woman could have moved the body unless she had an accomplice. Mr. Ferris said he delayed coming to us because he tried to figure out who would conspire with Ella Conklin...who had a motive."

"Another rival masseuse?" I asked. "Were other masseuses employed?"

"Three employed, Mrs. DeVere. There was Fiona Peebles, Ella Conklin, and one other young woman...Ramona...." He looked at his notebook. "Ramona Smith, but doubtful that she was involved. Mr. Ferris says the vicious rivalry was between Fiona and Ella. And he figured out how the body got moved."

The chief sat back and folded his arms across his chest, waiting for one of us to ask the leading question. I said, "Please tell us, Chief Fitch."

"A wheelbarrow, Mrs. DeVere. Mr. Ferris guesses she pulled the limp body out of the water and into the wheelbarrow, wheeled it away, dumped the body in a field and brought the wheelbarrow back to the camp. We are talking... two or three hours at the maximum."

I glanced at Roddy, remembering the wheelbarrows by the camp's cook stove.

"And Mr. Ferris deeply regrets that he did not hire a nighttime sentry for the whole summer. He said that this health camp business has never before been dealt such a body blow."

"That was his word, a 'body blow?'" Roddy asked.

He nodded. "Mr. Ferris invites us to search the records of the business...Health and Wealth, is it? They operated in California, Arizona, and Florida prior to coming to Ulster County. A clean slate, he assures us, and Miss Zee will be happy to talk with us. Mr. Ferris says she is most alarmed and fears for her reputation in public."

Roddy said, "The deceased young woman...Fiona Peebles...she was photographed before interment, for your files. And you have her ring."

"Which I did not show to the man who called himself Roy Peebles," the chief snapped, "and for good reason. The grifters show up at police stations and funeral parlors with cock and bull stories about long-lost dead relatives. They beg to see the valuables and put on their 'grief' act. Women are good at it, but men too. We got suckered, but Chief Wicker laid down the law. Proof is required."

"But Mr. Peebles deserves to know that his daughter is...no longer living," I said, "and that she was drowned...."

The chief smacked his palm on the tabletop. "By a killer who did not change her name, Mrs. DeVere. A killer who guessed that Ulster County is far away from Daytona Beach,

Florida, where Ella Conklin is wanted for attempted murder. Now she is upstairs." He pointed to the ceiling. "Inside a brand new cell, and we got a matron on the spot."

I looked at Roddy, who did not return my gaze. "She is jailed," my husband said, "until she can be returned to Florida...?"

"And because she is under suspicion of murder here... suspected of drowning Fiona Peebles, whose body was dumped on your property."

"And she turned herself in?"

He scoffed. "We did not wait for that, Mr. DeVere, not when Mr. Ferris told us enough of what we call proximate cause. I personally went to the camp with two officers to make the arrest and apprehension...found her in a tent, banging on a man half-naked on a cot...massaging his legs, she said. We made the arrest and brought her in for questioning. We are holding her."

"And did she confess?" I asked. Roddy shot me a look. In criminal law, as he told me countless times, confessions are rarities for good reason.

"She claims to be innocent in Daytona and innocent in Ulster County."

The chief flipped his notebook pages.

Roddy sucked his cheek. "Chief Fitch," he said, "About Mr. Ferris's charge...I understand that he came to you as a concerned citizen?"

"And a business owner, Mr. DeVere, no matter what you think of the health camp business."

"And you, Chief Fitch, visited the Kiddwood Country House?"

"Looking for you, Mr. DeVere, because you are the property owner. Lucky you told me you and the missus were guests out there...on the fourteenth, our log says. And you saw me the next day, the fifteenth, to confirm the property ownership and discuss the burial of the body in the Kingston public cemetery. Mr. Kidd told us you went to the city for a few days, tending to business."

The chief rubbed his bristly cheeks. "Mr. Kidd seems surprised to hear about the Health camp. Looks like he doesn't know what goes on right next door, so to speak."

I looked at Roddy, who stared straight ahead for a long moment, then thanked the chief and said we must be going. I began to fold the newspaper.

"A few more minutes, if you will," the chief said, reaching for a pencil in his tunic pocket and once again flipping the notebook pages. "One other thing," he said, "...the cloudy part of it." He glanced my way but looked at Roddy with a raised eyebrow. "Under interrogation," he said, "Ella Conklin tells us that she saw you at the camp."

"What?" Roddy lifted his chin.

I crinkled the newspaper.

"Chief Fitch, my wife and I inspected the property and saw the camp on Sunday...the eighteenth of this month. The camp managers, Mr. Ferris and Miss Vanessa Zee, both spoke to us. Whoever was on the campsite could have seen us...employees and others."

"She did not see you just once, Mr. and Mrs. DeVere. Ella Conklin says you came twice. The second time, she watered your horse."

"Oh," I said, "the young woman in the white robe."

"Watered your horse and said the name, Fiona Peebles. Do you remember?"

He gave no time for response.

"...because Ella Conklin claims she tried to enlist you to help her, both of you. If that is your recollection, I will record it in my notes. If not, I will record that you do not recall the exchange." He paused. "We anticipate additional questioning in the coming days. Perhaps you would like to delay your answer until we can arrange an official proceeding."

Chapter Nineteen

THE KIDDS' BROUGHAM SPED us to Kiddwood without a moment's time to think or talk. We held hands.

I tried to recall the young woman in the white robe. Except for darting eyes and large hands, no physical feature of Ella Conklin came to mind. Did she kill Fiona Peebles? In jealous rage, did she lure her to the pool and force her under the water until her lungs filled and she drowned? And with a warrant for her arrest in Florida too? Ella had pressed the wad of wet fabric into my hand last Sunday afternoon, and I joked about the smeared writing on it. Cassie did not touch it, though its nearness in the phaeton summoned the otherworldly vision that troubled both of us.

I asked myself, was the young woman with the water bucket a murderer? Did she press the wet wad in my hand to involve us in her plot? I brought it with me in the little valise, a ripped rag among snowy handkerchiefs.

The carriage turned all too soon into the hard-packed lane, and Kiddwood's lighted windows and tinkling piano intruded in the dusk. I jammed the Kingston newspaper under my arm just before stepping onto the veranda, ushered inside by the Kidds' butler and greeted by Sadie in a frosty welcome.

"The prodigal DeVeres," she trilled, "yet once again at our dear Kiddwood." Her jeweled rings clawed my fingers, but no apology this time. "Roderick, you scamp," she continued, "up to new tricks, it seems, and we are owed a confession about the secrets of the DeVere property, are we not? An explanation? First thing this evening without fail, and I have broken my cardinal rule. Because of the disruption, dinner will be delayed." Sadie beckoned a footman. "Show the DeVeres to their rooms. When they are dressed, show them to Mr. Kidd's card room. We will await them."

We hurried past the foyer where formally dressed guests sipped wine, chatted, and apparently ignored Jack Barrott's robust piano chords. I glimpsed Alf talking with the young couple from the steamboat. He caught my eye and glowered. Our Health-to-Wealth secret was out and we owed him and Sadie an explanation.

We did.

Inside my room with Roddy, I opened the *Freeman*, and we read the account of Ella Conklin's arrest for the murder of Fiona Peebles in "darkest woods" beyond the Kingston city limits. The short article was a stream of headlines. "Jealous rage incites murder... Fears roused in Ulster

County...Assistant Chief of Police Clyde Fitch affirms officers vigilant...Jail completed in record time for record murder... Free Love possible motive...."

"The massages..." Roddy said. "I'd bet the massages roused suspicion that Health-to-Wealth is a traveling brothel, and the *Freeman* sold lots of papers."

"But it says nothing about massages."

"Maybe next issue. It's a weekly."

I looked for a reporter's name. No name. "Roddy, the newspaper is useless." I stuffed it under the mattress. "There were two women in the lineup for watermelon last Sunday," I said, "but the massage women did not participate. They were not part of the ritual."

"No, they were not." Roddy bit his lip and narrowed his eyes. "Think back to our first time at the camp, Val. Cedric led us into the grove, and the campers were just going into the bathing pool—"

"—except for two women in white robes. One of them is charged with murdering her rival. Roddy, we must see Ella Conklin right away...a jailhouse visit."

My husband raised an eyebrow. "Not just yet, Val, because the Kingston jail visit will not be private. Our talk will be witnessed, most likely by Fitch. We want to be prepared, especially since the Conklin woman hints that we were involved in Fiona Peebles's death." Roddy paused. "Or else, the police chief heard what he wanted to hear. In any case, we will prepare ourselves. Chief Fitch named a third masseuse beyond Fiona and Ella Conklin...Ramona...."

"Smith," I said. "We will talk to her...somehow."

"But first," Roddy said, "let us talk to Cedric Ferris."

"And Vanessa?"

"And Vanessa. But right now, dress quickly and prepare for the Kidds' questions." He winked. "Call it our 'Third Degree.'"

Willa pinned my hair and hooked me into the dinner dress and aquamarine jewelry. Satin pumps on, I joined my tuxedoed husband, and a footman marched us down the hallways into a card room, where Sadie and Alf, both dressed for dinner, sat at either end of a Chesterfield sofa—and a tuxedoed Clarence on a Hepplewhite chair looking most distressed. He avoided our gaze.

Sadie pointed us to a loveseat that faced framed paintings of the Brooklyn Bridge and of *Liberty Enlightening the World*, more often called The Statue of Liberty.

Short pleasantries began when Roddy pointed to the pictures and asked, "Did not Kidd and Company's cement hold up Miss Liberty in the New York Harbor? And the Brooklyn Bridge too?"

"Don't think you can butter me up, Roderick," Alf said, sounding pleased nonetheless. "I admit," he said, "that without Kidd cement, the bridge supports would collapse and the statue topple from its base. Brooklyn would go back to ferries, and Ellis Island just another rock in the harbor. Those new buildings they call sky-scrapers...?" He arched his bushy eyebrows. "Not one goes up without cement in the concrete. So, limestone for cement is our Ulster County treasure, worth its weight in gold."

He sat forward. "Now, let's get down to cases. We had a visit this afternoon from the Assistant Chief of the Kingston Police, Clyde Fitch. He came with a patrolman looking for you, and I told him you and Mrs. DeVere would arrive on the West Shore line from the city. We had a short conversation."

I deliberately kept my gaze from my husband, who said, "I hope you found Chief Fitch to be helpful?"

"Roderick, do not try lawyer tricks with me...or Sadie. I already guessed that tramps or hoboes infested the DeVere property this spring...vagabonds, Sadie would call them. The juggler that one night...amusing, but let nature take its course, I decided. Hoboes move on. They find a rail yard and ride off in freight trains. Time was on our side, as my missus said over and again."

Sadie straightened her rings. "I refused to let Alf go by himself to see about the water situation on the DeVere property." She touched her neck. "...snakes and who knows what those vagabonds would be up to?"

"But Clarence volunteered, didn't you, son?" Alf said. "You geared up and bushwhacked in...and got yourself lost."

"Lost," Clarence said. He sounded choked.

"Could not find his way to the water," Alf said. "Clarence heard it trickle but could not quite find it."

"Because I left the path," Clarence said dully. "I left the path and doubled back on myself, got lost and ended up back at the fence." He looked at Roddy for the first time. "The broken fence, Roderick. You know that fence."

I dared not look t my husband. Clarence's boldfaced lie was stamped in every word.

"And poor Clarence," Sadie said, "came down a bad case of ivy poisoning."

"So, you see," Alf said, "as far as the DeVere property goes, we have been short of water and left in the dark." He clenched one fist. "Now, we learn from the police what fools we have been. You have tricked us, Roderick. Deliberately tricked us." He thrust his fist toward Roddy. "Chief Fitch says there's a money-making operation on the DeVere land, and some sort of bathing pool."

"Men and women bathing naked," Sadie said, crossing her arms, "with rub-downs and tents." She nearly shrieked, "Canvas tents!"

"Now, dear...we agreed," Alf said softly to his wife, who moved next to him. Clarence gripped the chair arms and seemed to sink into his dinner coat. "I will do most of the talking," Alf said, "but now let's hear what Roderick has to say for himself. Let's hear it, Roderick."

I doubted that my husband would expose Clarence's lie, and I was right. Roddy's steady, poised calm in the next moment was tactical, as I well knew. In heated moments, his quiet demeanor let another person's words ricochet right back. In moments, Alf scratched at his whiskery white beard and said, "I admit, Roderick, that the water arrangement is traditional. And tradition does not mean ownership."

"But our families have been so close," Sadie said plaintively. "...even closer since your parents favor Bar Harbor over

Newport. Eleanor tells us they plan to build their country house because Kiddwood inspired them."

I bit my lip. The Mackle Trust from Papa's fortune "inspired" Rufus and Eleanor.

Alf tapped a knuckle against a front tooth. "The fact of the matter is, Chief Fitch says the DeVere property is a campground, and he seems to think it's on the up and up. It sounds to us like humbug."

Roddy stole a glance at me. The police chief had spoken solely of the Health-to-Wealth camp, nothing more. If the Kidds had learned about Fiona Peebles's death, we would know it by now. As for the murder charge, the Kiddwood guests knew nothing at this time, and *The Kingston Weekly Freeman* was tucked under the mattress in my guestroom.

For the first time in the cardroom, I felt slight relief and sat back as Roddy folded his hands and nodded gravely, a posture to command respectful attention. He looked earnestly at Sadie and Alf and began, "I regret to tell you, my friends, that the DeVere property is temporarily under legal contract from this month through the end of August... and now, if you please...."

Alf and Sadie held one another's hands and looked dazed as Roddy unfolded the woeful tale of summer, 1899, in Ulster County. As if for the first time, I listened to my husband describe the senior DeVere's' well-intentioned attempt to manage the property, then recount each event linked to businesses that responded to America's enthusiasm for healthful outdoor life as a pathway to prosperity.

Health-to-Wealth, Roddy declared, would decamp at summer's end, with police escort if necessary. At present, my husband would take advantage of the Kidds' hospitality to make arrangements for the early September trapping of beavers and the demolition of their lodges. In the next few days, this would require visits to the campground and to Kingston. In addition, Roddy hoped to prevail on Alf and Sadie to allow him to be excused from Kiddwood's delightful amusements, as much as he lamented absence from the sparkling company.

The Kidds nodded as though hypnotized. Hearing Roddy's rich tenor voice momentarily halt and rise for emphasis, I, too, was nearly held spellbound. In part, my husband's speaking style explained his courtroom triumphs, when the Temperance offenders were found guilty, the cafés and taverns exonerated.

For the moment, Alf and Sadie seemed appeased, and I was lulled too. It felt as though we would all stand, clasp hands, and rejoin the guests, until Roddy said he hoped that over the next few days Clarence might participate in the water planning.

Whatever spark flared from his son's name, we could only guess. In that instant, Alf sprang up and shook both fists at Roddy. "How dare you, Roderick DeVere," he roared. "You let a fly-by-night bunch set up tents and steal our water. You smooth talked your way with excuses and now dare to drag our son into your mess." He glared at Roddy. "What do you think you are doing to us? We are in dire need of water here. What in damnation are you doing?"

❦

I had no appetite, dreading to smile through the dinner that began just minutes before nine o'clock. Alf toasted the DeVeres' return in tones so jolly that no one would guess about his fiery, sudden outburst. For our benefit, he introduced a new arrival, a weak-chinned bachelor and the steamboat twosome who were engaged to be married, Miss Lucy Craig and her fiancé, Henry Rawlins. Along with Miss Craig's great-aunt Philomena, they had traveled on the *Mary Powell* to Saratoga Springs to decide whether the Springs qualified for next summer's nuptials. They returned from Saratoga to Kingston on the steamboat and had much to say about their wedding plans.

"After the wedding, our guests could enjoy the horse races and perhaps take the waters," Miss Craig ventured, and her betrothed added that the gaming tables would provide amusement if Lady Luck smiled.

"And we have another idea," her young man chimed in. "The wedding party could reserve the *Mary Powell* to travel from the city to the Springs."

"Very nice," Edna said.

"The steamboat gives away punch," the young woman said, "and now there's entertainment."

"What sort of entertainment?" Jack Barrott asked. "Music? A pianist?"

"It's a juggler," Miss Craig replied.

Alf cocked an eyebrow. "Juggler, is it?"

"Sounds like a carnival act," Edna said.

"No, he's really good. He juggled empty punch cups and the men's hats too...even lumps of coal from the crew. He's amazing."

Roddy said, "I believe we might have been passengers together on the *Mary Powell* just a week ago. No one was juggling."

"He's new," the young man, Henry, said. "The steward said he got aboard somewhere and perked up the top deck, so they hired him."

Sadie shrugged and said, "Interesting."

Roddy met my gaze. We knew better than to prod the couple about the juggler at this moment. If only Sadie or Edna would ask the couple about him. Or Alf. Where did he board the *Mary Powell*? What did he look like? Both women, however, chatted about Miss Craig's trousseau and the wedding plans.

The topic died as the courses continued, plates yielding to plates from the soup and fish to meat, salads, asparagus, and, at long last, tarts, cheese, and coffee.

Nausea had taken hold of me. Roddy looked tight at the jawline. The guests, I assumed, would now amuse themselves, while Roddy and I obligingly socialized.

All eyes on Sadie for permission to rise from the table, but Alf called out, "Roderick DeVere, the ladies will welcome liqueurs, but the gentlemen anticipate an after-dinner cocktail by the one-and-only maestro. This is June the twenty-first on the calendar, and we must celebrate the summer Solstice, longest daylight of the year. And so...if you will, good sir...prepare to show us your stuff!"

Alf's twinkling eyes looked like cut glass. "A cocktail," he said, "but no water or ice...your challenge, yes?"

The table quieted, every eye on Roddy, who bowed to our host. Sadie looked impatient, as if the drink demand was no part of their plan.

"Might a footman take a request?" Roddy asked. A footman was called and sent to the kitchen with whispered words. "Of Kiddwood's many bottles," Roddy said, "I hereby lay claim to *Bénédictine* and a martini glass for one and all."

"All?" Edna Rossiter's voice pierced like a piccolo. "'All' means cocktails for the ladies, Roderick, and surely you do not—"

"—ah, but I do," Roddy crooned. "And if Mr. Barrott will favor us with piano melodies while preparations are underway...and if our hostess will excuse me?"

Sadie glanced at Edna, who nodded approval. Our hostess rose to signal that dinner had concluded. Briefly off balance, Alf blinked. Across from me, Clarence looked wary, and the steamboat couple seemed game for whatever was in the offing.

Roddy's suave manner was confusing and troubling. My husband seemed to be fencing with our host, making it worse for us. We were to be contrite, subject to Alf's temper.

My hands turned clammy as Clarence sidled up as we left the table. "Roderick's effort to sustain the evening is commendable, Mrs. DeVere," he said, "but probably doomed."

All I could manage was, "We shall see."

The piano broke the tension with *Yankee Doodle,* and the weak-chinned bachelor sang, "stuck a feather in his cap, and called it macaroni." The steamboat couple briefly tried polka steps. Roddy uncorked two bottles of *Bénédictine* and measured the liqueur into each glass. By my count, every gentleman—and lady—could be served whatever cocktail he had conjured.

"Valentine DeVere," Edna said, stepping alongside me, "do I detect a conspiracy between you and Roderick?"

"What conspiracy?"

"Don't be coy, dear. You told me, in so many words, that one day soon the ladies will be free to elect the President while quaffing whiskey."

"I didn't exactly say...." I began, but a footman appeared with a glass bowl filled with puffy white...meringue?

"Whipped cream!" the steamboat fiancée cried.

Right she was, for Roddy deftly spooned a dollop of whipped cream onto every glass, a topping on the *Bénédictine.*

"What have we here?" Alf demanded. "What sort of cocktail is this?"

The guests flocked to the table, each man taking his martini glass by divine right, but hesitating to sip. Should the gentleman defer to the nearest lady? Should he actually offer lady a cocktail? Did the mixture in the martini glass qualify as a *cocktail*?

"Roderick," Alf boomed, "What is it? What do you call this?"

"Everyone must think of the hotels in the city," Roddy said. "The names of New York City's hotels are…?" He looked at the elderly man with military medals on his lapels. "General Coleman, please start us off with a hotel…?"

"The Brunswick," the general barked as if issuing an order.

"The Fifth Avenue," chimed Henry, the steamboat fiancé.

"Hotel St. Stephen?" murmured a debutante in an uncertain voice.

Alf's irritation surfaced. "Get on with it, Roderick, or we'll be here all night."

Roddy held up both palms. "Ladies and gentlemen," he said, "I will provide a hint in one word, and one word only. The word is 'hyphen.'"

Stroking his silken moustache, Clarence gazed above everyone's head and said, "Roderick, how droll of you to think of the Waldorf-Astoria."

The fiancée, Lucy, pouted and admitted confusion. Clarence said, "Waldorf, hyphen, Astoria. In other words," he continued, "the hotel nickname is Hyphen."

"And tonight's cocktail," Roddy announced, "is the Waldorf-Astoria, which appears on the hotel menu. Liqueur and cream, my friends, so let us toast Sadie and Alfred Kidd and enjoy ourselves, one and all."

The gaiety, the bright piano tunes, the laughter and dancing that broke out gave Kiddwood the atmosphere of a festival. The guests mingled, ladies and gentlemen newly discovering one another's charms. Smiles prevailed, except for Sadie and Alf, who looked befuddled.

It took Roddy's elbow and sharp glance to wake me to the fact that we had held our own in the face of a young woman's murder just over the property line…a murder in which Roddy and I were thought to have played a part.

Chapter Twenty

WILLA WAITED TO UNDRESS me, but I excused her for the night and asked Roddy to unclasp the necklace and unhook my dress. We huddled in my guestroom to talk. Roddy shed his tuxedo coat and turned back his shirt cuffs. I slipped into a robe.

"Remember to speak softly, Val. These walls have ears."

"Just tell me why you put on that cocktail show, Roddy?" I whispered. "Alf wanted to lord it over you, the repentant guest. You upstaged him, and everybody knew it. Alfred Kidd strikes me as a man who keeps score and obviously has a fiery temper.

My husband rubbed his sideburns. "Val, it's important that I hold my own. The Kidds must realize that Roderick DeVere is no longer a young man in school. The weekends at Kiddwood were good times, but as boys, Clarence and I were put through Alf's drills. The man always liked to be jolly, but at times I thought he missed his calling in the Marine Corps.

I can't blame Clarence for living across the ocean. Maybe he will patent the cigar lighter and show up his father."

"But why did Clarence lie? We know he saw the camp and met Cedric. He told you so. Why is he lying to his parents?"

"I don't know. Something to do with his father."

"And why are you protecting him? He skulks as though he's frightened, but he's waspish too. Your boyhood loyalties are a thing of the distant past, Roddy. You are both adult men and ought to...to...."

"To act our age?"

"I didn't mean...or maybe I did."

We sat in tense silence.

"Val," my husband said at last, "I do not know why Clarence is lying, but Alf can be a tyrant, and his son might be trying to keep clear of him any way he can."

Roddy stroked his chin. "You and I have different ideas about what's best, Val. For me, it's clearing the DeVere property of scandal. When the Health-to-Wealth fiasco is over and done with, I will urge my parents to reconsider their country house idea. Perhaps they can be persuaded to sell the property."

Hearing this, I wanted to applaud. The DeVere tract, however, had become far more personal to me. The Health-to-Wealth carnival, the legal contracts, the water issues, and the beaver dams and lodges all dwindled when set against the young woman whose father came in search of his daughter...the daughter who had been murdered and lain dead in a field.

And Roddy and I were linked to her death by the woman jailed for her murder—outrageous.

"Roddy," I said, "your word, 'fiasco,' sounds exactly right. I want to go to the Kingston jail and confront Ella Conklin, and I don't care whether Chief Fitch hears every word and takes notes. But we do see things differently. The property matters, and I don't dismiss it. But for me, the young woman's death has unlocked feelings."

I reached for his hand. "Perhaps it's the naming, this coincidence. If I had not been born on St. Valentine's Day, my mama and papa would have named me...."

"Fiona," Roddy said softly. "The 'fair one.' I remember."

"And the father who came to Kingston in search of his daughter...searching and searching...." I worked to keep my voice low and steady. "Roddy, 'Peebles' is not a common name. The chief rebuffed the man, but the Roy Peebles who came to Kingston is no grifter. He is Fiona's father. He came from New Jersey. How can we find him?"

Roddy bit his lip. "First things first, Val. Let's not get ahead of ourselves. You kept that cloth scrap from the camp? Do you have it here?"

"With my handkerchiefs. Do you want to see it?"

"Tomorrow morning in the daylight." Roddy rubbed his eyes. "Another question...was the wet cloth Ella Conklin's idea, or did she follow orders from Vanessa?"

"Or Cedric? Or both of them? And why? Vanessa denied all knowledge of a young woman passing away on campground property."

"And just two days after our Sunday visit to the camp," Roddy said, "Cedric Ferris went to the police alleging that Ella Conklin drowned her coworker."

My husband folded his arms. "And another possibility you already raised, Val….that the 'vagabond' juggler committed the murder and fled from the camp. If so, Cedric might try to pin the crime on the masseuse in order to protect Health-to-Wealth."

"I don't understand."

"Quite simply, the publicity would ruin Health-to-Wealth if it became known that a 'client' was a killer. The customers would be deathly afraid of one another. Word would spread, and no one would sign up."

"So," I said, "it would be neater if employee rivals came to blows, and the juggling murderer out of the picture?" Roddy nodded. "And we heard about a new juggler on the *Mary Powell*. A mere coincidence?"

"Or a puzzle piece that fits…somehow…." Roddy rolled his shoulders. "We need to be careful, Val, and we need to work together. For now, let's try to get a decent night's sleep and make the most of tomorrow's visit to the 'grove.' The morning camp routine will be underway. We'll observe it in action."

We planned to leave the house before the Kiddwood guests appeared for breakfast. Roddy held the cloth scrap near the bedroom window's morning light and confirmed the letters seemed to spell 'Santa.' We both shrugged.

With the scrap tucked with handkerchiefs, I reminded Roddy that Cedric and Vanessa were frauds who might, to this day, torment animals for entertainment if it paid off. Roddy replied that perhaps they got wind of the upcoming *McClure's* exposé and jumped at the chance to dupe gullible people into spending ten days in the woods eating vegetables to make them millionaires. Aside from the legal contracts and promotion of Ulster County, neither of us could hazard a guess about Roland Keith's part in the Health-to-Wealth scheme.

Edna Rossiter seemed to patrol the breakfast pastry table. Her "Good morning, Roderick and Valentine" sounded accusatory. "And what are you two up to today?" She eyed my slate gray skirt, shirtwaist, and jacket.

"Miss Rossiter," Roddy said, "be assured that we DeVeres are in relentless pursuit of water for Kiddwood."

Edna invited us to join her before we could snatch a scone and be off to the stable and dogcart. The footman poured coffee and tea indoors.

"Just a quick morning bite," Roddy said. "And what new book do you recommend just now, Miss Rossiter?"

"Oh," she said, "if I could only recommend, but *When Knighthood Was in Flower* is pure drivel, complete non-sense." She reached for a butter knife. "The plight of a book reviewer...picture my summer in Saratoga, where I toil with my pen under the eaves of an inn, then take the waters at the Vichy spring...plentiful waters at Saratoga, Mr. DeVere. Perhaps we all ought to have chosen to go to Saratoga Springs. What do you think?"

Roddy had told me his parents once took him to Saratoga and forced him to drink mineral water that tasted like scorched eggs. "Miss Rossiter," he said, "I think the waters will flow at Kiddwood in due time."

"And when they do, Mr. DeVere, will you offer libations to the ladies as well as the gentlemen? Something heftier than whipped cream and liqueur? Something...."

Just then, loud bumping noises erupted from deep inside the house, then something scraped across floors and then shouts.

Edna laughed. "That deliveryman," she said. "Twice a week, he wakes the whole household. Alf tried to tone him down, and Sadie raised the roof. But Kiddwood wants fresh produce, and it's that deliveryman, worse than a crowing rooster."

"Hank...?" I blurted. "Is it Hank? ...do you know his name, Edna?"

She flashed a Cheshire cat smile. "My dear, we need not learn the names of deliverymen. Perhaps in the far West the customs differ, but in the East—"

"—if you'll excuse me....please." Roddy sprang up and disappeared, but the noise had stopped. He returned in several minutes, shook his head, and said, "Sorry, ladies," but did not sit down. "Miss Rossiter, I must ask that Mrs. DeVere join me. In the name of fresh water at Kiddwood, we must be off."

A quick smile for Edna, and we started for the stable at a good clip, though hitching the sorrel Granny to the dogcart took the groom forever, and the hard-packed Kiddwood roadway felt endless. On the tar-and-gravel county road at last, I asked, "Was it Hank Boynt? Did you talk to him?"

"It was Boynt, and I tried to talk, but he spit and cursed."

"Cursed at you?"

"Swore at his team, but the oath was meant for the world at large. He was shoving crates in the wagon and never once faced me man-to-man. I thanked him for spotting the body in a field that happens to be mine. He grunted when I asked how he spied it. He said a blindman couldn't miss that white 'hump.' When I asked about the state of the body, he said I had better ask Wall Street or the 'body snatcher.'"

"Meaning the police or...or what?"

"The undertaker. He wishes he'd passed by the body, let it rot like the lettuce in his wagon would rot if I kept holding him up. He spat, cursed, cracked his whip, and that was that."

"Ghastly," I said, falling silent. Roddy's fingers had tightened on the reins as he spoke, and Granny slowed just as we approached the very place where Fiona's body had lain in the field. The sunlight sparkled, the trees a leafy green, and yellow wildflowers bloomed at the roadside. One gray cloud far above looked ripe with rain.

I shut my eyes, jolted when Roddy reined us to a sudden stop at the turnoff to the hacked-out narrow road that led into the campground grove.

"Look down there...something orange and green. Looks like carrots."

"You're stopping for a bunch of carrots?"

"Carrots mean a delivery to the camp, probably earlier this morning before Kiddwood. They fell off a delivery wagon."

My husband gave me the reins, jumped down, retrieved the string-tied bunch of carrots, and put it on the seat between us. "If Hank Boynt supplies Health-to-Wealth, we can find out...but remember, the inquiry is solely in our interest as property owners."

"Property owners," I repeated, though tension inched from my ribs to my shoulders.

The foul vegetable odor assailed us as we tied Granny to the same sapling at the edge of the Grove. The horse turned her head to bite the carrots, but Roddy snatched the bunch away as we heard, "Not one for your faithful 'Dobbin?' Not even one?"

My husband whirled. "Mr. Ferris."

"Mr. and Mrs. DeVere, my pleasure." He bowed. "I heard the hoofbeats and expected a messenger about our camp rotation, which is due at the end of this week."

"So," I said, "the turnover must be very busy."

"Mrs. DeVere, we have learned that efficiency is our friend. Barring unforeseen events, one newly healthy group departs tomorrow for their future of boundless wealth, while another comes forth to us in two days for the Health-to-Wealth inspiration."

Wariness stirred behind the hang-dog eyes. He stroked his lantern jaw that begged for a shave. Today, Cedric Ferris wore blue denim pants, a chambray shirt, and sandals once again.

"So sorry," he said, "that obligations prevented welcoming you to the grove last Sunday, but Vanessa told me of your conversation. It's good to have you here this morning." He eyed the carrots. "A little gift for us at Health-to-Wealth?"

"Found on the roadway, Mr. Ferris," Roddy said. "We assumed they fell from a delivery wagon...the driver failed to notice."

"Quite possible," he said. "We received vegetables at dawn." Cedric glanced back and forth from Roddy to me. "So helpful that Kingston's greengrocer finds a fellow willing and able to drive a wagon."

"Is his name Hank?" I asked.

"Not quite sure," he said. "We wave, but he's a busy man, very reliable." He clasped the carrots and tugged his shirt collar. "How I wish it were equally true for women skillful at massage. If only the gifted massaging hands were plentiful...and I think you might understand that a terrible thing has happened to a fine young woman we employed.... I presume that your visit this morning is in connection with the recent death of Miss Fiona Peebles?"

Roddy and I nodded with downcast eyes. "As owners of this property, Mr. Ferris," Roddy said, "we would like to talk with you concerning this—"

"—tragic, pointless death, Mr. DeVere. A death ruinous to the victim and the guilty party, and we have no other way to put it. Won't you follow me to the larger tent? Let us ease our way around the grove so the morning's 'Reach-to-Rainbow' calisthenics will not be disturbed. Please follow me."

Single file, we walked behind him, glancing several yards to the left where two groups of campers stood on tiptoes, their arms raised high. One group was led by a slender woman in a loose gown with a white robe at her feet. Surely she was Ramona Smith guiding her group whose arms reached and arched to a count... "rainbow one and two...one and two...rainbow...." The group on the other side followed a woman wearing an identical loose gown and a nurse's cap pinned to her red-gold hair—Vanessa.

We entered the large tent with the deck chairs and sat down. Cedric set the carrots on a table and closed the tent flap. "Privacy," he said. "Privacy in a somber time."

"What can I tell you, Mr. and Mrs. DeVere? What can I say?" His cello voice swung into a low register.

Roddy said, "Mr. Ferris, are we to understand that the young woman masseuse, Fiona Peebles, was employed by the Health-to-Wealth organization? And that she was murdered by a co-worker on this property?"

"As reported in yesterday's Kingston newspaper, Mr. DeVere. Perhaps you read the shocking report, sir...ma'am? I saw the bombastic headlines yesterday afternoon in Kingston. I needed the use of the telephone and Western Union to place calls and send wires in search of skilled masseuses who can fill in for us without delay. I also made a few inquiries for a Kingston masseuse, and I sent a wire to Mr. Roland Keith, who I trust will be helpful to you."

He frowned and shook his head. "To be frank, Health-to-Wealth could be crippled by the 'unforeseen event' that I ought to have seen coming. Whenever possible, I spare Vanessa the matters of management, but two masseuses we hired in Florida became rivals, and their rivalry intensified here in Ulster County. I blame myself for failure to heed the warning signs."

"Both young women were hired in Florida?" I asked. "Fiona Peebles as well as the accused?"

He nodded. "A John Harvey Kellogg instructor was teaching in the St Augustine area, and Miss Peebles told us that she came from the Northeast to study the Kellogg method."

He swallowed and touched his throat. "Unknown to me," he said, "Miss Ella Conklin, likewise a skilled masseuse, used her talent to escape the law in Florida, where she is wanted by police for attempting to murder a young man."

He looked from Roddy to me. "Be assured, we recruit each masseuse with utmost care. Vanessa oversees every applicant and requires a demonstration of the Kellogg method, which is rigorous and technical. Both Miss Peebles and Miss Conklin passed with flying colors, and we counted our blessings. We had no idea...."

He broke off to offer us water from a pail with a dipper. We thanked him but refused.

Roddy said, "Mr. Ferris, can you say what happened? To the best of your knowledge, sir? I ask as the property owner."

Ferris helped himself to a dipper of water. "Miss Peebles went missing, simply disappeared last...June the eleventh, as I recall. We assumed she had run off without a word to anyone, probably homesick. We were puzzled but too busy to ask many questions. Miss Smith and Miss Conklin took on extra massages, and Vanessa herself stepped in."

"So, you had no inkling that Fiona Peebles had died?"

"None, Mr. DeVere, until the regular deliveryman who brings us vegetables told me what he saw on the property. He was aghast. Needless to say, we were equally aghast. I feared for Vanessa's health. She has been in torment, blaming herself, and I calmed her as best I could. All the while, my own recent suspicions came to a head, and I went to police headquarters in Kingston. I had no choice."

He looked soulfully at each of us. "You understand, no choice...but then, to my horror, the police chief found a warrant for the arrest of Ella Conklin. She is wanted for attempted murder in Florida, and the police came to the grove and arrested her, fortunately during the 'Hypnotical Hour' when clients rest with eyes closed inside their tents."

"So, your clients did not witness the arrest?" I asked.

"As far as we know, Mrs. DeVere, our clients did not learn that they were massaged by a murderess...and her victim."

I shook my head. Roddy rubbed his chin. "So, Mr. Ferris," he said, "you have notified Mr. Roland Keith."

"By Western Union, Mr. DeVere. I expect to hear from him. And Keith Property Management ought to inform you as well."

He cocked an ear, listening to voices from outside. "...rainbow...gold at the end...rainbow...."

"Ah, Mr. and Mrs. DeVere, I do believe that our 'Reach-to-Rainbow' session is concluding, and we will proceed to lunch. Would you care to join us?"

"Thank you, Mr. Ferris," I said, braced for the vegetables. "And does everyone dine together?"

His wary eyes flickered, and the cello resumed. "Mrs. DeVere, I sense that Health-to-Wealth intrigues you, and you are welcome to dine with our clients. If you wish to visit with Vanessa, however, she will kindly postpone her midday fare to have a word with you." He turned to Roddy. "And you, sir, might be interested in today's menu?"

In moments, Roddy was swept toward the cookstove, while Vanessa joined me in the tent, breathless as she perched on the blanket-covered cot, slipped off her nurse's cap, ran a hand through the red-gold hair, and refastened the cap. "Our 'Reach-to-Rainbow' mornings are exhilarating," she said, "but taxing for me since our recent...adversity. I believe Cedric has told of our need for new employees who are certified in the Kellogg method."

"He has."

"...every part of the human body, Mrs. DeVere, from the scalp to the toes. For example, the hand." She eyed my hands. "Dr. Kellogg is detailed on the 'pronation and supination of the hand,' which must be demonstrated to our satisfaction before we employ a masseuse."

"The late Fiona Peebles," I said, "she was trained—"

"—in St. Augustine, Florida, the poor dear, but she came from New Jersey, which we learned only when she so reluctantly relinquished a piece of jewelry to our safekeeping."

"You have her jewelry?"

"Of course not, Mrs. DeVere, but the Kellogg method requires the masseuse or masseur to remove all impediments during treatments...no bracelets, no finger rings, nothing decorative at the ears or neck. So, we secure our masseuses' jewelry during working hours." She leaned toward me. "Imagine, if you will, the abrasion of metals and gemstones during treatment."

"Unpleasant," I said.

"Ruinous," she countered. "I presume that Miss Peebles has been laid to rest with her ring."

I repeated, "Ring...."

"A yellow gold ring set with a ruby, as I recall. It bore an inscription. She told us her father is a jewelry worker. I presumed she was torn between devotion to her father and eagerness to make something of herself in the wider world."

Vanessa wiped at a tear I could not see. "Regrets for my haste just now, Mrs. DeVere, but the body must be nourished. When next you visit us, I dearly hope Health-to-Wealth has resumed its true rhythms. Take care on our roadway, won't you? A dogcart can be a very wobbly ride."

Chapter Twenty-one

WE LEFT THE GROVE at Granny's slow walk, then picked up the pace on the county road. The trees blurred as I pictured Fiona's ring and inscription "*from Papa.*" It felt invasive that Vanessa had handled it. Had Cedric also held it in his fingers? Tried it on his pinkie? Ready to tell Roddy what I learned, I waited for his word about the lunch.

"Collapsed vegetation, Val. A wooden bowl and spoon, and so we 'dined.'"

"You ate it?"

"Nothing else to eat, except bread that looked like plaster. The meal tasted medicinal, and we took our doses, all the men and the two women. Chances are, Cedric and Vanessa very carefully gauged ten days for endurance. Another day or two, the 'clients' would surely call it quits. If Health-to-Wealth fails, I predict their next scheme will be the same program to guarantee reduced bodily flesh, but under a new brand name."

My husband shifted on the dogcart seat. "I lunched with a haberdasher and a leather goods merchant, both small businessmen with grandiose ideas."

"And they are true believers? No wavering?"

"Both dead certain that Health-to-Wealth will bring them mansions, thoroughbreds, the whole kit and kaboodle. They agreed the best part is the massages. They love lying on their cots while the young masseuses fuss over them."

"They said 'fuss?'"

"They said they feel rejuvenated when the masseuses work them over. They agreed it's worth the strange meals and the ice-cold pool to have the massages."

"And perhaps the masseuses sneak snacks into their tents? Did you ask?"

Roddy chuckled. "They would be shocked. I might as well have asked whether George Washington was a patriot. The massages are on the up-and-up, they both said so."

"Roddy," I asked slowly, "did you ask about the disappearances? About Fiona?"

He shook his head. "Check your calendar, Val, because Fiona Peebles disappeared before the current crop of Health-to-Wealth 'clients' arrived. For this bunch, it's about Ella Conklin."

"But did you ask?"

"I did, and it made them uneasy. The haberdasher excused himself, and the leather goods man talked about a squirrel chased from his tent by a 'client' in the business of vermin extermination."

"They know that a masseuse is suddenly gone, but know nothing about her arrest...or jail?"

"Apparently not."

"And they know nothing about Fiona."

Roddy took my hand. "To the present group," he said, "Fiona does not exist."

I bit my lip and blinked back a tear.

"I'm sorry, dear. I should have spoken more carefully."

"Never mind, Roddy. Somehow, her name still affects me." I looked at the cloudless sky and swatted a bee. "This morning," I said, "we heard Cedric present the same story that we heard from Chief Fitch, but I learned something new about Fiona's father. Vanessa says he is a jewelry worker."

"Ah," Roddy said, "then it is Newark."

"What about Newark?"

"Remember," Roddy said, "Chief Fitch mentioned the Roy Peebles who came looking for his daughter came from Newark, New Jersey. The city is a hub of jewelry production. The brooch you like so much? It came from Newark."

"The diamonds with pearls?" He nodded. The brooch featured nubbly pearls, uneven freshwater pearls I liked better than the perfect ones. "Roddy," I asked, "how many jewelry companies in Newark? I have a good idea...."

He put his hand on my shoulder. "Val, we will not take a flying trip to Newark." He paused. "But here's what we can do. I can request that one of the younger attorneys approach the Newark jewelry concerns to inquire about an employee named Roy Peebles. Young Matthew Harding is a diligent attorney, and he'll welcome the task. But remember, Val, that a low-wage jewelry worker would be hard-pressed to purchase an expensive ring."

I nodded, imagining the gold ring with a ruby and, best of all, "*from Papa.*" We neared the place where Fiona had lain in the field, both of us quiet as the sorrel horse clip-clopped, insects buzzed, and the slain young woman filled my thoughts.

Could a name alone link the dead to the living? I was not superstitious, not like Cassie, but the near coincidence felt uncanny. Born just hours shy of St. Valentine's Day, I would have been Fiona Mackle, a Gaelic "dear one." The slain woman's Papa's spoke in engraved gold, and mine in an Irish brogue.

Ulster County was death to Fiona, who had made her way to St. Augustine, got trained in massage, took a job, and was murdered in this place—which was alien to me. In the West, Papa would call on the sheriff now and then to help rout gangs near the mines. He was friends with the sheriff of Storey County, Nevada, and called him by his first name.

In New York, Roddy and I had come to rely on a certain policeman when crimes struck our Upper East Side neighborhood, especially Central Park. The city was booming and expansive, and Detective Sergeant Colin Finlay was honest and forthright. We trusted his skill and his insight.

"Roddy," I said, "I wish Detective Finlay was here."

"I understand," he replied.

"But you agree, don't you? Admit it, Roddy, you would rather rely on Detective Finlay than put your trust in Chief Fitch."

"Assistant Chief Fitch," Roddy said. "Clyde Fitch is the *Assistant* Chief of Police."

Such precision was Roddy's way, but his undertone sounded grim. I let it go at the time.

The sun was past its meridian, and still we drove on. Lunchtime had come and gone at Kiddwood, but the footmen would serve me a plate. Roddy said he had no appetite. "Val," he said, "the *Mary Powell* ought to be on her way back to Saratoga. I want to find out when she'll next stop at Kingston."

"To see about the juggler?"

"As described to us by Miss Lucy Craig and her fiancé."

"And we think he's probably the 'vagabond' who showed up at Kiddwood? Because if he is..." I shivered despite the warmth of the day. "If he is, he might have killed Fiona."

"And ran because he killed her," Roddy said. "In any case, if the juggler on the *Mary Powell* is that 'vagabond,' we need to know who he is...and why he fled."

Quiet with our own thoughts, we turned into the Kiddwood drive, where sounds of outdoor laughter and voices mixed with a metallic *clink*.

"DeVeres..." Sadie called, "just in time to pitch horseshoes. Lunchtime is over, but the footmen can fix plates for you both."

Roddy said no thank you, but a footman was dispatched to bring me a lunch of cold lamb, rolls, and sliced pears. My husband asked a footman for a time-table schedule of the steamboats just as a new *clink* brought cheers and applause for Jack Barrott. Alf was not in sight. In minutes, I sat on a latticed bench with my plate while Roddy stood with a leaflet and studied the steamboat schedule.

Edna stepped close to eye the leaflet. "Going up to Saratoga for water, Mr. DeVere? I recommend the Vichy Spring."

Standing by her friend, Sadie grinned. "And will you fetch water from Saratoga Springs because the beavers did not make way for you and Lady Valentine DeVere this morning? Or did the beavers disappear underwater? Could we say they set up a sort of...camp? Would it be a camp?"

The two women had malice in their eyes, Sadie no longer the *Ladies' Home Journal* homemaker and Edna her willing partner in devilry.

I put the plate on a nearby wicker table, my appetite vanished.

Roddy simply said that he had legal business on the *Mary Powell* and that we would meet the boat at its 4:10 p.m. arrival at Kingston and return promptly to Kiddwood.

"Promptly for the Cocktail Hour, Roderick," Sadie said. "We expect you. Alf will take it hard if you are gallivanting in Kingston instead of tending the bar here at Kiddwood."

"My business should not take long," Roddy said.

"Ah, always business, which my Alf knows too well," Sadie continued, "spending this lovely day in the library with Kidd & Company cement, when he would so much like to tramp to the old iron mine." Her eyes narrowed to a cold glint. "You do remember the mine, Roderick? You went with Clarence quite some time ago. Remember? I'm sure you remember...."

Roddy blinked. "Indeed, I do."

"Then consider this...unless you are here promptly for the Cocktail Hour, Alf might ask you to go with him again to the mine. And if he does, you might say that it will be like father, like son."

❧

Roddy and I did not discuss Sadie's dismal hints. My husband muttered that he would not be threatened by the Kidds but said no more. In Kingston, we allowed ample time to send the Western Union wire to Matthew Harding, Esq. and watched the *Mary Powell* come into view on the Hudson at 4:00 p.m., steaming its way to the Kingston Point Park that was dotted with picnickers and filled with cheerful cries from the penny arcade, along with rifle shots snapping from the shooting gallery in the amusement area.

We waited dockside with passengers who were eager to reach the Saratoga gaming tables. The *Mary Powell* tied up on the minute of 4:10 p.m.

Roddy asked to see an official, perhaps the purser or Mr. Thomas Kelton, the vice-president of the company. Eager to look for the juggler, I felt tied down at a deck railing while my husband insisted that we first speak to an official who could vouch for Mr. Roderick DeVere, Esq. who had legal business involving the damaged saloon.

The wait was annoying. The *Mary Powell* would stay at Kingston for just thirty minutes, departing at 4:40. Minutes ticked by as passengers in finery and crewmen in striped jerseys and white duck pants swirled about us.

At last, "Mr. DeVere...and Mrs. DeVere. How do you do?"

"Mr. Kelton, good afternoon," Roddy shook hands with the thin man in a gray pinstriped suit. He bowed and invited me to join him and Mr. DeVere to inspect the new repairs in the main saloon.

However, I announced that the fresh air on the open deck was too tempting to pass up. Roddy gave me a fish-eyed glance as I rattled on about fresh air in the late spring, smiled, and fanned my fingers.

Looking back, I would say that, at that moment, my husband knew me better than I knew myself.

I did not intend to deceive Roddy. Until my husband joined me, I planned to keep an eye out for a man carrying juggling balls or clubs. Amid the passengers in holiday finery and busy crewmen, however, no such man came into view. A few passengers already sipped their free punch. Each minute was precious.

I recalled that at dinner, Miss Craig and her fiancé described juggling on the topmost deck. "The juggler...is he up there?" I asked a crewman, ready to start for the stairway and up two flights.

"He starts his act when we're underway, ma'am. He comes out when we're on the river."

"Then, where would I find him just now? In a cabin?"

Wariness crept into the crewman's pale blue eyes.

"We're a day liner, ma'am. No cabins on the *Powell*. You'll see him soon enough."

"Oh, do let me explain," I said. "My husband is aboard with an official...making arrangements for a private party next month...a birthday party on the top deck. We are eager to have the juggler perform, and I hope to have a word with him before he begins his...performance. Can you help?"

I had tugged at his jersey without meaning to, but the crewman seemed more amused than annoyed when he called, "Ray, how about show the lady to the closet?"

"The 'nut' closet, is it?"

"The very one."

They winked at each another, and I was led to the stern where a bulkhead door was shut tight. "Filbert," the crewman named Ray called out, pounding on the door. "Filbert, a lady passenger to see you. Open up, man. Open up, Filbert."

The crewman had gone about his business when the door cracked open an inch, and the risk of my rash move became clear only now, facing the black slash of a barely open door. In the daylight, I was exposed, but whoever was behind the door was hidden.

Was a killer behind the door? I let my guard down amid the mirth and high spirits of the steamboat passengers. No weapon was at hand, not even a hat pin. The door did not open wider.

Fiona was held under water...physically. Could I be pulled into the pitch-black space and restrained, yanked into the darkness and discovered sometime later? My pulse raced. I could run. I could scream. Instead, I took a step back, half-crouched, then lunged to kick the door, full force.

The bulkhead door yielded so easily I almost lost my footing, then faced the man who had stood behind the door, a portly, short man in trousers, an undershirt, and stocking feet.

"Oh..." he said. "Oh, dear."

My glower became confusion. I blurted, "Are you the juggler?"

Goggle-eyed, he grabbed behind him for a coat, rammed his arms into the sleeves, buttoned up, and said in a thin voice, "I am Bert Filbert."

"Filbert," I repeated.

"Like the oval, edible nut," he said.

"But are you the juggler?"

He did not answer at once. Pink-cheeked and nearly bald, he smoothed wisps of hair and touched the trembling chin he tucked into his neck. Behind him, a bed palette, wall hooks, a washstand, and a crate with balls and rings—the basics of a juggler's living quarters. Was the *Mary Powell* his home?

"Juggler?" I asked a third time. The man looked confused.

He swallowed and stood on tiptoe. "What's this about? What do you want?"

I put out my foot as a doorstop. In careful tones, I said, "Health-to-Wealth, Mr. Filbert?"

"I don't owe them a cent. Not one cent." His cheeks flared scarlet. "Let them sue me."

"I am not here about money," I said.

"They'll get nothing else. They got it all."

"Who got it, Mr. Filbert?"

"The one in the nurse outfit. She's in tight with that Cedric Ferris," he said, "and the property man too. I could have my academy up and running."

"What academy?" I asked.

"The 'New York Academy of Juggling and Magic,'" he said. "But the lying property man's trick lease has my name in ink, and the rest went to the Wealth camp...every nickel from my Uncle Gus. And they wanted more."

"And so..." I said, "you left the camp at night because of financial stress?"

"Thought I'd freeze to death," he said. "...half the night in the woods until that house showed up, all lights and nice people. So yes, I juggled, and they clapped and let me stay all night. I hitched into town on a vegetable wagon."

He stopped and caught his breath. "And here I am, bed and board on the Hudson River...broke."

A steamboat whistle blew, and a calliope tune began.

"The music...we're off in two minutes," he said. "You'll see the best juggling this side of the Mississippi, balls and rings and clubs. I got to get dressed."

"Mr. Filbert," I said, "one more thing. Were you massaged at the camp? By a young woman named Fiona?"

"Oh yes, Fiona," he said. "Everybody wanted her in their tent. She was good at it...scared too. I could feel 'scared' in her hands. A juggler feels these things."

"What was she scared of?"

"Big man that came nights," he said. "Not one of us in the tents, and he wanted Fiona. One day, she was gone. I don't know where she went. I thought, good for her. That camp...it's no good. Costs way too much."

Chapter Twenty-two

BREATHLESS, I RAN TOWARD the gangplank. The frenetic calliope, the steam whistle, and the quivering deck underfoot meant the *Mary Powell* was leaving the dock. And no Roddy.

Men's hats, women's feathered bonnets, and no sight of my husband as I dashed forward. The paddlewheel churned... too late, I was too late.

Then, I was not. At the gangplank Roddy stood with arms akimbo and feet planted wide to block two crewmen who handled chains and cables. I sped toward them until my arm was grabbed as my husband hustled us down the gangplank onto the dock, where people waved goodbye to the *Mary Powell*.

"Catch your breath, Val." Roddy scolded in a clipped voice. Despite his pique, the juggler was my headline, my *find*. "Over there...." Roddy pointed to a wrought iron bench several yards from the amusement park area. We took a park path between groups of children who turned cartwheels on the grass and squealed in delight.

I felt pleased with myself. Roddy's jaw looked blunt. We sat.

"Are you ready to talk?" he asked.

"Are you?"

A full minute passed before Roddy gave a curt nod. "I suppose you have a reason, Val," he said, "...but you were nowhere to be found, and I thought, 'Here we come, Saratoga.' In case you care, Val, Captain Anderson has a reputation for speed and service. The *Mary Powell* arrives and departs on time."

I looked down at pigeons nearing the bench.

"So, let me say," Roddy continued, "that after inspecting the saloon repairs, I brought up the topic of the juggler, which was my plan. I talked at some length with Mr. Kelton and learned the man somehow got aboard here in Kingston without a ticket. He looked like a tramp but begged to show his juggling before they put him off the boat."

"And he impressed the officials?" I said.

"Nothing of the kind," Roddy said. "If you'll let me finish...?"

Back to the pigeons.

"It seems a crowd gathered and applauded, and the purser got the idea of entertainment on deck. The *Mary Powell* crew cleaned him up for a trial run, and he proved very popular with children and adults too. The crew found him a mop-and-pail closet big enough for a hideaway. He's hired for the summer season, mostly room and board, but they got him a decent suit of clothes and a set of balls and rings. Mr. Kelton says he's reclusive as a hermit unless he's on the top deck, juggling. I understand he earned an off-beat nickname. The crew calls him Mister Nut."

"Because his name is Filbert."

Roddy glared as if I had played a trick. "I found him," I said in a flat voice, "in the hideaway. The crew took me there, and I talked to him."

I reached for Roddy's hand, but nothing doing. "I did not know that you planned to ask Mr. Kelton about the juggler, and I did not intend to wander off," I said, "but time was so short. You were in the saloon inspecting woodwork repairs, and I just thought...."

"Thought you would strike out and find the juggler who might be a killer."

"Roddy," I said in my most somber voice, "The juggler is no killer. Bert Filbert did not murder Fiona Peebles. I'd bet my life on it. Let me tell you...."

I profiled Bert Filbert From his stocking feet to his money woes, omitting the terrifying instant at the bulk-head door. "So," I concluded, "Health-to-Wealth siphoned his every last dollar, and it looks like Keith Property Management is somehow involved."

"Roland Keith," Roddy said.

"But the main discovery," I said, "is that Fiona was a sought-after masseuse and that a 'big man' came to her in the night. The man was not a Health-to-Wealth 'client,' and Fiona feared him."

"That's all of it?"

"Except that Bert Filbert believes she escaped from the camp. He said, 'Good for her.'"

"He has no idea that she was...that she died."

"No. And I did not tell him. The whistle blew, and I ran to find you."

Roddy took my hand. "Val," he said, "I should have told you that I planned to bring up the juggler with the steamboat official."

"And I saw you frown to warn me to stay put," I said. "But Roddy, I am who I am." Tempted to say more, I tossed my head. "The question is, what now? A 'big man' at night in the camp might be the 'Santa' on the cloth scrap, but both are 'scraps' for us. What should we do? Chief Fitch thinks we are part of Ella Conklin's plot to kill Fiona. So, suppose we go to the chief with the cloth scrap and tell him what Bert Filbert said about the 'big man' in the nighttime?'"

Roddy gave me an indulgent look and shook his head. "I would like nothing better, if we had confidence in the assistant chief."

"So...you think Chief Fitch is corrupt?"

"Not the usual graft, Val. But Clyde Fitch has bought the story that Ella Conklin killed Fiona. By rights, he ought to send the woman to Florida for a trial, but I'd guess that he plans to have her tried here first. I think ambition has got the better of him. The 'big man' in the camp at night does not fit Fitch's idea of the case, and he would dismiss it out of hand. He resents Kiddwood and privileged lives, and I think he would like nothing better than to see us on a witness stand as accessories to Fiona's murder."

"Ridiculous," I said with more bluff than belief.

"The point would be, to smear our names," Roddy said. "To put us in bad odor and cast suspicion on Kiddwood, the Kidds, the 'between' seasons, the whole shebang."

"Then," I said, "we are stuck with useless information in a pointless pursuit. So, Roddy, can't we go home? If the young lawyer finds Fiona's papa in a Newark jewelry works, we can help him bring her home to a proper resting place. We can make those arrangements from home. And can't you arrange trappers for the beavers and workmen to smash the dams when the time comes? Alf offered dynamite, so maybe you could make an agreement?"

My husband stroked his chin and stared into the distance. "Tempting," he said, "except...."

"Except what?"

Roddy's eyes narrowed. "For one thing, Ella Conklin might be innocent."

I swallowed, barely able to recall the woman now jailed just blocks from this park, this bench. What did we owe her? What was Roddy thinking? She had thrust a wet wad into my palm and told police she saw us twice at the camp. She did not tell us her name, and my husband was not a criminal defense lawyer. Besides, the deceased Fiona had touched my heart, not the accused masseuse in the jail cell.

"Roddy," I said, "the woman is wanted in Florida for attempted murder."

"A wholly separate legal matter in another state, Val." He added, "This jurisdiction is Ulster County."

Hateful place. Somewhere, a bell tower clock struck five p.m., and the Kiddwood cocktail hour loomed. Roddy appeared strangely somber as evening drew new strolling groups to the park paths.

"Another problem if the case goes according to Assistant Chief Fitch, Val," my husband said, "is the potential damage to my reputation as an attorney."

The moment hung. Why did I not think that far? As a witness or accessory to Fiona's murder, I would be "that Annie Oakley woman," but Roddy could be professionally smeared.

The evening sun flared to mock my gloom when I said, "Roddy, we are boxed in."

"Not necessarily, Val. Consider this...the Chief of Police will soon return to take charge in Kingston, and he might be open to new evidence. Chief Wicker outranks Fitch, and he could go aboard the steamboat to question Bert Filbert about the 'big man' at night in the Health-to-Wealth camp. The cloth rag can be useful, but it needs to be shored up, if it is really evidence. I suggest we spend the next two days trying to bolster evidence. If we don't succeed, we will have tried our best."

"So...we go back to the camp to talk to the third masseuse?"

"Ramona Smith," Roddy said, "but not at the camp. The day after tomorrow, Saturday, the Health-to-Wealth turnover lets the masseuse enjoy her free day at the amusements...." He pointed to the arcade and shooting gallery. "Over there."

"But Saturday will draw a big crowd, especially if the weather is good," I said. "It sounds like a needle-in-haystack day, Roddy. And meanwhile, do we pitch horseshoes at Kiddwood? Spar with Edna Rossiter? Placate Alf and Sadie? And hadn't we better get going? They will be—"

"—not just yet, Val. You asked about the *McClure's* reporter, Lincoln Stephens?"

"The one who goes to strange cities and noses around to pick up evidence of crimes...?"

"He's the one. Let us spend tomorrow doing exactly that...talk to local folks...eyes and ears open, both of us. Maybe there's a beauty parlor you can visit. For me, a bootblack and livery stable, and the lumberyard. We'll ask whether a local Kingston man plays St. Nicholas at the holidays, and whether a local character fits the bill in general terms. We can both visit the greengrocer to ask about the deliveryman."

"The cursing Hank Boynt," I said.

Roddy nodded. "But right now, a head start...." He gestured behind him at the nearby commercial district. "Let's walk to the Bauer Hotel. You can take a seat in the lobby while I go into the bar. The bartender ought to remember me from restocking a few days ago....thanks to the Cleveland Bay horse."

I shuddered. "Sweetie."

"Maybe Alf did me a favor," Roddy said. "The smashed bottles in the ditch make a good story, so give me thirty minutes in the Bauer Hotel bar with the bartender. I'll buy replacements for the liquor I bought last Friday. If we're a bit late, Sadie and Alf will be happy to see an armload of new cocktail liquors."

My husband's own spirits seemed buoyed by the plan. "Roddy," I said, "I am famished…."

"Come to think of it…." Without a second's delay, Roddy nodded, stood, eyed the amusements area, dashed off, and returned with snack boxes.

"Cracker Jack for us," he said. "Let's go."

"Roddy, I'll wait here. Right here on the bench."

"Of course not." My husband's eyes widened as if I shocked him.

Etiquette dictated that a lady must not be left by herself in public, meaning outdated chivalry twisted into women's restrictions. As I was learning, the loggerheads of our marriage often meant one partner's trifle was the other's grave matter. Roddy had been alarmed last winter when I defied the rule to walk up Fifth Avenue with Velvet in a freezing cold morning. I was in high fury at the the time, and my husband feared my fine fur coat would make me a victim of theft, if not violent crime.

"Val, what are you saying?"

"Just that I will sit here and enjoy the snack on this Kingston Point Park bench instead of trudging to a hotel lobby. The grass is lovely, the children are turning cart-wheels, and friends are strolling on the paths. There is no reason to go into a dreary hotel lobby. I promise to stay on the bench. I will keep company only with the pigeons. No Cracker Jack for them."

My smile met Roddy's frown. I dug in on this park bench. If Roddy insisted on the Bauer Hotel, he must go without me. I had no more to say. Ravenous, I devoured the caramel corn mix, heedless of the pigeons.

Chapter Twenty-three

IN SECONDS, MY HUSBAND turned on his heel as the slanting sunlight cast the broad parkland in deep greens, while the lampposts on the pathways bloomed with the first electrical lights of the evening. The thirty minutes began pleasantly with views of children at play, much as my friend Cassie's son and daughter would turn cartwheels and somersaults on this grass. If she were here, Cassie would join me on the bench and speak of her latest letter from Dudley and his hunt for fossils in the South Sea Islands.

Soon, I will hear her latest news in our upcoming summer weeks in Newport, but not soon enough for a final exit from Ulster County. In a pinch, I would walk the distance, as I had walked the rocky trails in the Colorado mining camps with Papa.

I had just finished the Cracker Jack when a shadow blocked the sun, and the bench jolted on its concrete base.

"Good evening, Miss."

A man sat himself down on the bench. This bench, my bench.

"I say again, 'Good evening, Miss.'"

I nodded without speaking. A heavy man, he left just inches between us. My quick move to the very end of the bench and "cold shoulder" did not budge him.

Should I spring up? Walk away? A quick glance showed his stubby nose, a carroty moustache, and wooly hair the color of a calico cat. He wore a block-check suit in orange tones and glistening black boots. Holding a paper cone of peanuts, he opened a newspaper...the *Freeman.*

I stared straight ahead.

"I see you go in for Cracker Jack," he said. "Not enough peanuts for me...too much popcorn."

I kept silent. Perspiration prickled my neck.

His newspaper rattled. "Did you see this? Young woman got herself killed...murdered."

I held my place. I got here first.

"Outside Kingston, but killers can strike right here in the city. You live in Kingston, Miss?"

At his second "Miss," I crossed my left hand over my right to display the wedding band. Which made no impact.

"Can't be too careful," he said. "Broad daylight, you never know."

I took short breaths. Peanut shells fell on the concrete base.

"Then again...." I felt him lean toward me, his voice honeyed as he said, "Maybe you are looking for a special

Cracker Jack tonight? Your own 'Jack'...? Maybe you just got off a boat here, so you are new to the park?"

My cheeks felt scorched. I did not look his way.

"If that's your game," he said, "here's a favor for you, no charge." His lips smacked. "Madam Dwyer," he said, "she's got the market cornered, if you know what I mean. Treats everybody good...buyers and sellers too. Beats a park bench. You'll find her on Pearl Street."

I was sure he winked at me. Furious and stubborn, I froze, not moving a muscle as endless minutes passed while peanut shells cracked. Finally, the sound of glass bottles clinked in the distance behind me...at last, Roddy whose familiar footsteps and the chiming bottles sped me from the bench and up the path where he cradled wrapped-up liquors close to his chest.

"Val, good of you to meet me halfway. Your cheeks, dear... are you all right? Too much sun today?" He quipped, "I hope your bench was pleasant," then took my arm and said, "The dogcart is ready, so here we go. My conversation in the Bauer Hotel bar is worth its weight in gold. I have several leads for us."

Roddy's firm, warm arm against mine and his tenor voice felt both close and somehow remote. He was pouring out names I could not remember, a barber and a bootblack, a stable hand and lumber yard boss. "All for tomorrow's foraging for evidence." He named a beauty parlor operator who also went out of my head.

We had reached the dogcart, and Roddy helped me up, put the package on the seat between us, stepped up, flicked the reins—and said a street name that knifed into my mind and stuck when he murmured, "...a business for you to see about, Val...here in Kingston, on Pearl Street."

The Kiddwood cocktail hour was brightened by rye whiskey and the maraschino cherries that Roddy purchased at the Bauer Hotel. Sadie forgave our lateness when Roddy's Old-Fashioneds became Alf's and General Coleman's favorites. Lucy Craig sipped her fiancé's drink, pronounced herself "naughty" and sipped again. Roddy advised that authentic maraschinos ought to be a dark purple. Jack Barrott's piano tunes and a discussion of cocktail garnishes took us to the dinner table.

Once again, the footmen in full livery served as though we dined in a royal palace. I would later blame the several Old-Fashioneds and wine refills for the outburst that stopped all light conversation just as we were offered a dish that was announced to be *Champignons Sautés.*

Edna grinned at me. "For those of us who have not dined in Paris, *mushrooms.*"

Alf abruptly bellowed, "Paris to perdition, I'm talking cement." He slapped his palm on the table. "Limestone for cement, and mushrooms be damned."

"What rooms?" the dark-haired debutante asked, but the square-jawed man silenced her with a frown.

"Mushrooms in the limestone caves," Alf boomed. "Ridiculous! I won't have it!"

The table fell silent, and the footman halted midway with the offending dish. Throats were cleared with ahems. and light coughs could be heard from one end of the table to the other. Alf's face was beet red, and Sadie's white as a sheet. Jack Barrott's fingers tapped the table as if searching for a keyboard.

At that moment, Clarence arose from his place between the debutante and Edna. He raised his wine glass high and spoke in silvery tones. "May I propose a toast to my father, who shows us exactly what the French like to say, *À chacun son gout*...everyone to their own taste. In honor of Alfred Kidd, let us all drink to each and every taste, whatever it may be."

Glasses raised, we sipped in relief while avoiding glances at one another. Alf managed to smile. No one accepted the proffered mushrooms, and the footman beat a hasty retreat. Light conversation resumed, stilted but fluid, and Sadie proposed that after dinner, we all gather in the drawing room to read a classic old stage play aloud, each of us reading lines in turn from scripts kept at Kiddwood for just such evenings as this one.

"Shakespeare is much too much at Kiddwood," she said, "but *The Country Wife* is a comic delight. So, Valentine...," she continued, "I can imagine you in the role of Mrs. Pinchwife, and Roderick, surely you are the perfect Mr. Pinchwife. And Jack Barrott, you will be Mr. Horner, so the piano is silenced tonight." She smiled stiffly at the guests and promised everyone would take turns reading the parts. "Lines for one and all," she chirped.

In the drawing room after coffee and dessert, a footman handed out dog-eared scripts, and every guest surrendered to an evening that put a stop to chit-chat that might otherwise light a fuse and set off an angry blast before bedtime.

Roddy and I got to our rooms after midnight, both feeling we had played parts in a Kiddwood drama, never mind the scripts. In nightclothes, we sat in my room and kept our voices down, mine with effort.

"Roddy, everyone at the table really and truly raised a glass to Clarence for helping us get through that dinner. Clarence was amazing."

"Didn't think he had it in him."

"Sulking and hanging back...and lying," I said. "But he took over at the perfect instant with that inane toast to his father. If only we weren't roped into that play."

"Sadie's idea to quash more disruption," Roddy said. "And it worked. We played our parts."

"But mushrooms...." I shook my head. "Why would mushrooms set Alf off? Did he once get sick from poisonous ones?"

"Something to do with limestone," Roddy said. His eyebrows lowered into a frown. "Something to do with cement...something...."

A clock chimed 1:00 a.m. We agreed to get a few hours' sleep, but not before I brought up a touchy topic about tomorrow. "Roddy, the street in Kingston where you expect me to pay a visit?"

He looked up and stifled a yawn. "Nice name," he said. "Pearl Street."

"Do you remember what sort of business it is?" I asked.

"A boarding house," he said as he stood to kiss me good-night. "I understand Pearl Street is a boarding house for women. Sounds perfect for our purpose, doesn't it?"

Friday, June twenty-third, dawned with a sky that flared pink. No guests appeared at the breakfast pastry buffet, not even Edna, and so we sipped a quick coffee and tea, snatched scones, and left a note for the Kidds, saying Roddy would pursue water-related arrangements for the DeVere tract, while I sent Western Union wires concerning property managed for me in Virginia City, Nevada. We would return to Kiddwood as soon as possible.

The clocks chimed 8:00 a.m. when Roddy suggested that we leave by the back door on the chance that Hank Boynt might appear with a delivery of produce. "Maybe he'll be decent if a lady is present, Val. Maybe we can arrange to talk to him."

At the kitchen entrance, however, stacked crates of fresh vegetables meant the wagon had stopped here earlier. Roddy cursed softly and murmured that we might find time to visit Wall Street today, since Chief Fitch had vowed to question Hank Boynt further about Fiona's body and possible jewelry.

"But we will not request a jail cell visit with Ella Conklin," I said.

"Not until we are ready."

We tiptoed to the stable, where the groom hitched a dapple gray named Dimples. "She's tried and true, Mr. DeVere...and missus...good for a dogcart."

We reached the Kingston commercial district as shops were opening for the day. A boy sweeping a sidewalk directed us to Pearl Street, which was lined with three-story houses of stone or brick with tall windows and shutters. Stately elms and hedges bordered the houses, which were set back from the broad street. A coachman on the box of a passing carriage tipped his hat. Otherwise, the street was quiet.

"Awfully sedate neighborhood for a boarding house," Roddy said. He reined Dimples to a stop in front of a red brick house with limestone trim, a pitched roof, and a cupola.

"This is it?" I asked. "You're sure?"

Roddy slipped a notebook from a coat pocket. "Number Seventeen, Pearl Street, this is it. I'll tie Dimples to a lamp post and escort you to the front door."

Going our separate ways, we had agreed to meet at a nearby church. The one of us who finished first would wait for the other, so I expected to sit in a pew of the St. James Methodist Church at a corner of Pearl and Fair Streets to wait for Roddy, who planned several stops. Surely a boardinghouse employee would walk me to the church, but we would make certain of it.

All the window shades at number Seventeen were pulled down, and blinds covered the front door's etched glass when we stood under the portico and rang the bell.

"Ring it again, Roddy." The bell sounded unusual, a musical motif. On the third ring, the door was opened by a dark-skinned man wearing a porter's jacket and holding a dustpan.

Roddy said, "Good morning. We understand this address to be a house for women?"

"Women, yes," he said.

"I have come to speak to someone in charge," I said, "someone to give me a few minutes' time this morning... and someone who can walk with me to a nearby church here on Pearl Street."

"To talk...and pray," the man said, shifting the dustpan. He gazed at my walking suit with a double-breasted jacket and onyx buttons. Small amber earrings fit the day. I had worn it to Poughkeepsie. Willa pressed it.

"I expect Mrs. Dwyer will see you," he said.

"Dwyer...." I nearly choked at the name that I heard on the park bench. Roddy did not notice my sharp glance when he said, "Excellent," and before I could say more than the name from the bench, Roddy said, "I will be on my way."

And he was gone. Frankly, I had a choice, and I chose to be ushered inside to a drawing room furnished with red velvet and satin-striped divans and loveseats in gilded frames. Aromas of perfumes and cigars filled the air, which was stirred by a lazy ceiling fan. Framed pictures of deep-bosomed women in French lingerie filled one wall, and another of gentlemen at a racetrack with horses in the distance.

Boarding house? Not a chance. I knew where I was.

The scene felt quiet as a crypt, and no clock visible, so time stopped until the swish of silk and a husky "good morning" brought me to my feet before a tall, full-figured woman who swept a curtain aside in a stage entrance. A robe of heavy powder blue silk outlined her figure, and her henna-tinted hair seemed hastily fixed in place with decorative ivory pins.

She thrust out fingers glittering with sapphire rings, and my practical nails met a manicure gleaming with iridescent polish. "Do sit down," she said in a husky voice. "I am Eileen Dwyer... Mrs. Dwyer."

I perched on a loveseat. "I am Mrs. DeVere...Valentine DeVere."

"So, I would guess your birth date falls in mid-February. Am I right?" Her voice seemed mismatched by the frank gray eyes, strong chin, and firm mouth that made Mrs. Dwyer seem all business. Probably in her late forties, she looked just rousted from slumbers but ready for this early exchange. "February the fourteenth...your birthday?"

"Yes," I said.

"And what brings you here at this ungodly hour, my dear?"

"My husband drove me here," I said.

She gave a tight smile. "Call him what you will, Miss Valentine, but let us face the facts of the matter. He no longer supports you, and you will now support yourself under this roof. Of course, such attire as this...." She waved at my suit. "...wholly wrong, but we can supply the negligees and hosiery, which will be deducted from your income." She looked at my midriff. "One question, and you must—absolutely must—be honest. Are you preggers?"

"I...no...not at this time."

"Because Madam Dwyer does not operate a home for the unwed. Do you understand me?"

I sat up straight and looked her in the eye. "Mrs. Dwyer," I said, "I am not looking for a job."

"So, then," she snapped, "you'll do factory work and starve to death? Or spend your days slaving in a maid's uniform?" She crossed her legs at the knee. "Or walk the streets? Do you know about our winters?"

"I don't think you are listening," I said.

"Listening? Let me assure you, Valentine, that employment by Madam Dwyer is safety itself. I pay watchmen and tolerate no client who misbehaves. The girls employed here are well paid, fed, and sheltered. It is men's cravings that support this enterprise. So, what do you say? If yes, I will offer you the best cup of coffee and yeast rolls in Kingston. If no...." She gestured at the hallway door.

I, too, crossed my legs at the knee and said to her, "Do not confuse me with a job seeker, Mrs. Dwyer. I am here in search of information about a murder victim...a young woman whose body was found on my property...property outside the city limits. She was forced under water and drowned. I want to know who killed her."

Eileen Dwyer stared hard, sucked her cheek, tapped her feathered mule slipper on the carpet, and then turned her head and called out, "Griff, coffee and rolls for two."

In the next minutes, we avoided conversation. She did not ask about me, nor I about her. Where we came from, how we got here, what we would say to one another...none of it punctuated the silence broken only by the slight whir of ceiling fan paddles. At length, a white-jacketed young man wheeled in a cart, placed a small table between Madam Dwyer and me, and asked how we liked our coffee. For both of us, black, and served in fine china. Today's yeast rolls, he said, were cinnamon with butter cream icing.

The robust coffee was delicious, the best since I left the West. The roll was too good to pass up, but I managed to nibble instead of wolfing.

"Have another," said the husky-voiced Eileen Dwyer. "I know hunger when I see it. It's in the eyes. I doubt you had breakfast. Go ahead."

I ate two rolls.

"Now then," she said, "what's this all about?"

What moved me to confide in the owner of a brothel and a complete stranger? Was it her feathered mule slippers identical to those I often wore at breakfast with Roddy at home? Or was it an echo from my past? In Virginia City, Nevada, a beloved 'Madam," Julia Bullette, was legendary for generosity and care for the miners, a sort of Florence Nightingale of the night. Everyone loved her.

Perhaps I wrapped Eileen Dwyer in the cloak of Julia Bulette. Or perhaps the need to seek shreds of useful evidence became urgent. Whichever it was, I told her about the field where Fiona's body was found by Hank Boynt, then described the Health-to-Wealth camp and mentioned Kiddwood.

Mrs. Dwyer sipped her coffee, nibbled a roll, and sipped again. She then put down her coffee cup, folded her hands, and said, "Hank Boynt is dangerous. Stay away from him at all costs. As for the Kiddwood estate...." A smile played at the corners of her firm mouth. "I'll just say, in season the country estates contribute a fair share to Pearl Street."

She tilted her head and nudged the ivory hair pins. "One final point," she said. "You might like to know that a woman paid a call here. She wanted to hire one of our girls to work at a camp giving massages. She would not tell her name. Her hair.... Mrs. Valentine DeVere, we could both envy hair like that. No henna rinse for that one. Her hair shone bright as polished copper."

Chapter Twenty-four

THE ROUGH GRANITE ST. James Methodist Church was softened inside by light filtered through two stained glass rose windows. I chose a pew at the rear of the sanctuary, my thoughts tumbling with Eileen Dwyer's revelations. Immersed in her words, I barely spoke to the young steward, Griff, who escorted me here at his employer's order, and clearly puzzled by the lure of an empty church on a Friday morning. Madam Dwyer seemed bemused by my destination but did not inquire. She offered further assistance in my "hunt" and said number Seventeen Pearl Street would open its doors to me, preferably not before noon.

Sharp as she was, Eileen Dwyer did not realize how much she had divulged. Bursting to tell Roddy, I fingered *The Methodist Hymnal* beside me on the pew. Wherever his rounds took him, Roddy could "leg it" for the better part of the day, as Papa would say, meaning move fast. Not too fast, of course.

If only I had thought to wear my lavalier watch. With no idea of the time, I closed my eyes and rehearsed Eileen Dwyer's words. Roddy must hear them. A distant clock tower struck eleven bells. Or was it twelve? Losing count, I opened the hymnal and scanned the order of service...the prayers, the anthem, the tithes and offerings.

Was Fiona worth my "tithe and offering?" I closed the hymnal. In another hour, the clock tower bell would ring again, and I would confirm the hour as high noon.

Or 1:00 p.m.

That bell had not yet rung when Roddy appeared in the church aisle, crooked his finger, and led me into the bright sunshine, where I squinted as he guided me to the dogcart.

"We'll drive around and talk before we return to Kiddwood," he said, "and I'll tell you what I learned." Assisted onto the seat. I reminded myself that Roddy mistook Pearl Street for a women's boarding house.

Dimples pulled us into quiet neighborhoods where modest bungalows and cottages lined barely paved streets. "Bumpy ride," I said.

"Smoother than tar-and-gravel to Kiddwood," Roddy replied. "So, tell me, Val, what did the boarders have to say?"

"The 'boarders,' Roddy, are ladies of the night."

"Ladies...." He gripped the reins. "You don't mean...?"

"But I do. Pearl Street is a brothel."

My husband winced.

"And far more helpful than a boardinghouse. The Madam hosted me over coffee and sweet rolls. She is a savvy businesswoman. Let me tell you—"

"—not yet, Val." He paused. "She thought you needed a job, didn't she?"

"At first."

Roddy's shoulders slumped. "My wife...." His voice choked. "What would your papa think? Patrick Mackle would turn over in his...."

Actually, I believed Papa would understand. And it pleased me to think of Rufus and Eleanor learning their Wild West daughter-in-law breakfasted with a "Madam."

"My parents...you do understand."

"I think so."

"So, let's hear it, Val."

"First of all," I said, "I learned that Hank Boynt is not a nuisance but downright dangerous."

Roddy nodded. "That's what a barber said when he gave me a trim this morning. Hank terrifies him every few weeks when he's in for a haircut and shave. He threatened the barber with the man's own razor."

"And he cursed at you last Thursday morning...hideous." I counted back to the morning at Kiddwood's back door when Alf presented Wellington boots for the trek to the iron mine. "Maybe Hank turns vicious when he's drinking, Roddy. He was nice as pie to Alf when he delivered produce."

"Because Alfred Kidd is an employer and a gentleman. A man like Hank Boynt knows whose boots to lick." Roddy turned the dogcart around a corner. "I still think we should try to talk to him."

I did not reply. The deliveryman lacked all respect for the body he had found, as if Fiona Peebles was not a human being but a carcass.

Impatient to leave off Hank Boynt, I said, "There's more to tell you, Roddy. Madam Dwyer...Eileen Dwyer... offered a keyhole glimpse of certain gentlemen from the country houses who visit her Pearl Street establishment... as customers."

"From Kiddwood? The guests?"

"She did not say, exactly, but Kiddwood was included in the country houses. I repeat, 'Included.'"

"I see." Roddy stared into the distance, seeming about to speak but held back. I did not probe. Our horse, Dimples, shook her mane and tail to shoo flies.

I had deliberately saved the biggest shock. "Worth the whole morning, Roddy," I said, "listen to this...a woman visited Pearl Street to hire prostitutes to give massages in the daytime. She has bright copper-colored hair. It has to be...."

"Vanessa Zee...Zelonski."

"And doubtless in league with Cedric," I said. "So much for the Kellogg system, another fraud in the whole bogus Health-to-Wealth camp. Vanessa and Cedric must be desperate without Fiona and Ella Conklin."

Roddy shifted the reins. "So, Val, when did Vanessa visit Pearl Street?"

"I assume in the last day or two, why?"

"If she came in the last couple of days, she would try to fill in for Fiona and Ella," Roddy said. "But early in the month suggests that prostitution was part of the operation from the start."

"Masseuses as...." I broke off. Had I been naïve? My mental portrait of Fiona had not allowed this possibility.

Roddy flicked the reins and turned another corner to circle the block. "When scouting a Health-to-Wealth location in Ulster County," he said, "did Cedric Ferris seek houses of prostitution as a resource? Did Roland Keith help?"

The questions multiplied, and the clock tower bell in the distance struck a doleful 1:00 p.m. as if it tolled for Fiona.

Or me.

If Roddy and I were at home, I would call our dog for a tug-o-war and feed her a bit of biscuit. At anxious times, Velvet gave me breathing space. Here, I must find it for myself. "Roddy," I quickly asked, "Where did you go besides the barber shop? Tell me."

He smiled. "After the barbershop, I bought five-cent cigars and drove to Webster's Livery and Boarding Stable on Mill Street. Then, I gave out the cigars and asked the stablehands to take a quick look at Dimples's front feet."

"What for?"

"For connection. We all decided her hoof walls were smooth and hard and her shoes fit, and then we talked about horses and the baseball season...one thing and another. And fortunate, Val, because I met Mr. Grove Webster, who has been Kingston's Treasurer and has just been elected Ulster County Sheriff."

"So, he knows Chief Fitch...."

"He knows everybody, and he likes to talk about Kingston. Lately, the city has had ups and downs, he said. The railroad yard is holding steady, and a big coal business is coming, but right now, cement is in trouble."

"Oh?"

"The demand is huge, and new machines can mine the limestone fast and effectively. Two companies compete with Kidd & Company, but they all have the same problem—supply. There's not enough limestone in Ulster County, and they're all fighting for it."

"No wonder Alf is ready to fly off the handle," I said.

"And I found out why the mushrooms set him off," Roddy continued. "Mushroom growers are leasing abandoned mines. They're damp, dark, and cool...perfect for mushroom farming. No more outdoor gathering in hopes they aren't poisonous."

"So," I said, "For Alf, the business that first brought his family its wealth was iron, and then to cement, and soon...mushrooms? No wonder the man's temper is on a hair trigger."

The dogcart turned toward Kiddwood, and I tried to feel more forgiving of our host. From iron to fungi, the descent would devastate a major player in a vital industry. And Sadie?

She had her pride. She could bask in her husband's glory as Mrs. Alfred Kidd, but if the name stood for mushrooms, Sadie would be mortified. *Town Topics* would print nasty lines on *how-the-mighty-have-fallen*, one of its specialties. I resolved to be kinder.

We arrived at Kiddwood in midafternoon to find some guests at croquet, while others struggled with paper kites that refused to fly in the light breeze. On the lawn in front of the veranda, Lucy Craig's fiancé jogged across the grass dragging a kite along the ground. Jack Barrott called, "Fly... do fly for Henry!" while the dark-haired debutante's giggles prompted croquet players to pause, ogle the kites, and return to their mallets.

We learned that Alf had taken Lucy to tour the old iron mine, so questions about the latest plan for water would wait until he returned. I fibbed that my Western Union wires to Nevada had been satisfactory. Sadie huddled with us to whisper that a Kingston policeman had stopped briefly at noon to leave a message for Roddy. ("Slipped under your pillow in a sealed envelope, Roderick, and no one the wiser. And your door is locked.")

Sadie was obviously curious, as was I, but before Roddy could see about the note, he was taken aside by Clarence.

"I must 'steal' you for a cocktail lesson, Roderick. When the *Fly Away* is launched next spring, I will offer my yacht's own drink for guests...the ladies as well as gentlemen."

He winked at me, and I resolved to feel kindlier toward the tremulous younger Mr. Kidd, whose bare ankles remained a harsh pink even as his cigar lighting gadget appeared useless. The two men went inside to the liquor area, and Sadie pointed me to the croquet court, suggesting I simply doff my jacket, since Edna and the other ladies wore skirts and shirtwaists with bowties.

Minus the tie, I took up a mallet and proceeded to amuse everyone when my ball went aloft...everyone but Edna, who chided that I might fare best on a polo field.

The afternoon spent, we all went indoors to change for cocktails and dinner. Willa laid out a sky-blue crepe de chine dress with a scoop neck and cap sleeves and was ready to assist me when my husband tapped at the door to our adjoining rooms and asked me to join him. "A few minutes, Willa," I said, going through the bathroom passageway into Roddy's room.

"Close the door, Val."

In formal trousers and shirt, Roddy held a folded paper and envelope. His face was as white as the paper in his hand. "The note..." I said, "the police...."

"The note is nothing...only a request to meet Fitch tomorrow."

"Roddy, that is not nothing," I blurted. "It gives us the perfect excuse to go...." I broke off because my husband looked stricken. He put the note and envelope on his bed. "Roddy," I said, "are you ill? The cocktail with Clarence... what did you drink?"

"Not what I drank, Val. It's what I thought...about Pearl Street."

"What?"

"Sit down."

We both perched on the bed. "What about Pearl Street?"

"It's Clarence...and his father."

"What about them?"

"I was careful, Val. I wanted to avoid trouble."

"What trouble, Roddy?"

"At all costs...no dredging from the past."

"What past?"

Roddy twisted his wedding band. "The men from the country houses...you learned where they go in Kingston."

I remembered Roddy's face in the dogcart. He almost told me something. Now I could guess. "They go to Pearl Street," I said softly.

"Clarence tried to tell me," Roddy said. "We were in prep school...different schools, but that summer, his father...."

"Alf," I said, careful not to push. "What about Alf?"

Roddy looked straight into my eyes. "I asked this afternoon to make certain, Val, and Clarence told me true. Alf took Clarence to Pearl Street. He said it was time to 'show him how to be a man.'"

"And he did?"

Roddy nodded. "Father and son both."

"And for Clarence...?"

"For Clarence, one of the worst times in his life."

Chapter Twenty-five

A "QUARANTINED" CLARENCE WOULD not appear with the guests tonight, he confided to Roddy after his humiliating admission. Roddy wished him peace.

We faced another cocktail hour, another dinner, another evening of games and piano tunes in a country house that sank us deeper into the Kidd family morass. In reality, the tuxedos and gowns were finery's camouflage, and the daywear let us masquerade as frolicsome guests. Both blended into a scene seething with betrayal.

So pleasant to the eye, this house, its veranda, its lawn and racquet courts, but they recalled a deceptively picturesque space from my girlhood in the mining camps. A smooth sandy beach by a river in Colorado looked appealing to prospectors who were desperate for respite and recreation. "It's quicksand," Papa was warned. One step, he was told, and it would open its mouth and gape wider and deeper until it sucked the light and air and left a body heaving and quivering to the last.

Kiddwood began to feel like quicksand. So did Kingston. So did the Health-to-Wealth camp on land that Roddy's parents owned, land bought with money my papa had earned with hard work, skill, and faith.

Land now defiled by murder.

I would not bring up Fiona's death at this instant, but the "quicksand" demanded that we reckon with a whorl of facts. "Roddy," I said, "we have spent much effort on the fraud and deceit on your parents' property."

"And on the water shortage problem," replied my ashen-faced husband, still appalled by his boyhood friend's confession. We sat together on his bed. When summoned, the Kiddwood valet would come to help Roddy dress, as would Willa to me.

"Let's take stock," I said. "For our sake, for us. We came here in good faith for old times' sake."

"For two families' long friendship," my husband said in solemn tones.

"Then, two days later," I said, "Alf's special horse nearly pulled you into a deep ditch. You narrowly escaped. That same day, he took me to the old iron mine."

"The customary tour for a visitor."

"But two visitors had to be pulled from the shaft by the Kingston police last autumn, Roddy. And I was almost Alf's next...." Could I say, victim? "His next dupe. Alf was about to push me into the mine. If I had not clipped him behind his knee, I would be this spring's contender for a police rescue."

"You didn't tell me."

"Because you had just come from the ditch with the smashed liquor bottles." I shifted on the chenille bedspread. "Roddy, the Kidds rely too much on their reputation for practical jokes. And Clarence relies too much on your goodwill. He lies."

My husband tapped a knuckle against the bed frame. "We know he lied about Health-to-Wealth, pretending he knows nothing about it."

"Suppose he is lying about other things?"

"Not Pearl Street, Val. He was sincere...he told me true."

I would not dispute the point. "Roddy, the question is, where do we go from here? For us?" I eyed the unfolded note paper at the end of the bed. "The message from the police...what is it?"

"A request to see Chief Fitch tomorrow."

"For what purpose?"

"It doesn't say. We don't know."

"That's the problem, we don't know. How many times in that Wall Street office already? Two?"

"Three. I also went the day after we arrived, remember?"

I did. Roddy had learned about the engraving that gave the dead woman a name. And a father. "So," I said, "we will appear in the morning. Unless the police investigation takes a new turn, we will be folded into the story Chief Fitch heard from Cedric Ferris—"

"—and acted on." Roddy bit his lip. "Which makes us complicit, according to the accused." He paused. "Or is it according to Fitch?"

"If it is," I said, "we have no choice. We must go on our own.." I pushed back a loose strand of hair. "Your law career befouled in a courtroom, your name headlined in the *Freeman*. Your reputation...your feelings."

The moment grew quiet. Roddy took my hand. "And your care that Fiona's life somehow be honored, no matter how it was lived."

Eyes downcast, I nodded. "No matter how...."

A clock struck the half-hour. "Let us agree," Roddy said, "to gather what is useful to us at the police headquarters. Fitch will be in charge...and possibly a county prosecutor too. But let us speak up and listen. And ask our own questions. Then, the third masseuse...."

"Ramona Smith," I said, "but we have no description."

"Never mind. If she is at the park tomorrow afternoon, we must find her. And then, the jail visit with Ella Conklin." He paused. "And one more character...."

"Hank Boynt?"

Roddy nodded. "The foul-mouthed wagon driver. He might know something important."

"If he'll talk."

"Well find out." Roddy leaned for a kiss. "Now, my dear, let us dress and socialize. I will mix a gin cocktail, and Jack Barrott's piano will quit at Sadie's "dot" of eight p.m.

We arrived at police headquarters just before eleven o'clock, tied Dimples to a hitching post, and were promptly led into

Clyde Fitch's office, where the Assistant Chief of Police bent over paperwork, waved us to the familiar round table, and finally took a seat across from me.

"Mrs. DeVere ...Mister...."

"Chief Fitch," my husband said.

So much for pleasant *Good Mornings*. The chief's neat goatee was expanding into a beard, perhaps for dignity. The brass buttons on his uniform shone bright as coins.

"Rumor has it that Saturdays and Sundays will be called the 'week-end' one day soon," he said. "For now, thieves go to work while churchgoers worship, and our one day of rest is shot to pieces."

"Difficult," I said, "to plan a schedule." My small talk sputtered. What did he want from us today? This Saturday morning did not feel like the "official proceeding" we were warned to expect. Roddy explained on the way here that the "proceeding" could be a deposition conducted by the Ulster County prosecutor. Chief Fitch would be present, but the prosecutor would ask the questions. No such official was here.

"Appreciate you coming in from your country house... taking time. You'd be hard at play out there, I'd think."

Roddy stopped my protest with a flinty glance. "Chief Fitch," he said, "I am hoping to clear up confusion, as is Mrs. DeVere. But the reason for this meeting was not stated in the message sent to Kiddwood yesterday."

"No, it was not."

"Deliberately," Roddy said, "to avoid misunderstanding?"

The chief folded his arms. "Ever hold an envelope up the light to read what's inside? Curiosity gets the better of somebody, and it gets messy."

"We appreciate the consideration," Roddy said. "Perhaps you wish to provide new information today?"

"Of a sort," the chief said. "Old to me, new to you." He looked toward the file cabinet, then at me. "Mrs. DeVere, as I recall, you agreed to examine the ring found on the body of the deceased Fiona Peebles."

"I did."

"To determine whether it is familiar to you."

"Correct."

"But you have not come forward for the last week to request a view of the ring."

Was the man accusing me of negligence? Trying to put me on defense? My papa warned not to get my dander up. "Chief Fitch," I said, "I believe you intended to question the wagon driver, Hank Boynt, to make certain that he did not steal other jewelry from the body. As I recall, you were also to investigate whether Mr. Boynt had pawned stolen jewelry. Am I correct?"

Without an answer, he went to a file drawer, brought a small envelope to the table, and poked with his thumb and forefinger. "The ring, Mrs. DeVere, that was found on the deceased's middle finger."

Here it was, the gold ring with a dark red ruby, and smaller than I had imagined. It lay on the envelope the police chief pushed toward me on the table.

"Ever see this before?"

I did not touch the ring but moved the envelope to see the engraving in delicate script—*Fiona from Papa*. A relic of a lost life.

"Familiar to you?"

I slowly pushed the envelope back across the table, raised my eyes and said, "I have never seen this ring."

Except in my mind, ballooned in my thoughts. I blinked back tears, clenched my teeth, and asked, "Chief Fitch, is this ring the only jewelry found on Miss Peebles's body?"

Steely-eyed, he nodded and said, "We are satisfied that Hank Boynt told the truth this time."

"Well and good," Roddy said. "But the deceased was also photographed, so perhaps this would be the time...."

The chief flushed, stuffed the ring into the envelope as if to pocket it, then left it on the table and said, "I regret to say the photograph ...problems developing the film."

"So, you have no picture." I said it softly without accusation.

"The Kingston Police Department has no budget for frills," the chief said.

"Then, the examination of the ring is the sole reason we are here this morning?"

He avoided my gaze. "The attorney of Ulster County advised that you be shown the ring."

"The county prosecutor," Roddy said.

"Yes, sir. He planned to be here but is delayed."

"But your investigation proceeds," Roddy said, "in accordance with Mr. Ferris's complaint?"

"It does."

"And Miss Conklin maintains her innocence?"

"Like a newborn babe, but the Kingston force is nobody's fool." He stroked his new beard. "The county attorney advises that you visit with the accused, which is permissible."

"Possibly," Roddy said, "before Ella Conklin is remanded to Florida."

"She will be tried in Kingston first, Mr. DeVere. Kingston has first call on her, and City Hall has been alerted."

Would the trial be a local spectacle? Promoted in the *Freeman*? A boost to his career?

Roddy tilted his head. "It sounds police leadership is a seven-day-a-week job."

"It's eight days' work in seven, Mr. DeVere."

"Then, you must look forward to your chief's return. Do you know when Chief Wicker might take up his duties in Kingston?"

Fitch rubbed his jaw. "Well, we don't know for sure. Chief Wicker...a lot depends on health. Lung trouble...we don't know."

Roddy showed no emotion, but I could read his mind. If Chief Wicker did not return soon, the case was frozen fast. Ella Conklin's prosecution would go according to Cedric Ferris's complaint, Roddy's name would be dragged into the trial, and Fitch would be lionized. His beard and shiny buttons took on new meaning.

They signaled ambition.

All the more reason that Roddy and I must act on our own.

"Since your visit to the upstairs cell is not for today," Fitch went on, "I will let our matron go home for lunch." He pushed back his chair but waited for me to stand, his courtesy to the lady. "Busy Saturdays this time of year," he said. "Folks go out and forget to lock their doors. They ignore thieving pickpockets in the park and cry to us when their purses come up empty."

I stood, and he gestured to the doorway. "So, Mrs. DeVere, a word to the wise. You watch yourself. There's times the police need hankies for the crybabies."

My fury stayed contained until we reached the dogcart. "How dare he?" I brushed away Roddy's arm and hoisted myself onto the seat. "Crybaby, indeed!"

"Val, he saw you start to tear up over the ring. Clyde Fitch did not rise in the ranks without seeing—"

"—the obvious? The weepy woman?"

"Now, Val."

"Do not 'Val' me, please. I need a few minutes. That man is crude and cunning."

"Qualifications for the job."

We rode in silence to Kingston Point Park, where the adults and children gathered in numbers that moved me from anger to despair. How could we possibly find Ramona Smith, the third masseuse, in this crowd of women in spring fashion's full skirts and sunbonnets? They clustered at the amusement area, many arm-in-arm with men in straw skimmer hats. Children thickened the scene, including infants in bulky prams. Laughter mixed with birdsongs, and somewhere a steam organ piped wheezy melodies.

In sheer numbers, our task seemed impossible.

"Are you hungry, Val?"

"Not for Cracker Jack."

Roddy bought two bars of sweetened chocolate at a snack stand. We opened the wrappers, bit the chocolate, and scanned the crowd.

Roddy reached to take my arm, but I said, "We must separate. If we hope to find Ramona Smith, we must each go a different way. Don't worry, Roddy, I'll be fine."

Etiquette gave way to necessity. We agreed to meet at the refreshment stand when the clock tower bell struck 3:00 p.m. Meanwhile. Roddy would go to the carousel and bowling alley. He put dimes and pennies into my palm for the arcade, and I slipped them into a skirt pocket. In minutes, my husband was out of sight.

Scanning the crowd, I saw nothing of the "bench man" in the orange checkered suit. Nor was any woman conspicuous as a masseuse, no white-robed young woman to knead muscles.

Ramona's most recent Health-to-Wealth clients were now on their way home to become millionaires...unless a man became infatuated and made a date to meet her here this afternoon. So, certain couples needed attention, especially if the man were older. Then again, fathers and daughters could be here for the afternoon. And grandfathers and granddaughters...uncles and nieces.

No end to this fool's errand, this needle-in-haystack. I ruled out the women pushing prams and the tight circles of girlfriends. Pausing at a rubbish can, I tossed away the chocolate wrapper, closed my eyes, and tried to imagine where this sprawling scene might include Ramona Smith. A young woman whose two co-workers had met terrible fates...where would she go to take her mind off Fiona and Ella Conklin?

Perhaps her own fears?

My first thought, *distraction.* The penny arcade had games but also Edison Kinetoscope machines that entertained with ninety seconds of tiny, two-dimensional humans in motion. Would those miniature, black-and-while figures take Ramona's mind off things? Barely bigger than insects, the figures would be intriguing, but for how many repeats? Inside the arcade, I watched the lines for the Kinetoscopes move quickly. In just ten minutes, youths and couples with children spent their pennies for ninety seconds and walked away. The novelty did not satisfy for long. If Ramona put pennies in the slot, she would not stay.

Outside the arcade, I eyed the bandstand, where a semi-circle of women tuned their banjos. Women's banjo orchestras were a novelty, but would a performance distract the masseuse from Health-to-Wealth troubles? Would Ramona join the audience for an afternoon banjo concert?

Or was distraction too single-minded? Too passive? A masseuse worked actively, hands-on. What amusement demanded action in this park? Where could a woman take her mind off perilous thoughts? Maybe the bowling alley, where Roddy might find her.

Or the shooting gallery. The snap and bang of firing bullets drew me to the wood-framed little rifle range, where young men lined up a a counter, shouldered .22 rifles, aimed, and fired at tin targets shaped like eight-point bucks in a deer hunt.

At the end of the counter, a young woman handled the rifle as though trying to manage a foreign object. With light hair and freckles, she wore a pale blue cotton dress, gathered at the neckline and tight at the wrists, the best dress of a nanny or a servant on a half-day holiday.

Or a young woman masseuse hired for the season at a camp in the woods?

I watched, waited, barged in when the space beside her opened up, and then put down dimes from my skirt pocket. "Ten rounds," I said, counting the bullets the attendant put on the counter for the bolt-action, single-shot rifle. Easily handling the bolt and bullet, I raised the rifle, took careful aim, and felled a silhouetted buck. And did it again, aware of the young woman watching beside me.

I pretended to examine the rifle, glanced her way, and smiled.

"You sure know how to shoot," she said.

"I grew up in the West. Most everybody learns firearms."

Her eyes widened. "Like Annie Oakley."

"A crack shot," I said, "with the Buffalo Bill show. She travels far and wide. And earns a pretty penny too."

"Must be nice."

"Nice," I said, "to have a day off work." I slipped a round into the chamber. "Is this your day off?"

"Every eleventh day," she said. "Ten days on, the eleventh day off."

"That's not very often," I replied. "My name is Louisa."

"I am Ramona."

"Pleased to meet you," I said. My heart thumped. "And would you like a few suggestions about the rifle?"

She would. I showed her how to snug the butt against her shoulder and brace the barrel with her left hand on the forestock. I told her to squint and sight a deer at the end of the muzzle. I told her to squeeze the trigger. "Squeeze, but do not jerk," I said. "And your shoulder should feel the kick."

She jerked, missed, and said, "Ouch."

"Great beginning, Ramona," I said. "How's the shoulder? I bet you could use a massage."

Her eyes flashed with fire and ice. "If you knew...."

I shrugged, nonchalant. "Maybe a massage parlor here in Kingston...? I heard about a special kind...named 'Kell' something."

"Kellogg?"

"That's it."

"Stay away from it. I had friends, girlfriends...but the boss...." She shuddered.

"Oh," I said, "I hear awful things about bosses. Sometimes a woman...."

"There's a woman boss," she said, "but the man is the one...he never left my friend alone. Nighttime, you know. We came from Florida."

"A long way."

"I'm going back. I count the days." She grew silent.

"Would you like to shoot again?" I leaned closer to her. "Sometimes, we pretend to shoot somebody who's giving us trouble. Just pretend...."

She raised the rifle. "He came after my friend at nights. I opened my eyes to see the sandals on his feet. Now she's gone forever. And the other girl...big trouble. He handed her off...."

"The boss?"

"To jail. They put her in jail." She raised the rifle. "One more time with this gun, I'll shoot at him. I wish somebody shot him a long time ago."

Chapter Twentyfive

"RODDY, I FOUND HER."

"Where have you been?"

The clock tower bell tolled three p.m., but I dared not leave the shooting gallery until Ramona fired her final shot, thanked me for the lesson, and hurried to meet a wagon driver who she said "burned" her ears with curses when he drove her back to work on her days off. I asked his name, but she disappeared into the crowd.

The tower bell struck four as I joined Roddy, breathless from hustling and bursting with the news. "Found her."

"Then, where is she?"

"Gone...but I learned...learned absolutely everything."

My husband's eyebrows creased in doubt.

"Everything," I repeated.

Roddy's glance turned to concern. "Val, let's sit down. Would you care for ice cream?"

"Ice cream?" I nearly shrieked.

He pointed to a vacant bench. "Sit down, dear, and let me get you a dish...vanilla, I think."

Ordered to the bench. I drummed my fingers, tapped a foot, and craned my neck, bewildered at my husband's notion that I somehow needed a frozen treat.

The "why" of it came clear with the weight of hair against my back. Reaching up, I found my hairpins gone and my hair straggling loose and wild. Brushing my cheek, my hand turned soot black. Another swipe, and I realized the cheap rifles were probably wiped with stove blacking.

To cry or laugh over the dish of vanilla ice cream coming my way? I soon blackened Roddy's handkerchief with my fingers, then spooned each bite while he looked on. Finally, I reached back to twist my hair into a semblance of a braid.

"Roddy," I said in a voice striving for calm, "we have a great deal to discuss. We need to speak privately, and no one must overhear what I have to tell you."

"The dogcart, Val...no, let's walk along the riverfront. No steamboats just now, and no people."

Roddy took my arm and led us on the shortest path to the river. The water smelled fresh. "Roddy," I asked, "how tall is Cedric Ferris?"

"How tall?" My husband's cooing tone meant he still thought me unnerved. This riverfront was Roddy's idea of a therapeutic walk. I had leapt too fast. I must go slow and steady like my lawyer husband when he told the Kidds about the camp.

"Roddy," I said slowly, "I figured that Ramona Smith was either at the bowling alley or the shooting gallery. I found her struggling with a .22 rifle, and I bided my time and saw an opportunity. Here's what happened next...."

As I spoke, we soon walked in step, back and forth past the place where the steamboats docked and the river lapped in wavelets. I recounted each detail of the afternoon. "The sandals," I said, "told me everything. No one else wears sandals. It means the 'big man' in the night is Cedric...Cedric Ferris."

"And that is why you asked about his height."

"Yes."

Roddy gazed across the river at the distant shoreline. "So, we have been misled about 'Santa' and your wet rag... whatever that is supposed to mean."

I nodded. "The fact is, Cedric Ferris forced Fiona from the masseuses' tent in the nighttime. Ramona said he 'never' left her alone. When she finally resisted him, he killed her. That's what I think."

"And Ramona was awake when he came at night?"

"She was."

Roddy said, "In court, she could be a most persuasive witness."

"At Cedric's trial," I said, "with both Ramona and Ella Conklin witnesses against him. Let's hope Chief Wicker comes back to Kingston soon."

My husband bit his lip. "As to that," he said, "discouraging news from Fitch this morning. You heard him refer to Wicker's 'lung trouble.' That means consumption."

"Tuberculosis," I said.

"Same disease, Val, but it means monthslong treatment in a sanitarium. A patient seldom regains full health. When he returns, Chief Wicker is likely to retire."

"And his successor…Clyde Fitch."

"Most likely."

We were back to the question I dreaded to ask. "What should we do?"

"Pay a jailhouse visit to Ella Conklin tomorrow. Unannounced."

"On a Sunday?"

Roddy's smile was grim. "To make certain that Chief Fitch's day of rest is 'shot to pieces.' Now, let us drive Dimples to Kiddwood at a decent trot."

⁂

Roddy's Old-Fashioned cocktails, then dinner and evening games of Bingo took us to the Kiddwood Saturday night "curfew," when Sadie called the footmen to switch off the electrical lights and snuff the candle flames.

Not a minute too soon for Roddy and me. At dinner, Alf inquired about Roddy's progress with the water and beavers but seemed distracted. His trek to the iron mine with Lucy Craig had halted at the marsh, where Miss Craig refused to continue, fearing to "drown in that swamp." Her request was quickly granted for tonight's dinner on a tray in her room. At the table, her fiancé seemed embarrassed to enjoy dinner when his betrothed was indisposed.

Clarence was conspicuous by his absence. Sadie regretted that he was feeling unwell but agreed his evening of "quarantine" best protected family and friends. She was certain her son would attend church in the morning, the Old Dutch Church in Kingston featuring a stained-glass window by Lewis Comfort Tiffany.

Clarence was nowhere to be seen on Sunday morning when the Kidds and guests departed for the Old Dutch Church. It was assumed that Roddy would kindly escort his Irish wife to Sunday Mass at St. Mary's Roman Catholic Church. (Nor did I say that Papa and I filed into Presbyterian pews in Virginia City, Nevada.)

Roddy and I again took a dogcart, this time hitched to Granny, and church bells summoned all Kingston as we neared the Wall Street police headquarters and jail.

Inside, a young desk officer with scant blonde whiskers and one lazy eye received us in surprise that bordered on alarm when Roddy asked about the jail's visiting hours.

"Sir, we have no such hours."

"Then, eleven o'clock on Sunday morning is perfectly convenient," Roddy replied. "We are here to visit Ella Conklin, who is charged with homicide."

"Oh, that one...her." The officer yanked his whiskers. "I don't know...can't permit you...Chief Fitch isn't—"

"—I am an attorney." Roddy whipped out his card with "Roderick W. DeVere, Esq."

The officer laid the card on the desk behind him, seeming unsure whether to hand it back. "Sir," he said to Roddy, "the matron doesn't come on Sunday."

"Which is why Mrs. DeVere is here today."

I gave a prim nod, my expression as matronly as the tan skirt and jacket minus jewelry for exactly this occasion.

The young officer shifted a brass ring of keys from one hand to the other. "I will need to telephone Chief Fitch…"

"By all means," Roddy said. "But to save time, if you lead us to Miss Conklin's cell, I can proceed, and Chief Fitch will meet us in the visiting room."

"There is no visiting room."

"Then meet at her cell."

We three climbed two flights to a hallway that stretched between two bleak rows of empty jail cells and smelled of lime and washing powder.

At cell number Eleven, the officer called out, "Visitors" in imitation of Chief Fitch. The keys clanked, but he made no move to unlock the cell door. "Talk through the bars," he said. "I have desk duty. I will telephone Chief Fitch."

"Please do."

He walked off.

The woman stirred from a metal bunk at the rear of a tight space. She did not come forward. "Miss Conklin," I said, "Ella Conklin?"

"Who is it?"

Under Fitch's questioning, she identified us twice at the camp, but our names seemed meaningless. "The couple with the horse," I said. "You saw us at the Health-to-Wealth grove. You watered our horse."

She still did not come forward. Should I talk about the wet rag she put in my palm?

"We would like to talk to you," Roddy said. "We would like to help."

The minute dragged, but she came out of the gloom, her dark eyes in a narrow face as wary as trapped wildlife. A coarse cotton shift hung loosely on her frame, prison garb for Ulster County. Her hair had been cut short.

"Miss Conklin," Roddy said, "we understand that you worked from the first of this month at the Health-to-Wealth camp? And before that, Florida?"

She hesitated as if fearing a trick. "What about it?"

"Your massage skills," Roddy continued, "did you learn them in Florida?"

"St. Augustine," she said. "They teach you, and they get you a job."

"So, at first you worked in Florida?" She nodded. "And you became acquainted with Fiona Peebles in Florida?"

Her strong fingers suddenly gripped the bars, a reminder that the masseuse was accused of murder here...and wanted for attempted murder in Florida.

Roddy's tenor voice became soulful. "Miss Conklin," he said, "can you tell us what happened in Florida? Was it in St. Augustine?"

"Daytona," she said, "people drive on the sand, horses and carriages on the sand. Bicycles too. Put down a blanket, and a person can get a massage."

"And you worked on the sand...the beach?"

"For a while, it worked out good. No rent for a massage parlor, just the blanket. I worked for a man that handed out the blankets. Then a fellow...a client...got fresh on me and then got mad. He pulled a knife."

She moved her hands away from the bars and motioned with her fingers and wrists, as if massaging the air. Her lips moved soundlessly.

"What are you saying?" I asked.

"'Manual mobilization,'" she said. "The Kellogg way...shoulders, the inferior and superior lever, and so I got the knife, but he cut himself. The blanket man called the cops, and the rest is...."

She wiped her eyes on the sleeve of the prison cotton. How many times had her white robe sleeve dried tears at Health-to-Wealth?"

"That's how the charge against you in Florida came about?" I asked.

"I wanted him to get off me. He cut himself, it wasn't me."

"But you are wanted for attempted...."

Roddy's hand on my wrist stopped the next words. He said, "Your acquaintance with Miss Peebles, Fiona...where did you meet her?"

"Massage school at St. Augustine. The school got her the Health-to-Wealth job."

"In Daytona?"

She nodded. "Vanessa Zee hired her right away. But Health-to-Wealth needed another masseuse when business on the beach got so good. Vanessa stood up on a chair and promised miracles. And he gave out the handbills."

"Cedric," I said.

She shut her eyes. "Wish I never...."

"But they hired you," I said.

"Vanessa, yes, but Fiona helped. I told her about the knife, and she stood up for me with Vanessa. We both came up here to the woods."

"Then, Fiona was your friend?" Roddy asked. "Not your rival?"

She shook her head. "We split the money three ways. This other girl, Ramona, worked with us. We were all friends."

"Until Fiona..." I said.

"I thought she ran away." Ella gripped the bars again. "I thought the nights drove her off."

"What about the nights?" I asked softly.

"Cedric," she said. "It was him. He'd come almost every night, and she had to go. Ramona was asleep, and I pretended to sleep, but I saw his feet."

"What about his feet?"

"Sandals, like in Florida. He wears them in the woods."

Roddy took a half-step back to give her space. "Miss Conklin," he asked slowly, "why would Cedric accuse you of murder?"

"I should've known." She leaned forward, pressing her face between the bars as she stared straight at me. "It's Cedric, but something else. It's six months to Christmas, but at night in the tent, he'd whisper, 'Santa...Santa time.' I tried to tell you. I ripped a white shirt to tell you. Health-to-Wealth got like a prison, and here's jail. Feel these bars. Feel them."

I touched the cold iron.

"You read 'Santa,' didn't you?"

I nodded, my fingers curled around the bars.

"And I said to you, 'Peebles.' I said her last name. Did you hear me? Or not? If you heard, you need to find out about him. Or they will call me guilty. They say in New York, a person can die in a chair that's electrified. Do you know about that? Cross my heart, they say it's t truth."

Chapter Twenty-seven

ONCE OUTSIDE, FRUSTRATION MADE me want to shout or stomp or throw a rock. But Kingston's streets and sidewalks filled this midday Sunday with churchgoers who were sent into the world with blessings. Surrounding us, they looked serene.

Their faces greeted a world I did not inhabit. "Roddy," I said, "every Kingston citizen is suddenly in a carriage or walking toward home."

"Not everyone, Val. Look who's coming."

On horseback at a fast trot, Chief Fitch rode toward us in a dress uniform with knee-high boots, spurs, and a badge that shone like gold. He saluted carriages and sidewalk groups in passing, but he dismounted in front of us, held the reins of his horse, and glowered. There would be no Sunday greetings on this walkway.

"Just what do you think you are doing?"

Roddy spoke in his lawyerly steady voice. "Chief Fitch, we have just completed the jailhouse visit that you advised us to undertake. We have spoken to Ella Conklin, who answered a few of our questions."

"Your questions...yours?" His nostrils flared.

"As the trustee of property on which Miss Conklin allegedly committed homicide," Roddy continued, "I have concerns." He added, "...naturally."

"Do not pull 'nature' on me, Mr. DeVere. "Survival of the fittest, is it?"

"I would not put it—"

"—that way? The way of the world, Mr. DeVere. I informed you the Kingston police put lead weights in our nightsticks...to be the fittest. Your property is your property, but Ulster County is ours, and I hereby forbid you to set foot in the jailhouse unless accompanied by me...and the Ulster County attorney."

The chief leaned closer to Roddy, ready to issue another order, but his horse suddenly shied with a sideways jump. In the next minutes, Chief Fitch grappled with the reins and fought for the stirrup. Mounted at last, he spurred the horse to a trot and left us without a backward glance.

"Fuming," I said, "but after the fact. Isn't that what lawyers say, 'after the fact?'"

"Usually in reference to a crime, Val. But our visit to Ella Conklin was no crime. Fitch was embarrassed, but if he or the county attorney had been at prison cell number eleven, the conversation would have been very different. As it was, however...."

Roddy did not continue. His troubled expression matched my thoughts. Ella Conklin confirmed Cedric's guilt, but her words brought up 'Santa' and the ripped cloth, which muddied the case, as if a clear pool turned cloudy. We turned toward the dogcart and the sorrel, Granny, waiting patiently to take us to yet another Sunday dinner at Kiddwood.

Actually, we arrived at the country house before the Kidds and guests got back. It seems that Lucy Craig and her fiancé, Henry, insisted on an abrupt departure, along with their chaperone. Immediately after church, they wished to be taken directly to the steamboat dock to await the southbound *Mary Powell* or the *William F. Romer* to return to the city. They requested that the Kidds' servants see to their luggage, preferably by rail, but they wished to travel by boat "calmly," Henry said, in order to "quiet" his fiancée's nerves.

The Kidds and the guests were tight-lipped about the sudden decision, though Edna told me she was sure the Old Dutch Church sermon was to blame for the couple's bad manners.

"A Tiffany window is too high a price to pay for fire-and-flood from the pulpit, Valentine," she said. The minister took his sermon from Joshua, the Old Testament prophet on the waters of the Jordan River."

"It sounds elevating," I said.

"You would think, but he went on darkly about waters that come down and stand on a "heap." And banks that rise up and overflow. He meant to be instructive, but Lucy was still recovering from her visit to the iron mine with Alf."

"But she did not see the mine."

"The marsh, Valentine, the marsh she called a 'swamp' and feared to drown."

"And dined in her room," I said. "So, Edna, who else has yet to go to the old mine with Alf?"

"Alicia," she said, then saw my confusion. "The young lady you call the 'dark-haired debutante,' Valentine. I needn't tell you how important to learn everyone's name. Now, let us go in...to dinner."

It seemed to me that a mahogany leaf had been removed to shorten the dining table. The guests clustered closer, and the room looked larger. Alicia, the dark-haired debutante, asked Sadie whether Clarence felt well enough to dine, and Alf excused himself to "inquire" about his son's health.

We waited and waited. Jack Barrott offered to play, but Sadie said after-dinner would be time enough for tunes. Gossip about the engaged couple's extremely rude departure would enliven the scene, but the topic was forbidden by eitquette, so we limped along chatting about the weather and the upcoming summer at Bar Harbor and Newport. Edna invited everyone to visit her at Saratoga Springs and drink the Vichy water.

The word, "water," turned all eyes toward Roddy. At that moment, fortunately for my husband, Alf entered the room with his son, who looked bedraggled. Clarence's hair was mussed and his silk scarf wrinkled. His coat looked large for him. Was he losing weight?

"Apologies, friends," he murmured with downcast eyes, then slumped at the place set for him beside Alicia, who looked delighted. She hoped he would offer a toast to his mother, since his previous tribute to his father had been glorious. Clarence stood as if hauled up by the scruff of his neck, lifted his glass, and muttered, "To my mother, Mercedes, whose name in Latin means 'mercies.' May she be merciful to one and all."

We touched glasses at the strange mixed message, and footmen rushed in with tomato aspic that barely survived the delay. Course after course from the entrées to dessert measured the afternoon whose remaining hours were to be spent at everyone's liberty. Sadie's "what you will," meant no organized games. Jack Barrott covered the piano keys and sat down with a novel. Everyone but General Coleman retreated to change into informal clothing.

Inside my room, the door locked, Roddy joined me to reexamine the cloth rag with "Santa" in in hand printing that had smeared when the rag was wet. "Ella said she ripped a shirt." I said.

Roddy fingered the cloth. "Could be." He put it on the bed, and we stared as if it would speak to us.

In a way, the cloth had already spoken in the phaeton carriage when Cassie envisioned a person lying near water and grass. Those who came too close to the person, she said, would become like stone.

Should I bring that up? Cassie's strange "spells" were long familiar to my husband, who dismissed the stone as a lady's gem.

Which made rational sense. Touching the cloth at its ragged edge, I felt nothing. Roddy held it up, looked closely, and shook his head. "Put it away, Val. It's meaningless."

"Not to Ella Conklin."

"No, not to her." Still peering at the cloth, Roddy loosened his necktie. "At the shooting gallery, are you sure that Ramona said nothing about a nighttime 'Santa?'"

"She did not. She saw a man in sandals. It has to be Cedric, but why call him Santa, unless the masseuse job was a gift, like Saint Nicholas for the summer?"

"A long shot, but possible," Roddy said.

We peered at the cloth on the bed. It shouted in code.

"Val, there is one person who might shed light on all this...if he would talk."

"Hank Boynt," I said.

Roddy nodded. "He goes to the camp with deliveries, and a predawn hour could be mistaken for the nighttime."

"So," I said, "he might know what happened to Fiona."

"Or he might have killed her."

"Killed...." My ears pulsed, and my mind fought for the logic. "Your mean, as a favor to 'Santa' Cedric when she resisted him?"

"That's my guess."

The air felt sucked from the room. Roddy's face looked grim, and mine like clay in the mirror. I started to say, "Suppose we tell Chief Fitch...." then broke off. Impossible.

I jammed the cloth in the handkerchief drawer. "Roddy," I said, "if Hank Boynt talks to us, he could incriminate himself, and Cedric as well. Suppose Alf would arrange a meeting? Nothing formal, just a chat at the back door early in the morning, something like a week ago Friday when Hank delivered produce, all friendly the back door with Alf."

Roddy stroked his chin. He would not be rushed.

"How about it? Hank Boynt would not dare curse at Alf."

"True...." Roddy rubbed his hands and finally cautioned me with his ground rules. "We will not detail our suspicions to Alf. We will tell him that we believe the produce wagon deliveryman might remember further details about the body he discovered on my parents' tract. That's all."

"That should do it." In the next moments, I slipped out of the tan suit and chose a navy skirt and a blue-and-white striped shirtwaist. Roddy decided on flannel trousers and a corduroy sport coat.

The guests had scattered, but we found Alf in the library sitting by himself poring over business documents at a table across from the glass-front cabinet with the iron miner's tools. Looking up, he raised a bushy eyebrow and startled us both with a sharp challenge. "I have been expecting you two since dinner." He roared, "What kept you?"

"Kept us?" Roddy's tone stayed mild.

"What do you mean, kept us?" My strident tone surprised me and Roddy too. "Apart from a short flying trip, we have been Kiddwood guests for nine days." I repeated, "Nine very long spring days."

Alf abruptly stood, slammed the library door shut, and motioned us to chairs on the other side of the table. "In these nine days, Valentine, you spent a great deal of time in Kingston, but it seems you paid no attention whatsoever to the streets."

I froze. Pearl Street raged in mind. Did he know of my visit? "What streets?" I asked.

He swiveled to Roddy. "And you, Roderick, a smooth-talking liar."

"I don't understand…" Roddy began.

"Don't understand the whereabouts of the Old Dutch Church? Let me enlighten you both.…"

He halfway stood and pounded the table. "The Old Dutch Church is located at number 272 Wall Street," he boomed, "the same street as the new Ulster County Jail and police station a few blocks further at number 285. And what did I see in front of the jail at noon today, but my dogcart with my old horse, Granny! And who did I see after church in my carriage with Mrs. Kidd and our guests? Who was outside on the sidewalk with a uniformed police officer in front of the new jailhouse? Tell me, who did I see?"

White foam gathered at the edges of his mouth as Alf lashed at me, "The Catholic church, Valentine, is on Broadway, where you pretended to go to Mass this morning."

He shook his fists. "Liars, shame on you!"

I did not look at my husband, who must handle this. It would be useless to point out that my Irish immigrant Papa and I were parishioners at the Presbyterian Church on "C" Street in Virginia City. It would do no good to say the Kidds "pigeonholed" me.

At the end of the library table, a pitcher half full of water and small glasses let me move to give all three of us a drink. Pouring small amounts in each glass, I tried to signal that the topic of water was Roddy's best bet to calm the situation.

I sipped, as did Roddy, who shot me a swift glance. Alf's water stood untouched as my husband began to unwind a tale about the police chief and the discovery of the body by the wagon driver who also made frequent deliveries of produce to Kiddwood.

"You ask, why Sunday?" Roddy posed the question as an attorney might do at a hearing or in court. "Sunday," he continued, "because the police are less in demand for their workaday duties. So, on this Sunday morning, the young officer at the desk agreed to telephone the chief of police... the Assistant Chief of Police whom you met, Alf, when he came to Kiddwood early last week.

"Fitch."

His grudging voice was a good sign, I thought.

"Chief Clyde Fitch," Roddy went on, "who obligingly met with us this morning and escorted us outdoors at noon. But the reason for the discussion is legal clearance for the property...the one-and-only essential concern being water at Kiddwood."

Roddy reached for his glass, took a long, slow sip, and kept the glass in his hand. He looked earnestly at the hulking man across from him. "The police investigation must conclude, Alf, before we can deal with the beaver lodges and the water flow. We simply cannot have the Kingston police interfering in our plan for water." He sipped again.

Alf glanced sideways, eyed his own glass, and almost touched it. "The police are finished, then?"

"Except for one other matter that might, possibly, cause an unfortunate delay...." Roddy paused and put down his glass. The room felt at a pivot point.

"What delay?"

"It seems," Roddy began, "that the police have a record of run-ins with the wagon driver who found the body on my family property. He delivers fruit and vegetables here at Kiddwood."

"Hank," Alf said. "His name is Hank."

I stayed quiet.

"We were thinking," Roddy said, gesturing to include me, "that a police interrogation can make a man freeze-up and forget important details. We think that it could be helpful to talk to Hank informally...casually."

"What for?"

"To put to rest any concerns about the body found on the property. To be honest, Alf, I tried to have a word with Hank last Thursday morning at your back door."

"Oh? Really?" In that brief instant, Alf's eyes widened in a look that was new to me. Neither jolly nor angry, he looked off balance.

"We were up early having a bite with Edna," Roddy said, "and I heard the wagon, but the man cursed a blue streak. He would not utter a civil word. Not one single civil word."

At that, Alf let loose a burst of hard laughter that filled the room. "So," he said, wiping his eyes, "you want to talk to Hank, and you think I can put a civil tongue in his mouth?" He laughed again, but somehow without merriment. "Roderick, leave it to you. And Valentine, you are one for...for the books."

Fitting for the library, but his words were no compliment to me. I sat still as he folded his arms across his chest, smoothed his white whiskers, and looked at Roddy with a sly gaze. "Tell me, Roderick, can you mix a cocktail that is heavy on beer or ale...no hard liquor?"

This time, Roddy looked off balance, but he said, "The Shandygaff."

"Well, then, here's what we'll do, Roderick," he said. "You mix the shanty-whatever-it-is, and we will drink it on the back porch with Hank first thing tomorrow morning. Do we have a deal?"

Roddy would have shaken hands, but we watched Alf gulp his water and throw his glass into the fireplace. He might have hoped to cause a crash, but the glass was swallowed softly in cold ashes.

Chapter Twenty-eight

HOW "EARLY" WAS A question unanswered when we left the library. Tomorrow morning's timing on the back steps remained vague as the afternoon slid toward evening. Sadie made the rounds from the drawing room to the veranda to apologize for her "hermit" husband who found it necessary to "hide out" in the Kiddwood library because business affairs had unexpectedly "called" him. She added that Alf wished everyone most pleasant "idle" hours but asked that no one seek reading material from the library.

Guests strolled the grounds or played board games. Clarence was not in evidence, but Roddy and I joined Jack Barrott in pick-up sticks, which the musician won handily. At another table, the square-jawed man and the dark-haired Alicia competed at tiddely winks. Edna offered the winner her copy of *When Knighthood Was in* Flower.

"Ruinously popular," she declared, "but as the French say, 'À chacun son goût.'" She turned my way. "To translate," she said, "'to each his own.'"

"Or hers," I said.

Roddy took my arm to guide us inside toward the butler's pantry, where he asked a footman about beer steins. The butler was consulted, and three mug-like steins were retrieved on Mr. Kidd's order, as Roddy emphasized. He added that Mr. Kidd had also requested bottles of ale and ginger beer be provided to Mr. DeVere.

In our adjoining rooms, we soon had the ingredients for the men's morning drinks with the deliveryman. Roddy planned to be at the back entrance with the Shandygaff cocktails by five o'clock a.m. unless he heard otherwise from Alf, who did not appear at the Sunday buffet supper. Nor did Clarence, to Alicia's obvious dismay. Jack Barrott was pressed to play old favorites and complied at Sadie's insistence. Several guests retired early, as did we.

"Roddy," I said when we returned to our rooms, "it occurs me that Jack is like the vagabond on the steamboat. He entertains for room and board, a guest in name only. Do you remember him here from years ago?"

Roddy shook his head no and recalled that Sadie hoped Clarence would study the piano seriously. "She did her best, but her son would not budge."

"It seems to me," I said, "that the younger Mr. Kidd's refusal is a lifelong habit."

My husband did not disagree. He put the bottles into the bathtub. "The Shandygaff makings for tomorrow," he said.

"What, exactly, is that cocktail?" I asked, staring at the bottles in the tub. Roddy told me and, for once, I did not feel eager to sample the beverage. Not ever.

The Shandygaff

Ingredients:

- ½ Pint English bitter or pub ale of choice
- ½ Pint Ginger Beer

Directions:

1. Fill a pint glass or stein halfway with the ale.
2. Fill to the top with the ginger beer and serve.

"Roddy, whenever did you drink this?"

"A favorite from college days, my dear. Soon coming to the Kiddwood back entrance. I'll want to rise by 4 o'clock to mix the drinks. Can you help?"

We mistrusted the ornamental bedroom clocks, and borrowing an alarm clock under any pretext seemed unwise. We would set our internal body clocks.

Which meant we hardly slept at all. The sky was ink dark when we both rose, Roddy stepping into trousers and pulling on a flannel shirt, while I slipped on a robe to watch him uncap and uncork the bottles, pour the contents into the steins, and tiptoe out with a kiss.

"Wish us luck."

"Shamrock," I said, "four-leaf clover."

Too wakeful to sleep, I lay down and imagined the scene at the back steps when the delivery wagon rumbled to a stop. Alf would call his greeting, and the deliveryman respond with a salute. He would prepare to unload the crates and bushel baskets and be surprised at the requested pause. The invitation to join the men would stir Hank's uncertainty, even suspicion. Perhaps his pint would need to be taken to the wagon seat—if so, by Roddy.

Or else the deliveryman would be persuaded to join the men on the steps. The three would touch their steins to toast the morning—a toast by Alf or Roddy. They would sip or quaff their drinks. A few minutes of small talk would follow, very few because the driver had other scheduled stops. Chances were, he had already delivered vegetables to Health-to-Wealth.

The one-and-only question was: would the cocktail in the informal setting loosen Hank Boynt's lips? If so, what would he say about anything he might recall leading up to the discovery of Fiona Peebles's body? He drove the tar-and-gravel road often and observed goings-on at each location on his route. Would he incriminate himself? Or Cedric? Or both? What could he remember? What would he say?

My thoughts strayed to Pearl Street, where Eileen Dwyer and her "girls" would bed down after their lucrative night shift, while Ella Conklin would rise for the day in her Wall Street jail cell, perhaps roused by the women's matron and terrified by the upcoming trial for the murder of her friend and coworker. At the Health-to-Wealth camp, Ramona Smith could count one day less until she fled to Florida, but not before she was called as a witness in her coworker's defense. She would face Cedric Ferris from the witness stand.

And Cedric, wily Cedric? Was he sleeping soundly these last few nights? Was he? My thoughts roamed to a courtroom in Kingston and pictured a squirming Cedric facing his accuser. Or would he try to appear unfazed, barely blinking those hang-dog eyes?

These notions ceased when Roddy burst into my bedroom clasping the three steins, his face a dark scowl.

"What? What happened?"

"He did not show up."

"Hank?"

"No sign of him."

I sat up. "Maybe he got here earlier, before you and Alf... no, today's vegetables would already be at the rear entrance."

Roddy set the steins on the bureau. "We finally gave up. The cook said Hank's deliveries have been on time all this month. She says her best recipes call for onions, and she fears the 'Missus' will not understand. Alf assured her that he would speak to Mrs. Kidd and would send a cart into Kingston to the greengrocer for onions and other vegetables she might need. He was so very kind to her, Val...the Alf that we haven't seen lately."

"But the cook will keep a lookout?"

"And do her best to delay Hank long enough for us to question him, but I am not optimistic. Hank Boynt might be sick from drinking too much last night, and I doubt Alf will agree to rise once more before the rooster crows to humor me, despite his claims to be an early riser. I think he likes solitary walks with no need to talk to guests...or family."

Roddy ran a hand through his hair. "As for Shandygaffs at dawn...Alf poured his into the dirt. I took a few sips and gave it up. One advantage from the hour on the Kiddwood back steps...Alf became philosophical."

"About Clarence?"

My husband's glance verged on a smirk. "My dear, we could wait until Clarence's *Fly Away* sets sail and never understand that father-son mystery beyond what we already know. We know quite enough as it is, don't we?"

"We do."

"Then, listen to this surprise about the DeVere property. Alf offered to take it off Father's hands."

"To buy it?" I swung around to set my bare feet on the floor. "Alfred Kidd talked to your father about buying the DeVere tract?"

"At the 'between' season last autumn," Roddy said. "That's what he told me."

"But why? For the water?"

"Alf said he wanted to simplify the situation. He rambled on about Ulster County as his homeland and said that he and Sadie would welcome the DeVeres...roll out the welcome mat for Rufus and Eleanor and for us too." Roddy pulled up a side chair and faced me. "I think he wanted the limestone."

"Or wants it now? Didn't you hear about a shortage?"

Roddy nodded. "From the livery stable owner. Mr. Grant Webster told me three cement companies compete fiercely for the diminishing limestone, which is their raw material." He winked at me. "Your papa would call it ore."

He would indeed. I might have reminisced about the West, but the prospect of ridding the DeVere family of its hundred-acre tract made me giddy.

"Roddy," I asked, "What did you say to Alf?"

"I told him my parents are set on building a country house. I told him they have an architect designing plans. "

"What did he say?"

"He said blueprints are only paper, but I repeated that Father and Mother are committed to their own country house on the property."

I tightened the collar of my robe. "Roddy," I said, "your parents listen to your advice. They need persuading, but they usually do come around." I paused for a full minute, then said, "Suppose you could persuade your father and mother to let it go."

"Sell the tract?"

"Why not? Let it be freed from your parents...and us. The Health-to-Wealth scam will end, and the criminal trial will expose Cedric Ferris's nighttime forced intimacy with Fiona."

"Only if Ramona Smith cooperates," Roddy said sharply, "and Chief Fitch stands aside to let the Ulster County prosecutor develop his case."

"A case against the man who drowned Fiona Peebles," I wailed. "And Hank Boynt called as a witness or accomplice...

and an official courtroom witness instead of beer on the back steps."

Roddy's knuckles whitened on the chair arms. My toes dug at the carpet. He stood and grasped the steins. "I'll give these to a footman and call the valet for a shave. You will...."

"Get dressed by myself for another day in the promised land of Kiddwood."

We eyed one another, preparing to face the day, constantly on watch and not once guessing the explosive news to come just hours from now.

❧

By 9:00 a.m., we joined Edna at the pastry table, where she chatted with Alicia, who hoped that Clarence might be at breakfast. Edna advised her to "go fishing in the sea of bachelors who swim 'toward' young ladies."

I ignored the exchange and nodded good morning as the footman poured coffee. Roddy would join Jack Barrott for steak and eggs. The day was to be quite warm for late June in Ulster County, said Sadie, who lamented that Alf had once again "burrowed" into the library on matters of business.

It was nearly 9:30 when the Kidds' butler hurried toward Sadie and whispered something that sent her off without a word to anyone. For courtesy, I was ready to take a seat beside General Coleman but instead strolled to the doorway where Sadie had disappeared. Roddy's breakfast had been served, but he, too, had seen Sadie hasten away and met my gaze as if to say, pay attention.

For several minutes, nothing happened. The square-jawed man entered the breakfast space, and Alicia joined him. Edna had observed her friend's hasty exit and tilted her head like a bird about to take flight. Voices then rose approaching the breakfast space, both Sadie's and Alf's that sounded blustery.

Sadie looked flustered, and Alf annoyed as he waved "good morning," went to Roddy, tapped his shoulder, eyed me, and crooked his finger. The guests raised eyebrows, but footmen are trained to take no notice unless called upon.

Roddy's "excuse me" to Jack meant that we would follow Sadie and Alf to the Kiddwood foyer, where a uniformed police officer stood with a stout man in an oatmeal-tan business suit and trousers stuffed into knee-high calf-skin boots.

Alf dismissed the butler and took charge—or tried to, but the businessman recognized Roddy and said, "Mr. DeVere, I believe."

"Mr. Webster," my husband replied. The two shook hands, and Roddy introduced the owner of Webster's Livery Stable who had recently been elected Sheriff of Ulster County. Alf congratulated the incoming sheriff, who replied that he would not take office for several days but appreciated the good words. The policeman stood silently at attention, introduced by Mr. Webster as Officer Saunders of the Kingston Police Department.

Alf blustered on, "Mrs. Kidd tells me the Kingston vegetable wagon has disappeared. Is that it, disappearing vegetables?" His rubbed his whiskers, and a smile played at his lips. He winked at Roddy.

"Mr. Kidd, we regret to disturb you," said Mr. Webster, "but a wagon and team has returned to my stable without the driver."

I flashed Roddy a quick glance. His shoulders tightened.

Alf's voice rose, "Is that so? A well-trained team with no need for a driver? Somebody is saving wages, I would guess." He sounded like a carnival barker.

The stable owner touched his sandy short beard and narrowed gray eyes at Alf. "Mr. Kidd, if I may say, this matter is no trifle. The driver handles my Irish Draught team in agreement with the Kingston greengrocer...good draft horses to pull a wagon of produce on a regular route outside of the city."

"But the driver did not return?" Alf asked, sounding newly incredulous. Sadie frowned and touched her throat.

In the next moment, the officer stepped up and spoke in a fact-flat voice. "We are searching for the missing driver identified as Henry Boynt. Chief Fitch has detailed two officers to conduct a search along the delivery route."

"And the wagon came back empty this morning?" Roddy asked. "Or was it full?"

"Half and half, Mr. DeVere," said the stable owner. "Some vegetables had been delivered, it seems, but bushels of produce and sacks of onions remained in the wagon."

"Well, let us clear up some of your puzzle, Mr. Webster." Alf grinned. "Very early this morning, Mr. DeVere and I waited for the wagon because the DeVeres here...." He nodded to me. "Our guests, the DeVeres, wanted a word with the driver. So, Mr. DeVere and I waited a good long while, but the vegetable wagon never arrived." He chuckled. "Seems the DeVeres thought I could help the driver speak plain English."

The policeman blinked, and the stable owner winced. "Henry Boynt...Hank tends to be foul mouthed," Mr. Webster said, "and he leaves a trail of roughhousing in Kingston. But the man can handle a team, and he works hard these days. Some of my draft horses need exercise, and he is at liberty to drive them after hours. His life is now on the straight and narrow. When I take office as Ulster County's Sheriff, I will promote the idea of mending lives."

"Then you must look to the Kidds to support that campaign," Alf boomed. "Meanwhile, I will send a cart into town for onions and whatever our cook might need to keep Kiddwood well fed." He pulled a gold watch from his pocket. "Mercy, it is the middle of the morning. May we offer you both an early lunch? A libation?"

Officer Saunders looked baffled. "Libation, sir?"

"Something to drink?" Alf winked at the policeman. "Or to eat?"

"Thank you, but no, sir."

"We will be off," Mr. Webster said. "Your information has been helpful. Thank you for your time."

"Happy to meet with you, Sheriff Webster, but my bet…." Alf cupped his hands and stage whispered to all of us. "My bet is that you will find Hank Boynt sleeping it off by the roadside. My wager is that a liquor bender got the better of him. In my business of cement, I have learned to take the measure of a man. You had best find a wagon driver that can handle his horses as well as his liquor."

Chapter Twenty-nine

HANK BOYNT'S BODY WAS found at 2:44 p.m. today, June 26, by officers Earl Steere and James Gordon of the Kingston Police Department. The officers reported seeing the body lying face-down in a pool of blood in a roadside ditch approximately one-eighth mile from the Kiddwood property entrance. From observation, both officers determined the probable cause of death to be a fatal blow to the back of the skull and loss of blood. Officer Steere secured the area while his partner summoned Chief Clyde Fitch, who arrived at the scene at 4:16 p.m. with two additional officers and ordered the body to be taken to the Leahy Funeral Home in Kingston for verification of the cause of death. By 6:10 p.m., Mr. Joseph Leahy, Coroner of the city of Kingston, located two fractures of the skull by a forceful, blunt object or objects and concluded that death occurred when the arteries and veins running through the brain were severed by the sharp interior ridges of the skull. The death, Mr. Leahy concludes, is thereby a homicide. No identifying documents were found on or near the body, but Mr. Grant Webster, president of Webster's Livery Stable, identified the deceased as Henry (Hank) Boynt, an employee. Next of kin of the deceased are not known at this time. The case continues.

All this was told to us by Chief Fitch, whose 10:00 p.m. visit to Kiddwood put a stop to the after-dinner charades that Sadie and Alf promoted with the theme of "Kings and Queens." Clarence had excused himself after coffee and dessert, claiming to be "utterly useless" at charades. The rest of us endured guesses at King George III or "Crazy" King Ludwig before Edna proclaimed the square-jawed man to be Louis XIV. Applause sprinkled as the butler appeared, ashen-faced, to whisper to Alf, who whispered back, then set us all free by declaring that charades were cancelled for tonight.

Roddy was asked to mix nightcaps, but Alf beckoned us to follow him and Sadie to the card room, where Chief Fitch had been led by the butler. His hat off, the chief stood awkwardly to apologize for intruding at this late hour and hoped we would understand his decision to post an armed officer at the entrance to Kiddwood, for the night.

Sadie clutched her throat and Alf raised an eyebrow, quickly inviting the chief to be seated. "Take that loveseat, Chief...and let's all sit down."

Roddy and I chose two accent chairs at opposite sides of the room. We were here last Wednesday when Alf charged us with deceit over the Health-to-Wealth camp and Clarence lied through his teeth, not to mention Alf's angry outburst when Roddy hinted that Clarence might participate in the water plan.

As before, the Kidds sat side by side on the Chesterfield sofa. Facing them on the loveseat, the police chief would see the framed paintings of the Brooklyn Bridge and Statue of Liberty if he gazed at the wall above the sofa.

"Now then," Alf said, "what's all this about a Kingston gendarme posted here at Kiddwood tonight? Another 'vagabond' on the loose?"

His chuckle stopped when the chief opened a notebook and proceeded to recount of discovery and identification of Hank Boynt's body, pronouncing each name with care, from the police officers to Mr. Webster, and timing to the minute.

The four of us stared, both dazed and anxious for more information when the chief snapped the notebook shut and repeated, "So then, this is a homicide."

The room was deathly silent until Alf thundered, "Murdered...the fellow was murdered."

"By all indications," Fitch replied.

Alf's voice rose in rage. "A sneak attack? No chance to defend himself?"

"By all appearances, sir, the deceased was taken by surprise...unaware."

"By a coward!" Alf pounded the sofa arm, so heavily upholstered it barely thumped. "When did it happen?"

"The time of death," the chief said, "is not known exactly. The blood pooled, and the body very stiff...." He broke off when

Sadie gasped. "Pardon, ma'am. Just to say, the death had most probably occurred several hours before the body was found."

"And you think a killer is loose in this area?" Alf took his wife's hand. "A lunatic with...a hatchet? An axe?"

Sadie squirmed. The chief wet his lips, and I glanced at Roddy, who did not appear ready to ask a question. Nor did I. We were probably invited into this room because the DeVere property bordered Kiddwood.

And because Fiona Peebles's body was found two weeks ago on the neighboring property...found by the very man now attacked and murdered.

A coincidence?

"Sir," the chief began, "we have no information on the murder weapon. Mr. Leahy determined a fatal impact by blunt force. As to the possible presence of the perpetrator in the vicinity of your property, I wish to take the utmost precaution."

He paused at the word, precaution, patted his new beard, and said, "My jurisdiction does not extend to this area, but Mr. Webster will take office as Sheriff of Ulster County in a few days, and cooperation will benefit the city and county too. Mr. Webster agrees that a police officer posted where the public road abuts the entrance to your property best serves the interests of safety."

"For one night only?" Sadie almost squeaked. "Just this one night?"

The chief's cheeks flushed. "Ma'am, let us proceed one day and night at a time. If a deranged wrongdoer is afoot in this area, we will find and arrest such person."

He tucked his arms close to his sides and widened his eyes at Sadie. "On the other hand, we know Hank Boynt was disliked and had troubles with the law. It is possible that someone who knew his delivery route attacked him... possibly a grudge, nothing in relation to others in the area."

"Oh, we do hope so." Sadie fanned her fingers.

Roddy sat forward. "Chief Fitch," he began, "you have explained, sadly, why the wagon and team returned to the stable without the driver, which we learned about this morning when Mr. Webster and a police officer called upon Mr. and Mrs. Kidd."

Roddy rubbed his hands together. "...and therefore the delivery wagon did not appear here at Kiddwood this morning, as expected. Mr. Kidd and I waited outdoors from about 5 o'clock at the rear entrance. We hoped to have a word with Hank Boynt."

"A word?" The chief blinked.

"A query from Mr. DeVere about his property, with the idea that I could curb the man's salty tongue." Alf sounded nearly playful. "Hank sometimes drove up at the crack of dawn to find me walking about, and his 'good morning' was easy as pie. I never knew the man's last name until today. 'Boin'...did I get it right?"

"Boynt, sir." The chief spelled the name, and Alf nodded so vigorously his snowy hair fell across his forehead.

"But we also learned, Chief Fitch," Roddy said, "that some of the produce was probably delivered before Hank Boynt was attacked." My husband locked his gaze on the chief's steel-gray eyes. "Isn't it likely that the delivery was made to the Health-to-Wealth encampment?"

Fitch returned a wary look. "On your property, Mr. DeVere?"

"Temporarily under contract to an outdoor company, as you know," Roddy continued, "and under the direction of a man known to you, Chief Fitch, a man named Mr. Cedric—"

"—Ferris." The chief clawed at his hat. "Be assured, Mr. DeVere, that we will speak to Mr. Ferris first thing in the morning. But safety here is our utmost concern. The Kidds' residence is highest on my list."

"And our appreciation, Chief Fitch, is beyond words. Is it not, my dear?"

"So grateful," Sadie whimpered.

Alf's eyes glittered. "Chief, we must not see you off without proposing a nightcap." He pointed two fingers at Roddy. "Mr. DeVere can mix a most suitable beverage."

"Thank you, but I will say goodnight." The chief shifted on the loveseat and moved his hat. "Officer Steven Cummins is standing guard at your roadway entrance, just in case."

"But our guests..." Said whimpered. "And servants' gossip...."

"Ma'am, consider this a private matter. Officer Cummins will not be in sight of your home, and your household need not be alerted."

Sadie rose, and I stood too. The men were on their feet when Fitch noticed the paintings and said, "The Brooklyn Bridge, unless I am mistaken."

"The very bridge, indeed," Alf said, "with towers supported by Kidd & Company cement, the world's finest from Ulster County limestone. And you see the statue?"

"The Liberty Lady?"

"Standing in the New York harbor on Kidd & Company cement." Alf gestured to the door. "We know you will solve this heinous crime, Chief Fitch. And when you do, Kiddwood will honor you with a toast in our home. Count on it! We will all raise a glass. Won't we, Mr. DeVere?"

I thought Roddy would offer a simple "yes" or perhaps an agreeable nod of assent. "Won't we, Mr. Roderick DeVere?" Alf repeated.

But my husband replied in four grueling words, "When justice is served."

Chapter Thirty

RODDY'S WORDS ECHOED LIKE a stone falling into a Rocky Mountain canyon, though I wondered why he did not simply go along with Alf's promise to toast the police chief. Both Fitch and Alf frowned at his words, and Sadie looked weepy. Why annoy these people with a high-flown saying?

In silence, the Kidds rejoined the guests, as did Roddy and I. The piano began to play, but liqueurs were already being dispensed. General Coleman had commandeered the bottles and was pouring everyone *crème de menthe* or Grand Marnier. The portions looked outsized. Several bottles lay on their sides, empty.

"Alfred, I took command," the general blared. "Thirsty troops this evening after that fool round of charades. On my orders, your butler and footmen are furloughed." He pointed at Roddy. "And you, DeVere, were in retreat, were you not?"

"Retreat...?"

"Or taken prisoner, sir. Either way, you are now free and entitled to your bonus, either mint or orange flavor. What will it be?"

Before Roddy could answer, a wine glass brimming with liqueur was thrust into his hand.

"And ladies? Your pleasure? Peppermint for you, Sadie? Or is it orange?"

Sadie mumbled, and Edna called out, "Orange, General... goes with her gown."

Edna was tipsy. So was the General. The guests who clustered at the piano began to sing, "Whiskey-O, Whiskey-O...." The piano seemed to search for the melody. The square-jawed man sang, "'Rise her up from down below,'" and the guests chorused, "'Whiskey-O, Whiskey-O.'"

Sadie blinked back tears, and Alf's face went nearly as white as his whiskers. "Roddy..." I began, just as a wine glass was handed to me by Edna, whose "cheers" sounded like "jeers."

"Val...." Roddy eyed the doorway, and I followed him slowly out of the party scene and down the hallways to our rooms. The maid, Willa, waited to assist me, but I wished her goodnight.

"Let's lock our doors," Roddy said. The skeleton keys turned the bolts.

"My room or yours?" I asked.

Roddy shrugged. We chose my room, put the wine glasses of liqueur on the dresser top, and sat down, Roddy on the bed while I perched on the stool of the dressing table.

"Tipsy," I said. "They are all tipsy."

"Drunk," Roddy said. He took off his coat.

"What's that song?"

"An old waterfront ballad, I think."

"The Kidds," I said, "are mortified."

"Awful for them," Roddy said, "but maybe a lesson about forced amusements."

"I don't suppose you saw Clarence?"

"Around the piano singing 'Whiskey-O?' Not my old friend's idea of worthwhile music. Or company." Roddy loosened his tie. "Actually, I looked for him."

"Keeping out of sight of the dark-haired Alicia,' I said.

"That girl has the wrong idea about Clarence," Roddy said. "But I'd guess he is mainly keeping clear of Alf."

"Hiding and more haggard by the day," I said, "and counting the hours until he can escape a 'between' season that is falling apart. And now, a second murder." I spoke in a taut voice, "Roddy, are we really safer because a policeman stands at the junction of the county road and the Kiddwood entrance?"

"I would guess the policeman was Grant Webster's idea," Roddy said. "And Fitch went along because he wants a good working relation with the man to be installed as Ulster County Sheriff. The Kingston chief who bitterly resents country houses would not be eager to protect Kiddwood."

"Or eager to face his huge mistake about Cedric Ferris.... It was Ferris," I said, "who killed Fiona. And now Hank Boynt...."

Roddy rubbed the side of his cheek. He did not nod.

"Don't you agree, Roddy? Remember the shooting gallery...Ramona Smith heard Cedric whisper to Fiona in the middle of the night in the masseuse tent. 'It's Santa time.' Don't you remember?"

"Of course I do."

"You said Ramona would be a good witness at Ella Conklin's trial. You said so."

"I did."

"Then why...? Or do you want to talk about Hank...the late Hank?"

Roddy pulled off his tie and laid it on the bed beside him. "Val," he said slowly, "Why would Cedric Ferris want to kill Hank Boynt?"

I began to toy with a hairbrush on the dressing table. "I was talking about Fiona's murder," I said.

"I know you were."

"Then, why Hank...?" I thumbed the bristles. "You want to talk about Hank Boynt? How Cedric would kill him?"

"Not *how*, Val, but *why*. What motive? What reason? The fellow delivered vegetables to Health-to-Wealth, every wagonload vital to the camp's operation. I'd say that Cedric has plenty on his hands finding a new masseuse for the summer."

I pictured Vanessa at Pearl Street, trying to hire Eileen Dwyer's "girls" for daytime service.

"Something else to consider, Val...the timing of Hank's death."

"Sometime last night," I said. "We heard Fitch say he was...his body was stiff."

"Consider 'timing' on a larger scale, Val." Roddy leaned toward me with a solemn stare. "Hank Boynt was due at Kiddwood to answer my questions about Fiona Peebles's body, supposedly to help me clear up any questions about the property."

"As we had planned," I said.

"But consider what else he could say at the back steps drinking his stein of ale? What could slip out? What could I hear from him?"

"But Alf would hear it too. Alf...." I stopped, my throat suddenly clamped. I managed to say, "Surely not," as the iron mine visit came into my mind. I had clipped Alf behind his knee at the moment he pushed my shoulder. If I had not acted...the pitch-black shaft. "Roddy," I said, "the ditch...that horse nearly pulled you in."

"Sweetie."

"Alf's favorite," I said. Just then, a mantel clock struck twelve tinny beats. "Roddy, suppose you were dragged into that ditch...badly hurt. Or worse."

"You needn't think—"

"—think the worst? Isn't that what we are doing? I never told you about my visit to the iron mine, my own close call. Tell me this, what benefit to Alfred Kidd if one of us were crippled? Or...worse?

Roddy bit his lip. At last he said, "Limestone."

"Stone," I echoed. Cassie's vision surged into my mind, her picture of a figure lying in grass near water, and those who came close turning to stone. Not gemstones as Roddy thought, but limestone. "How would that work?" I asked.

"My father would sign away the DeVere tract, Val. He would do it in a heartbeat."

"Then, we are talking about Alf as a cold, calculating man."

"We are."

"But murder? Would he go that far?"

My husband did not say no.

"Hank?" I said. "Why Hank Boynt?"

"Consider his occupation, Val."

"He drove a wagon...vegetables. With Mr. Webster's Irish horses."

"But he exercised different draft horses in his off hours. A wagon driver who could give rides...."

"To Alf? But where...?" Roddy narrowed his eyes. "To the camp? And back to Kiddwood? To Fiona...and back?"

"Val, where is that rag that Ella Conklin wadded into your hand?

"The 'Santa' rag? It's with my handkerchiefs."

"Let's have a look."

I went to the drawer, tugged, unfolded, and smoothed the cloth shred. Then I sat on the bed beside Roddy. "Same rag," I said. "Nothing new."

"Nothing except...this time we can see what we are looking at." Roddy touched the cloth. "Who looks like Santa

Claus, Val? Who has the white beard and whiskers? Whose laughter is jolly?"

The rag seemed to pulse. "'Santa,'" I murmured. "A nickname."

"A code name," Roddy said. "No one at the camp needed to know that the nighttime 'Santa' is the master of Kiddwood."

"But Cedric knew, didn't he? He woke Fiona and took her to...to him."

"Cedric knew," Roddy said, "and profited."

"And Vanessa?"

"They are partners." Roddy bit his lip. "Someone else also knew."

"Clarence...." My breath came in a rush. "The Kidds' son and heir. He lied to protect his father...and mother."

"Or his fortune at the shipyard...the *Fly Away*."

"Whatever it took...even when Fiona died." I clutched Roddy's hand. "Night after night, she endured Alf until she resisted. And then he killed her. Alf pushed her under the water, and she drowned. That's what happened, isn't it?"

Roddy nodded. "And that is precisely when Alf needed Hank Boynt the most."

"The wagon," I nearly gasped. "Hank took her body away in the wagon, didn't he? Hank dumped her in the field."

The moment was so quiet we heard the mantel clock tick.

Roddy said, "And that, my dear, is the reason the meeting on the back steps was too dangerous for Alf. So, he went to the roadway early and waited, then hailed Hank when he got close to Kiddwood."

"One eighth of a mile...that's what the police said. And Hank would not be suspicious, would he?"

"No reason to be. He would step down from the wagon... turn his head for just a minute...."

I clutched Roddy's hand. "And Alf bashed him with a rock?"

"We don't know, Val. 'Blunt force,' could be anything...a chair leg, a brass candlestick...anything. The question is, what to do. We are guests."

"And prey. We are prey, Roddy." I swallowed, my throat dry. "If Alf should guess that we suspect him...that we have any inkling...."

My husband quieted me with a gentle finger across my lips, then began to outline a plan. We would bypass Chief Fitch who was, as he said, both stubborn and weak. Instead, we would approach the incoming sheriff who seemed like a reasonable official who could be open to our ideas about two Ulster County homicides. For the moment, however, we would make every effort to behave like cheerful guests, with Roddy responsible for restoration of the water.

I nodded, numb and chilled too. On this night, I needed my husband's arms around me. Our separate beds were narrow, but by 1:00 a.m. we lay pressed together on my bed, yearning for the sleep that eluded us both and yet secure in the plan we thought best—a plan to be smashed to bits and nearly cost us our lives.

Chapter Thirty-one

A GRAY TUESDAY MORNING promised rain, but not a drop had fallen when Roddy and I entered the breakfast room at 8:15, where Edna said good morning and called the slate-gray sky a joke played on Kiddwood by *Dame Nature*. It seems the water shortage had reached a new crisis point.

"Barely a trickle," Edna said. "The kitchen is desperate. The butler has spoken to Alf, who is fit to be tied. When you see him, stand clear and give the man elbow room."

"Understood," Roddy said as a nervous footman apologized for the lack of coffee or tea this morning. The available beverage, he said, was bottled grape juice.

"It has come to this," Edna said, "Dr. Welch's unfermented grape wine. Sadie insists that Kiddwood keep it here for teetotaling guests." She pointed to a line of corked bottles on the buffet table. "Warm grape juice in the Hudson Valley's own Sahara."

Edna held her palm against her temple. "I dare not request an ice pack. Alf has ordered the ice melted and every drop of water saved. Luckily, all the guests will sleep until kingdom come. I tell you, last night was a riot, if you get the picture."

She touched her temple and winced, "Must speak softly... pounding headache...way too much *crème de menthe* last night." She poked a finger at Roddy. "And you disappeared before the battle royal...both of you."

"What battle?" I asked.

"General Coleman's war, the mint against the orange. We chose sides, and the battle was on. Not one full bottle was left at Kiddwood by morning. Roderick, you could be dispatched to Kingston for a new supply...or maybe a water wagon." She turned to me. "Isn't that a Western fix?"

"I think Texas, Edna...maybe Kansas."

I tried to appear amiable, sympathetic, and concerned. Roddy nodded yes to a muffin though the footman warned the pastries were yesterday's fare because of the water "situation." I did not mention the countless times I was ravenous for stale sourdough biscuits on a pack mule in the Rocky Mountains.

We sat nibbling the muffins and sipping sweet grape juice while Edna explained that a dentist named Welch thought up pasteurizing the juice for church services. "Now it is sold commercially, and...." She broke off at the sound of approaching voices in conversation...no, in rancor.

"Absolutely not," Alf barked. "Insane...I won't have it."

He pounded into the room with Clarence at his side... no, actually tugging the younger man by an ear. "Who ever heard of such a thing? Never..."

Clarence wrenched free and raked fingers through his tousled hair. He seemed not to notice his misbuttoned jacket. Father and son looked our way but stayed immersed in their quarrel.

"Who ever heard of such a—?"

"—Anthony Drexel, that's who. His *Margarita* has a working fireplace. Rosewood paneling and a working—"

"Fireplace on a yacht? Ridiculous."

"And Gordon Bennett has electric chandeliers in the *Namouna*, and Howard Gould's *Niagara* has a darkroom for guests with cameras."

"I don't give a rat's tail, Clarence. I draw the line at a fireplace. Why don't you do something smart with that plaything of yours...? Light another cigar with it, and you're sure to set a man's beard on fire...again."

"Never let me live it down, Father. Keep it up if you must, but you owe me...."

"Owe you? Owe you?" Saliva flew from both of their mouths. "That last Belfast shipyard bill...and you dare say that I owe you?"

"You know what I mean, Father. You know...." They glared at one another. Clarence's silken moustache had grown over his upper lip, and it quivered as he started to speak.

Suddenly, Alf noticed the three of us at the table with muffins and purple grape juice in crystal tumblers. He roared, "Son or a...."

"Now, Alfred," Edna purred. "We penitents are sipping at our leisure…hoping for rain, of course, but…."

"But nothing, Edna Rossiter. This is no springtime frolic. Skip your lady talk." He pointed to Roddy's glass of juice and glared. "You see what you have done."

"Sir…" Roddy began.

"Do not 'sir' me, Roderick. You were brought here to deal with the water from the DeVere property. Now the situation is dire. You must see to it at once. Find out what's needed, and I will send men with picks and shovels." He pointed at the footman. "I'll put you footmen into overalls, and you can blister your hands with real tools." The footman blanched.

Alf swerved at Clarence. "You go with Roderick."

"Father, my ankles…the poison ivy finally—"

"—to hell with 'finally.' You go together and report to me by midday. Both of you."

Roddy glanced my way, eyed Clarence, and marched off with him, leaving me at the table with Edna, who lowered her gaze until a fuming Alf stomped off with a disgusted, "Morning, ladies…."

I took a deep breath and sipped the juice.

"Don't mind Alf, Valentine. His bark is worse than his bite. Now and again, he needs to let off steam, especially these days."

"The water…" I began.

"Of course, the water shortage has everyone upset, but oh, that yacht…." She scrunched her neck. "I have been a bystander every step of the way. Once the keel was laid, there was no turning back. A grand gift to their son has become the Kidds' burden to bear. And recently Alfred's business has become frightfully competitive, which inevitably strains resources, everything *très cher,* if you understand."

For once, she did not translate the French.

"Their loving generosity will soon send the Kidds' son far away from his doting parents," she said.

"Unforeseen outcome, Edna," I tried to say it sadly. She nodded and nibbled her muffin. Edna had called herself Sadie's oldest friend and the "mortar" holding the Kiddwood season together. If she had an inkling that Alf patronized Pearl Street, she did not reveal it, nor hint any awareness that she knew he spent parts of these June nights at the camp on the DeVere property. Edna's idea of the man whose "bark" was worse than his "bite" apparently did not stretch to trysts.

Nor to murder. Two murders, the second to conceal the first.

Another question: did Sadie suspect her husband? Did she let her thoughts drift to the insomniac Alf's whereabouts while she lay awake in her suite? If so, did she bury all suspicions?

And if Clarence spoke to his mother about his father's nighttime jaunts, did Sadie dismiss the notion with a flash of her Cartier jeweled rings?

Questions not to be answered this morning, June 27, 1899, as I pondered what to do until Roddy returned with Clarence. Doubtful the two men would have any solution to the water woes. The Kiddwood atmosphere would darken by the hour.

"Edna," I said, "would you lend me a new book for a few hours?"

She grinned. "How's this sound...historical romance about a colonial Tory squire who falls in love with an indentured servant girl?" The nasty gleam in her eye told me that Roddy was the squire, and the servant girl yours truly.

"History," I said, "never fails to fascinate." With that, I accepted her loan of a new novel and sought an easy chair near a window.

Despite a novel packed with color and romance, I glanced up often in hopes of seeing Roddy. Instead, guests shuffled toward the buffet, one looking more dispirited than the next. Jack Barrott's hands trembled, and Alicia's rouged cheeks accented her pallor. I had not yet seen Sadie. When the light shifted, I moved my chair without troubling the anxious footman.

Just before noon, the Kidds' gaunt butler approached. "Mrs. DeVere, if you would be so kind, Mr. Kidd wishes to have a word with you in the library."

"With me alone?"

"If you please, ma'am. Mr. Kidd wishes me to show the way."

Off guard, I had no excuse except the return of Edna's book. The butler would gladly return the volume to Miss Rossiter, he said, after he took me to the library.

"If you please," he said again.

In minutes, Alf stood to welcome me to the library table he had pounded in fury last Sunday. He dismissed the butler, bowed, and kissed my hand.

"Valentine Mackle DeVere," he said, "I bow before you in humble apology."

"You needn't," I began, but he swept his arm toward a chair in a cavalier gesture. I sat on the edge of the seat to see him touch his whiskers and look baleful around the mouth.

"At times, Valentine, my temper gets the best of me. Too often this month, you have witnessed outbursts, shameful displays. Now I must tell you how very sorry I am. Will you accept my apology?"

Staged for my benefit, his contrition forced me to a short nod. The library with its fireplace, books stacked to the high ceiling, globe and cabinet of relics from the old iron mine—all made up Alfred Kidd's domain. Accepting his apology, would I be free to go?

What did he want?

Soon enough, I found out when he pointed to maps spread over the table. "Let us have a look, Valentine. These are surveyors' maps. Are they familiar to you from the West?"

My papa pored over maps of silver mines. He would point out the longitudinal elevation and the sites of rich ores found in different mines. Months ago, Roddy showed me a map of Manhattan and Central Park to show me a zoning scheme.

"Familiar to you?" Alf repeated with the slightest hint of impatience.

I rose halfway from the edge of the chair to peer at the tabletop and said, "Nothing like these, I'm afraid."

"Ah, well, then, let me explain." Sounding jolly, Alf ran a thick finger across property lines, pointing out the Kiddwood estate to the iron mine and across to the DeVere boundary. "Here's the Ulster County road…and here's DeVere property next to Kiddwood. You see the two properties, cheek by jowl, so to speak."

I expected remarks on the water shortage Instead, Alf sat back and stroked his white whiskers. "There are times," he said, "when a transaction is due…when it is time to put cards on the table."

What cards? What transaction? I tried not to squirm. Roddy ought to be here.

"And so, Valentine, cards on the table…I wish to acquire the DeVere property. I will propose a generous offer to you.

"To me?"

"To you, Valentine Mackle."

"*DeVere*, if you please," I said. "But Alf, the property is not mine to sell, even if I wished to do so." I tried to sound lighthearted.

"'If you wished to do so?'" He wet his lips. I instantly regretted my phrasing.

"Come now, don't be coy," he said. "The world knows it's your Mackle money at the source. Everybody knows."

I did not trust myself to reply, not then. A red rage swelled from ribs to my scalp.

"Let us be honest with one another, Valentine. Roderick's parents would sleep in a lodging house by the week if not for you. The DeVere fortune is your own. You have the right, and you have the power."

"I will have you know, Mr. Kidd," I said evenly, "that the DeVere property is funded by a trust that is not accessible to me. It would be against the law—"

"—the law? To quote old Vanderbilt, 'What do I care about the law? Ain't I got the power?'" Alf's eyes drilled at me. "You, valentine need not be troubled by the law."

"My husband..." I started to counter that Roddy was a member of the New York State Bar Association, but he would bat my words away. I sat still on the edge of the chair, wound up tight in this den, this lair.

How long we faced one another without speaking...was it minutes? I stared up at the clerestory windows and felt Alf's eyes gauge his odds of success. Neither of us spoke, and I prepared to go with a quick "excuse me" with my skirt gathered in one hand. I edged off the chair just as the butler opened the library door without knocking, pushed aside by my wide-eyed husband with his chest out and hands looking ready to grapple.

Roddy's glances darted from me to Alf and back again as I stammered my husband's name? Relief for us both when Roddy saw me seated safely with "Santa."

"Why, Roderick...do join us," Alf said smoothly, his well-oiled voice of apology now issuing an invitation. "Come to the table, won't you?" He waved the butler away and peered over Roddy's shoulder. "Is Clarence at your heels?"

Roddy said, "Clarence...I'm afraid he will see you later, Alf." He approached my chair, doubtless to escort me from the room. "About the water," he said, "we do not have a positive report."

"How could it be otherwise, Roderick? How could I expect two younger gentlemen to triumph over the elements?" Alf rose and bowed to Roddy.

Sounding humbled, he stood between my husband and me. "Won't you please take a seat? Your Valentine has graciously accepted my apology for this morning's outburst, and I cannot rest until I have your forgiveness."

"Quite unnecessary," Roddy said, "but about the water—"

"—not at this moment, Roderick. Kiddwood's thirsts will be quenched one way or another, but let me shake your hand in a token of our long friendship, the Kidds and the DeVeres. What do you say?"

The clasp looked strained on both sides.

"And now, Roderick, a few minutes at the library table, if you will?" Alf pulled out a chair, but Roddy sat beside me and took my hand.

Seated with the map in front of him, Alf spread his fingers. "Roderick," he said, "I invite you into a conversation just begun with Valentine as we awaited your return. We have been discussing your family property."

"Oh?"

"The property that I attempted to purchase from your parents, as you know."

Roddy nodded, his gaze wary.

"Without success at the time, Roderick."

The "time' was last year. At this instant, I vowed to correct Alf's version of our "conversation."

But he flashed a glassy smile and changed the subject. "When Sadie and I disagree," he said, "we thrash out our differences in private, and perhaps you DeVeres do so as well?"

Roddy looked at me and said, "From time to time." I nodded.

"Excellent," Alf said in his jovial voice. "The fact of the matter is this: I would very much like to purchase the DeVere property.... You both know this, yes?"

We waited for the hitch.

Alf rushed on. "I would never divide husband from wife. Never! So, whether you both feel the same way about the sale, you must come to an agreement. This library is my most prized room at Kiddwood, but I will leave you here to settle the matter of the DeVere property. Let me know when you have come to an agreement. For now, the room is yours."

With that, he stood, went to the door, closed it and left us alone.

Stiff as statues for a moment, we exhaled as if our breath had been held every second with "Santa."

Roddy whispered of his terror when told I was alone with Alf.

"He is desperate to get the DeVere tract," I said. "...his killing ground, Fiona drowned and dragged in the wagon... her body...."

"Val, stop. We need to think clearly. Alf could barge in any minute."

We both eyed the door, enclosing us in a killer's space and closing off my feelings...of Alfred Kidd forcing himself on Fiona, of the pool where he drowned her, of her father searching...searching.

I turned to Roddy. "Suppose we appease him until we can meet with Sheriff Webster? You can promise Alf that your parents will sell the tract, and I will bring up the Mackle funds."

"It won't work, Val. We would look like double dealers... accusing Alf of homicides and selling him property at the same time. And the new sheriff would listen to Chief Fitch's idea that we are somehow connected to Fiona's murder by the masseuse in in the Ulster County Jail."

"Ella Conklin," I whispered, "trapped in cell number eleven."

We clasped hands, and I closed my eyes to shut out Alfred Kidd, a futile and childish effort. So far, he had no inkling that we knew he was "Santa." If he knew, we would be his targets. Like Hank Boynt, we would need to be elim- inated. He would not waste time. The question was, how?

"Val, open your eyes. I have an idea." Roddy kept his voice low. "We will throw the dare back at Alf. We will tell him we ae eager to hear his best offer for the DeVere tract. We both agree to hear his offer. What do you think?"

"Stroke of genius," I murmured.

The relief was short-lived. We walked to the door, and Roddy rehearsed, "...your best offer." He gripped the knob once, twice, and again."

"What's wrong?" I asked.

Roddy wrenched the doorknob with both hands. Then, in a voice of disgust and disbelief, I heard these words, "Locked... The door is locked. We are locked in."

Chapter Thirty-two

WE DID THE PRACTICAL things and felt the predictable feelings—at first. "I'll knock for attention," Roddy said, rapping his knuckles against the mahogany door. He listened, paused, rapped again. We heard nothing. Roddy tried the knob once more. I said, "Let me give it a try." The knob did not budge.

How much time passed before we began to smell the smoke?

Half an hour?

One hour?

Soon enough, we would debate the fuel. Paper? Wood? Cloth? The debate, however, would start when the smoke began to seep from under the doorframe and the sensation of heat became palpable.

But not just yet.

"Did you hear the lock turn when Alf left?" I asked. Roddy shook his head. "Do you think he meant to lock us in?"

"Could be from force of habit, Val. Or a practical joke, like the barware that first time…stirring drinks with a kitchen spatula. Maybe he thinks it's funny to hold us captive in his library."

"Half joke," I said, "and half to lord it over us. But for how long? I'll call out," I said, and shouted, "Alf…Sadie. Hello? Edna? Jack? Do you hear me? Anybody?"

I pressed one ear against the door, then the other ear.

"Any footsteps, Val?"

"No."

Roddy's closed fist pounded at the door. "I'd bet everyone is at lunch," I said. "Including Alf."

"The buffet is at the other end of the house, Val. Too far for anyone to hear us knock or call."

"But maybe we'll be missed?"

"Or else thought to be in Kingston," Roddy said.

"Or maybe Kiddwood's guests are too preoccupied with hang-over remedies to give us a thought."

"So, we are to be kept here," Roddy said, "but not idle, so let's look for a spare key. A skeleton key ought to get us out of here."

Roddy rummaged through the drawers in a small chest. I scoured the library table, lifted the maps, moved paper weights and an inkstand. Then I ran a finger along the bookcase shelves and lifted the corners of an oriental rug. So far, our hunt for a key felt serious but not intense. We had our plan to meet with the new sheriff and played our part as cheerful guests, even while Alf raged about the water and presented his obnoxious bid to buy the DeVere tract.

When I stepped to the glass-front cabinet, however, my heart thumped and my hands suddenly got cold. "Roddy," I called, as if my husband were a mile away. "Roddy...Roddy...."

"What is it?" He was instantly at my side.

"There...look there." I was pointing at the display of old mining tools. "That space," I said, "beside the drill."

My husband peered through the glass. "What of it?"

"That space is empty," I said, "where the hammer ought to be."

Roddy nodded. He did not yet see what I saw.

"The day I went to the old iron mine," I said, "Alf brought me here to show off the miner's hammer and drill. They go together, Roddy...and the hammer is missing."

We stared at the drill and the space beside it. Roddy took my hand, "Val, your fingers are cold."

"Because...because of Hank Boynt's death."

In that silent moment, my husband blinked, swallowed, stared into the cabinet, and finally whispered, "The weapon... the murder weapon."

I nodded, just as Roddy pulled me away from the cabinet. "Step back, Val. Alf must not see us near it, nowhere near the cabinet." He tugged my arm. "Let's go back to the table."

We stood over the surveyor's map with heads together as if examining the Kidd and DeVere properties. My fingers felt ice-cold. "Why didn't he put the hammer back?" I asked. "Wipe it off and put it away."

"He couldn't, Val. Remember, he needed to waylay Hank before he met me on the back steps. His time was short."

"So," I whispered, "he hid the hammer, or tossed it away."

"To retrieve it later or let it rust away in the bushes," Roddy said. "He might not want the reminder of what he did, not in his 'office' space."

"Then," I said, "we can ask Sheriff Webster to arrange a search for it. Our case will be stronger, and...."

I paused as Roddy raised his head and sniffed. "Val," he said, "what do I smell? Do you smell it?"

I pulled back. "Something," I said, "is it...burning?"

Roddy answered in a taut voice, "Yes, something charred...burning."

We asked what it might be. A fire to take the chill off a room? Probably not at this time of day. A kitchen blaze seemed a remote possibility. "But not impossible," I said. "The culprit would be hot grease. Or live coals from the coal-burning stove. Then again, the drawing room upholstery fabric and a cigar not quite stubbed out."

"Smoldering nightlong," Roddy said.

The odor seemed to increase. Roddy coughed. I cleared my throat. A slight haze filled the room, and my eyes started to sting.

"Not one window to open," Roddy said. He craned his neck to look up. "Clerestory for light, but no ventilation." He coughed again, then grabbed a letter opener from the table and slipped it into the keyhole to twist it back and forth. The lock held.

"Handkerchief?" I asked. Roddy plucked a hankie from his jacket pocket, and I patted my eyes, then covered my nose and mouth and tied the handkerchief in back as we did when the Washoe "Zephyr" sand-and-wind storm struck in Virginia City. Roddy held his necktie against his face. He pointed to the bottom of the doorframe. Smoke was coming in....waves and puffs of light gray.

The haze thickened.

"Roddy, does it feel warm?"

He nodded. His eyes watered, and he pounded at the door. No one answered. Beside him, I pounded too.

The smoke curled at our ankles. The light gray darkened to a charcoal black. Somewhere inside the house voices cried out and something banged.

And then cracked and crackled.

At the table, I grabbed the map to scrunch and jam at the doorframe. Roddy snatched the inkstand from the table, stood back, and hurled it at a clerestory window. It fell to the floor. He picked it up and tried again. It struck a pane of glass and bounced off. On his third try, the glass broke.

The smoke came in faster.

Roddy stuffed his jacket at the doorframe. The smoke eddied and curled.

I touched an inside wall. "Feels hot, Roddy...hot."

He put a hand against the plastered wall and felt it up and down. "Hot!" was his muffled word.

Coughing, choking, we looked at each other with eyes streaming. "Fire," I said.

"House...." Roddy nodded.

"Can't...breathe, Roddy. I can't...."

He held a hand up. "No...."

The banging, the crackling...and shrieks. I heard shrieks.

"Drowsy..." I said, "can't...." My last word, and Roddy tried to hold me. He tried in the smoke and heat, and terror in his eyes. Helpless....

The bolt must have sounded, but I did not hear it. The key in the lock, and the opened door...to face a wall of black smoke. Two soot-black arms and hands clawed and clutched to pull us, Roddy and I both yanked stumbling and tripping with breath held, although every breath was gone. Swallowed in smoke, dragged through smoke, we somehow were left on the grass by the man in scorched clothing who ran back into the smoke.

Grass and air. We gasped and gulped, both sick on the grass.

"Get back...back!"

General Coleman gave the order just as flames thrust and roared through the rooftop with an ear-splitting boom. I drank air, gulped air, but a burning ember fell between Roddy and me on the grass, and we scrabbled our way back, behind the croquet lawn, the badminton court.

"Goner," I heard a voice say. "Goner for sure."

Was it a guest's voice? A footman? Roddy took my hand, and we retreated further back, panting and coughing with every step. The stable was far enough back to be untouched, though the coachman and groom stood outside, mouths open.

From behind the badminton court, I saw Willa huddled with the servants and the kitchen workers in their aprons, all agog at the sight of flames shooting into the blue sky and window glass bursting. The footmen lined up too, and the gaunt butler with them. One footman knelt in prayer.

The guests stood silent or talked with arms waving up and down, especially Edna whose words were snuffed in the roar and crash of timbers. I counted the guests, the square-jawed man, Jack Barrott, Alicia, the others...and Sadie, standing apart, stunned.

"All guests here, Val," Roddy said, "except...where's Alf? Do you see Clarence?

At that instant, as if cued, a disheveled man burst from the burning house, his clothes scorched, his arms soot black. "Clarence," I said.

"Clarence..." Roddy echoed, "...who unlocked the door, got us out." My husband took a few steps, seeming to count heads. A thunderous crash, and a front wall collapsed. "Not another living soul," Roddy murmured. "Somewhere in that funeral pyre," he said, "lies the body Alfred Kidd."

Chapter Thirty-three

WHERE WERE WE? AT home but not yet *really home.* This Thursday, June 29, found us once again at 620 Fifth Avenue in the Green Drawing Room in our favorite Bergere chairs. Recovering from Kiddwood would take time, but our servants did their part this afternoon, greeting us as if smoky apparel worn for days was as ordinary as a lack of luggage. My maid, Calista, promptly drew me a bath, as did Roddy's valet, Norbert. Bathed and dressed for dinner, we tried to relax. Our dog, Velvet, had welcomed us at first with warm licks and wriggles but now circled the drawing room at a stand-offish distance, as if our unexcused absence must be on canine record.

Roddy's wheeled bar cart beckoned with bottles, ice, and fruit for garnish, but I said, "Not just yet," and he agreed that clearing our minds of Kiddwood would take more than a bath, a change of clothes, and a cocktail.

"Val, would it help you to see the *Journal* or the *Times*?"

"Absolutely not."

Roddy had dutifully read the papers that were also delivered around the corner to his parents. In their apartment tomorrow morning, he would need to know exactly what Pulitzer and Hearst had printed about the fire in Ulster County. The *Kingston Weekly Freeman* went to press one day early to break the news, and Gotham's papers then dispatched squads of reporters to cover every angle in lurid detail.

"Let me guess, Roddy," I said. "The *Times* and *Journal* front pages reported a "blazing conflagration" and the "tragic" death of the president of Kidd & Company, along with photographs of the Statue of Liberty."

"And the Brooklyn Bridge," my husband said tartly.

"Plus, features on the guests and the servants...and the widow? I imagine Edna offered abundant quotes on Sadie's grief?"

"At length."

"And Clarence? The faithful son who helped one and all escape the flames but tragically could not save his father?"

Roddy hesitated. "We know the formula, Val. We needn't cynically replay the official version."

"Then, shall we speak frankly? We have not had a chance to say what we really think."

My husband glanced toward the window at the trees fully in leaf for the summer. The past two days had been a jumble of ad-libbing and action. All Tuesday afternoon, the Kiddwood house burned to the ground, and the servants and guests watched smoke gust from the foundation when the flames finally died. Hopes were voiced that somehow Alf had escaped or was not in the house when the fire started. Or that somewhere in the smoking ruin was a fireproof vault from which he would appear unscathed.

The sight of Sadie sobbing against Edna's shoulder had nonetheless sobered everyone, especially with Clarence at their side, his arms blackened and hair singed. The stone chimney ruins gave rise to murmurs about rebuilding, but self-interest came into play with questions about the night's lodgings and meals. The coachman readied a carriage to take Sadie, Edna, and Clarence into Kingston to the Oriental Hotel, and the groom hitched Granny and a horse named Snook to a wagon and offered the guests a ride into Kingston. The wagon filled up with the groom's promise to return for the last few of us. The servants whispered among themselves and set out on foot. Willa told me a cousin lived within a mile and would take her in. I asked for the address, not having one cent to give her at the time.

Nightfall found us with Alicia and General Coleman at dinner at the Bauer Hotel, where we made the best of the "calamitous day," as Alicia called it, voicing grief for Clarence and regretting the Oriental had no room for her. The general proposed that we all return to the city by an early morning train, but Roddy shot me a quick glance, and we murmured about tying up details here in Kingston.

One such "detail" was an early morning visit to City Hall to review property records. Lying awake in the lumpy bed of the Bauer Hotel, I entertained *eureka* ideas about the future of the DeVere tract and Kiddwood too. Hearing me at dawn, Roddy admitted he was intrigued but must first examine records pertaining to property transactions.

The future of properties, however, was nowhere in mind during our next stop at Webster's Livery and Boarding Stable on Mill Street. Seated in Mr. Grant Webster's corner office, we sat across from the sheriff-elect whose business suit and work boots signaled a stableman's grounding and a lawman's authority. He asked details about the Kiddwood fire and its probable cause, and we confirmed that Alfred Kidd had succumbed, fatally. Against a background of stamping hooves and odors of hay and manure, Roddy began to present our case. As I recall, we spent two hours with the incoming Sheriff of Ulster County.

"Roddy," I said, as we sat on the Bergere chairs, "I think the new sheriff was more horrified by the idea that Hank Boynt was bludgeoned to death. Fiona's drowning alarmed him, but he choked up when we told him about Alf and the hammer."

"Because Webster saw Hank as a valued employee. He believed in him." Roddy shook his head. "The man was also shocked to hear us say that a model gentleman and business titan was a killer."

"Twice a killer," I said. "Brute strength to drown Fiona, but a weapon to make sure Hank would die. Cross your fingers that Alf's hammer is lying in the bushes by the county road."

"Close to Kiddwood," Roddy said. "We told Webster where to find it, and he will get up a search party to scour the bushes."

"If I could have shown him the 'Santa' rag," I said. "If the fire hadn't...."

Roddy hushed me with a wave of his hand. "You described the wet rag, which will support inmate Ella Conklin's account when Webster visits her in the Ulster County Jailhouse." Roddy added, "Which he will do very soon."

"Escorted by Chief Clyde Fitch," I said. "And Fitch will fill his ear with 'proof' that Ella Conklin killed Fiona and that we are complicit in the crime."

Roddy shook his head. "We have debunked Fitch. His idea will make no headway with the new sheriff. You piped up at the right moment about the shooting gallery and he masseuse...Ramona?"

"Smith," I said. "Ramona Smith"

"Who will confirm that Ella Conklin and Fiona Peebles were close friends, never rivals. Webster will take her statement, and we heard him say that he will be accompanied by the Ulster County attorney. Anyway, my guess is that Fitch has earned a reputation as something of a rockhead. And Fiona Peebles's death is a case for Ulster County. Webster made that clear. The jurisdiction will be the county."

I folded my hands. "So, will Ella Conklin be released from the county jail?"

Roddy rubbed his cheek. "A good chance the charge against her in Ulster County will be dropped, but she'll face the attempted murder charge in Florida."

"A trumped-up charge by an angry man," I said. "And hasn't that charge been this month's gift to Alf...and to Cedric Ferris? The Florida warrant handed them their story about Fiona's murder."

Roddy had to agree.

"And Cedric will be right there when the sheriff questions Ramona at the camp. Vanessa too." I heard my voice rise. "And will Cedric be charged? He woke Fiona for 'Santa time' and led her to Alf in the middle of the night. He is a pimp. He knew that Alf killed Fiona. He helped a murderer, and he ought to be charged."

My lawyer husband tapped his thumbs together. "Ought, yes...but the murderer is dead, and a case against Cedric would be costly in money and time. Sorry to say, the prosecutor will calculate the odds that Cedric might not be convicted, and—"

"—drop the case? Let the Health-to-Wealth scam go on, week after week as if nothing happened?" My shrill voice stopped the dog in her tracks.

Roddy reached across our chairs to take my hand. "I expect Health-to-Wealth to shut down in a few days, Val. Rumors fly, and characters like Cedric Ferris and Vanessa... Zelonski, isn't it?"

I nodded.

"They smell trouble and slither off to their next bogus scheme. It's money they want, but not homicide. I also expect Keith Property Management will keep a low profile. Roland Keith will write off the DeVere property at a loss to keep clear of his legal troubles...that is, assuming that his client will cooperate."

I nearly uttered the name of the client, my father-in-law. Tomorrow, Roddy plans to take his best barrister's skills to his father, and his utmost charm to his mother. He will urge the senior DeVeres to seek a different Hudson Valley property for their country house but insist they first void the contract with Keith and sell the limestone-rich tract to a cement company. The senior DeVeres, we both agreed, will be enchanted at the prospect of a sum unthinkable for a merchant of beaver pelts.

Roddy tried to coax a still-cool Velvet to his lap. She kept her distance. "I wonder whether she's sniffing the smoke from Kiddwood. Could it be?"

I did not say no. The Kidds' acreage had also wedged itself into my mind in the Bauer Hotel room in the wee hours of Tuesday night and Wednesday morning. Roddy had slept soundly, but I tossed and turned, wide awake, my thoughts racing ahead of the fire and our near-miss in the library.

For certain, the surviving Kidds would want to rid themselves of Alf's homeplace. It had never charmed Sadie and grew barely tolerable to their continental yachtsman of a son. Cleared of the charred ruins and sold, the estate could find another purpose.

Perhaps it was the canvas tents on the DeVere tract that stirred my thoughts that night in the Bauer Hotel. Lying fully clothed on that narrow hotel bed, the mining camps of my girlhood pressed into memory...unbearable in winter, but the summertime winds often murmured, the streams sang, and young birds learned to fly. Those times lodged deep within, treasured over time.

Turning on that hotel bed, I pictured children enjoying nights in tents in a summer season outdoors. Which children? My New York life meant youngsters like Cassie's Charlie and Bea…and some others glimpsed when I went to meetings on the Lower East Side. I rarely thought about the ragged children at play in the tenement streets. As Mrs. Roderick DeVere of the Upper East Side, I told myself that Central Park was theirs all the year round, whenever they made their way uptown.

That night, lying awake in smoky clothes on a hotel mattress no wider than a cot, I faced a fact: for those children, Central Park might as well be another planet.

Suppose, however, that Kiddwood could be purchased?

Suppose I bought it?

Suppose it could be made into a tent camp in Ulster County for the children who never set foot in Central Park? Or any park? As for water, wells could be dug, and the cement company buying the DeVere tract could be required to dig wells as a condition of the sale. My papa would approve. I know he would.

Roddy had been interested when these ideas tumbled out at breakfast in the Bauer Hotel, which explains why we first stopped at Kingston's City Hall, where I also inquired about the regulations for removing a body from the pauper cemetery for reburial in a memorial garden in another state, possibly in Newark, New Jersey. I was advised that next-of-kin could hasten such arrangements, and I took the information with thanks. An afternoon train took us back to the city, and a hansom cab brought us here. One day, we might laugh about the train passengers who avoided the bedraggled couple who smelled like something burning.

And here we were in the drawing room, coaxing a reluctant French bulldog to allow us to pet her while avoiding the frank talk about arson and murder.

"Homicide," I said softly.

Roddy glanced toward the cocktail cart with a sigh. "Val, is this the best time...?"

"To ask whether Clarence set the fire, which he did. Or to ask whether Alf meant to free us from the library... because If Clarence had not unlocked the door.... And how did he know we were there?"

"He didn't, Val. He wanted something from Alf's library office, I'd guess stock certificates."

"But he pulled us out...we would have died by smoke inhalation."

"Asphyxiation," Roddy said.

"Which killed Fiona, didn't it? Death by drowning is asphyxiation, so it's possible that Alf meant to...." I swallowed. "Then again, did Clarence kill his father? The last one out of the burning house...everyone out but Alf."

"We will never know, Val, but if the target was Kiddwood—"

"—then the arson was itself patricide, no matter how Alf died."

Roddy nodded. The dog sat on her haunches and eyed us as if to make up her mind. "Maybe if I mixed us a cocktail? Velvet often sees me at the cart. I'm ready. Are you?"

Roddy went to the cart, chin in hand, and announced that this evening's cocktail would be The Ampersand. The sound of glasses, ice, and corks smoothed the moment, and I would every afterwards link this new cocktail with our homecoming.

Ampersand Cocktail

Ingredients:

- 1 ounce Brandy
- 1 ounce Tom Gin
- 1 ounce Italian Vermouth
- 2 dashes Orange Bitters
- 2 dashes coração

Directions:

1. Add ample ice to mixing jar.
2. Add Brandy, Gin, and Vermouth.
3. Stir moderately and add Bitters.
4. Strain into cocktail glass, top with curaçao, and serve.

"Salud, Val." We touched glasses. I sipped.

"What do you think?"

"Tangy," I said. "I like it, but why the Ampersand? It's a curlicue symbol for the word 'and,' isn't it?"

"That's what this month feels like, and, and, and...no end to it."

We sipped. Our dog took a few steps forward. "Let me add another ampersand to the month," I said. "About Ella Conklin...when she is sent back to Florida, she will need a good defense attorney...Daytona, isn't it?" Roddy nodded. "So, let us see that she has the best defense, and we'll pay the fees. Can you see to it?"

Roddy sipped. "After I talk to my parents in the morning."

And one more ampersand," I said, "about the young lawyer who's looking into the Newark jewelry companies? Do you suppose he has located Roy Peebles?"

"Krementz," Roddy said. "There's a message from Matthew Harding in the backed-up mail. A Roy Peebles is employed in the Krementz Company's Buffing and Polishing Section." My husband raised a hand when I started to speak. "No need to spell it out, Val. We are to contact Mr. Peebles about his daughter and have her returned to him in Newark, no expense spared."

"The least we can do," I said. "And the engraved ring must be returned to Fiona's papa. And now, Roddy, I have something else to bring up...another ampersand."

My husband sipped, blinking.

"Amanda Sterling," I said.

He blinked again.

"Or was it Mandy Sterling? The bachelor Roderick DeVere and the debutante of the year at Kiddwood?"

"Oh, my dear Val...."

"Edna told me how you called her hair 'spun gold tresses.'"

"Surely not." His tone was less than convincing. "Wait, I remember now," he said, "...a parlor game, charades....let down your hair... Rapunzel. That was it, Rapunzel."

My side-eye glance came with a wink, but Roddy leaned across to touch my hair. "Not one spun gold strand," I said, knowing my hair was called dishwater blonde. But my husband stroked my hair and surprised me.

"Val," he said, "it's time to have your portrait painted."

I nearly spilled my cocktail.

"We go to Newport in a week or so, and portrait artists work during the summer season." He suddenly looked shy. "It would be a gift to me."

"Roddy...I don't know, not sure." Just then, Velvet made her decision, ran our way, jumped and licked. I put my drink down and lifted her to my lap. "How about this, Roddy?" I said, "How about, 'Silver Miner's Daughter in Dinner Gown with Lapdog?'" We laughed brightly, little thinking that in weeks to come. such amusement as ours would take a dark and twisted turn.

ABOUT THE AUTHOR

Cecelia Tichi is a native of Pittsburgh, the steel city of the Gilded Age, and is an award-winning teacher and author of numerous books focused on American culture and literature. Her most recent titles: *What Would Mrs. Astor Do? The Essential Guide to the Manners and Mores of the Gilded Age* was followed by *Cocktails of the Gilded Age: History, Lore, and Recipes of America's Golden Age* and the sequel, *Jazz Age Cocktails: History, Lore, and Recipes from the Roaring Twenties*. The "Val and Roddy DeVere" mystery series premiers with *A Gilded Death*.

www.ingramcontent.com/pod-product-compliance
Lightning Source LLC
Chambersburg PA
CBHW021434310726
48971CB00005B/1359